homebody

ALEX DUNKIN

Buon-Cattivi Press
Adelaide, Australia

Published by Buon-Cattivi Press, 2016
Adelaide, Australia

ISBN 978-0-9953661-0-7

Book design and illustration by Andrew Crooks
Printed by IngramSpark

A huge thank you to Andrew, Greg, and Dylan for their support, inspiration and guidance while writing *Homebody*.

Foreplay

SWEAT DRIPS OFF Diego's muscled arms. His dirty singlet clings against his stomach and chest highlighting each bump of his six pack and pecs. Mike watches on as Diego nails the last piece of wood into the new decking.

The remnants of twilight fade into the darkening sky. Diego stands up and nods proudly at the hardened wood of mastery he hammered himself.

'Um—do you—um, would you like a drink?' Mike chokes out over the fluttering in his chest.

'Sorry, what?' Diego spins around to face Mike. His thick, dark locks twirl in the air as he moves around. Mike sighs at the sight of Diego's tanned skin. A dark shadow has grown across his face in a rough pattern of stubble from the full day since shaving.

'Would you like to come in for a beer?' Mike asks, glancing down at his feet.

Diego beams, his pearly whites shine brightly in the last flashes of daylight.

'Absolutely,' he responds with confidence. 'I'd love one. I'll be there in a second. I'll just take off these messy clothes.'

Mike begins to turn but halts at the view of Diego rolling his singlet up over his head. Diego's natural hairlessness leaves all his muscles exposed and shining. The last drops of sweat dry under the small tuffs of underarm hair. Mike feels a shiver of anticipation run up the back of his spine.

Diego clears his throat. Mike stumbles over his thoughts. He hadn't notice Diego look up from placing his singlet away in his tool box.

'So,' Diego begins, 'do you live here alone?'

'Yeah I do,' Mike responds sheepishly. 'I'm not seeing anyone. It's just me alone here.'

'Good,' Diego grins. He steps over to Mike. His hips sway seductively as he moves. He stands close enough for Mike to smell the manly scent rising from his body. 'I'm also available. So maybe we could have a couple beers and see where the night takes us—'

The oven's alarm blares a harsh interruption to his romantic fantasy, and the smell of freshly baked bread reminds him to put down the trashy novel and resume his humdrum of domestic bliss...

The Act

I.

His name is Aaron, twenty-six, Virgo, homemaker. He lives in wedded bliss with the love of his life, David, twenty-seven, Libra, banker. They met in high school, David spotting the gangly new kid at school across the yard. It didn't take long for David to reach out to Aaron, leaving behind his friends one lunch time and sitting next to him.

Since then it's all been like a dream for Aaron. For the rest of high school they were inseparable, their commitment to each other an icon for other students. Even for the year after David graduated, Aaron spent every spare moment at David's new apartment in the city, heedless of how his education suffered.

After they married they stayed on in David's apartment, as it has everything they need. Two bedrooms, one for when Aaron entertains David's guests, the other a primed and plush love nest. More and more Aaron finds the room has become his rather than theirs. The demanding hours David must maintain to climb his corporate ladder don't allow for the time together that they once had. The mere thought drags up the memory of the only time Aaron had called the office after hours pacing the kitchen waiting with David's dinner cold on the counter. The conversation with Timothy, David's nimble assistant, still seems fresh in his mind.

'He's in a meeting, Mr Jones, can I pass on a message?' Timothy chirped with a hint of contempt.

'No that's fine, I just wanted to know if he's on his way home,' Aaron said.

Aaron hears commotion in the background, bellows of 'Cut!' and 'Outrageous increase!' distinct above the general furore. He had cringed at the confrontation, his back tensing and pulling his ribs painfully together at the sound of David's raised voice.

'It's unlikely Mr Jones will be finished soon. I'll let him know you called.' Timothy hangs up swiftly.

The anger and disappointment in his husband's voice dig like nails into the base of Aaron's skull, then and now, and he blocks the echoing ache of memory from his mind. Aaron has never called again, as it won't bring David home any sooner. Aaron knows he'll return eventually, even if not until the weekend. In the meantime Aaron remains ready for him. He maintains a spotless apartment, making sure everything is in order. Not a single curtain fold is out of place. Each night, two plates of home-cooked food are on the table at seven, with more at the ready in case of dinner guests. Aaron has lost count of how many serves he's thrown into the compost. *It's all just in case*, Aaron tells himself as he scrapes off a fresh plate of food and runs the crockery through the dishwasher. *It's all for our relationship. David may need to host important clients at any moment. I have to be ready for that.*

※

Tonight, to test Aaron's ability to stretch a meal, David welcomes four guests to the dinner table heralded only by a snooty text message from Timothy late in the day: 'Six tonight. Preference for shiraz'. *It isn't the first time*, Aaron reminds himself. *I can do this. It's what we do best. I'm lucky to marry him, more lucky that I deserve.* Aaron suppresses his fretting to focus on producing six adequate meals out of four serves of mutton roast and vegetables with extra gravy and a pea purée.

'Can you believe that sudden drop in our stocks?' Aubrey asks, with a mischievous glint in her eye. 'All we did was shift our majority from City to West Investment Co., it's nothing out of the ordinary.'

'Nobody likes change,' David takes the bait. 'It's not the first time a bank like ours has swapped external firms. We all know it is down to whatever the banks are doing internally as to where we store the majority of capital.'

Jennifer, Aubrey's wife, places her goblet down and clears her throat.

'We all know that, David,' Jennifer announces confidently. 'The difficulty is the lack of understanding from external parties. We make these changes all the time, we make constant announcements through social media, yet the share price will drop as though all this jumped out of the mist.'

Aaron stands suddenly, his shoulders stiff and proud to emulate confidence as a host.

'May I grab extra shiraz for anyone?'

'Oh, yes please,' Aubrey exclaims. 'This is a fantastic vintage. Knowing David, he must have bought up every crate of it. Not because you intend to drink all of it, darling, though I know you'll try your hardest, but to keep it out of the hands of those with a less refined taste. So, I'll wager I can drink as much as I can stomach tonight.' Rather than bridle at the barb, David smirks in haughty satisfaction.

'Very good,' Aaron replies. 'I'll go grab a few more bottles. It won't take a moment to decant them.'

Aaron steps out of the dining room leaving David with his guests. Aubrey and her wife play merrily with the others. Their wit and skill at sniping and titillating debate are legendary at the bank, whipping their listeners into an electrifying passion much sought after among elite circles. Samuel and Randall are more reserved, a newlywed couple fresh at the game of dinner parties. Aaron chuckles to himself as he trundles down the hall. He remembers what it felt like to be the new entrant into unfamiliar territory, but with David's rapid rise inside the bank he has had to adapt just as quickly. *Married, supportive couples rise faster*, David constantly reminds him. Aaron makes sure their status as a couple is secure enough to meet all the demands of the bank, even though he's lost track of David's actual position. The title changes with the seasons. David's first role saw him at home a lot, buried behind piles of numbers and grateful for every meal pushed before him. But soon enough the ever-increasing seniority of his positions dragged David from the convenience of his home office into the trap of the lower executive wing.

Aaron steps into the chill of the apartment's purpose-built cellar, a status symbol David insisted was essential. Silence welcomes him like a dear friend. The ordered, enclosed room soothes Aaron, purging the rigidness of the dinner party. Each bottle, each vintage ever bought or gifted, is splayed before him. He runs his fingers over the label of each bottle, all carefully kept free of dust. He knows the exact location of the bottles he seeks, yet he lingers in the fulfilling comfort of an intimate knowledge of the racks surrounding him provide a fulfilling comfort. Aaron glides past the locked racks, each bottle a prized possession that entirely dwarfs the cost of the collection of bulk wine lying in boxes at the end of the room. Aaron digs three bottles out of the uppermost box and folds the lid back into place. While their guests are famed for their banter, their wine palette certainly isn't sophisticated in any way.

Aaron stands, a bottle in each hand and the third tucked under his arm, and moves back towards the door. Darkness smothers the room suddenly with a sad fizzle of the light blowing. Aaron sighs from the middle of the room, filled by a dull sense of obligation. The unwanted distraction of changing a light bulb darkens his mindset and into a pale shell of energy. He stands, dismayed. *At least it's a change in routine*, he thinks to himself. The slight boost in enthusiasm fails to tug him out of the dark spot he stands in. The darkness itself settles in, a soothing chill embraces Aaron in a comfortable hug, diverting his thoughts further and further away from the third act currently playing out at the dinner party. Images of himself as a child flash behind his eyes. Aaron recalls dreaming of a home like the one he now has, an escape away from his dads and brother. The isolation of the cellar would shelter him from the risk of an argument. The nippy air reminds him of winter nights, huddling under his quilt, reading to escape the persistent draft that always trailed through his dads' house.

A trigger fires in Aaron's mind. A trained impulse sparks him from the momentary lapse in focus. He steps towards the door and finds the handle at the first grab. Light seeps in as he pushes the heavy door out of his way. *I'll fix that light later*, he thinks to himself. A disturbance rumbles at that thought. A niggle of annoyance tickles behind his eyes. *Screw it! I'll do it now. Get it done*, he thinks. Aaron turns quickly to face back into the darkness. From his right a solid thud whacks into his arm. Aaron snatches at the instant sting on his elbow. In the blindness of the pain he doesn't notice the two bottles releasing from his hands until they shatter on the tiles. Red splatters soak into the hem of his pants.

'Aaron dear, is everything alright?' David calls from the dining room.

Aaron gasps through the sharp tingling that rushes up his arm.

'Yes,' he clears his throat. 'One of the bottles slipped. It's nothing, I can take care of it.'

'I heard a yell. Are you sure you're okay?'

'Yes dear. Just a bit of a start.'

Aaron straightens up, a hand still grasping his tender elbow. He hears the conversation at the table return to normal, confirming no-one will come to look at his mess anytime soon. Processes flash through his mind to prepare his next moves. *Serve, clean, fix*, he thinks. *Wine will keep them at the table*. He steps out to the kitchen with the one surviving bottle of wine. On the counter he sets out the smallest glass decanter they own. *I can't let it look too empty*.

The aerator gargles the wine down into the crystal decanter. The slurping and small bubbles create a blankness in Aaron's mind. Each hiss of the wine blends in with the thousands prior. The greedy aerator sucks eagerly at the thick liquid. After a last sad gurgle, Aaron taps out the final drops and places the aerator on the sink. He draws a heavy breath, hoists a smile onto his face and, with only the slightest hint of a grip on the decanter, he steps out into the dining room.

'How's everything going in here?' Aaron enquires in a perky tone.

'Splendid food as always, Aaron,' Jennifer responds.

'Oh lovely,' Aubrey says, holding her empty glass up at the sight of the red wine.

Aaron steps over and fills her glass far beyond decency, and an eager grin blossoms on Aubrey's face. Aaron conjures as much charm as he can muster into his smile and continues around the table topping up everyone's wine and clearing away tiny unnoticed crumbs.

'Excuse me for a moment,' Aaron says. 'I just need to check on something.'

The courtesy doesn't register with the guests, as they'd barely emerged from their conversation on economics and politics and drinking and economics again. Aaron escapes back to the kitchen, the comfort and security afforded by the shining surfaces a welcome respite. The meticulous tiling creates an effortless feel of distance and space. Aaron shelters in his kitchen dreamscape only a moment before he returns to the tasks he left behind.

Aaron grabs a tea towel and broom and heads towards the open door of the cellar. The light from the hallway would seem quite pretty as it reflects off the two spreading red pools on the tiles, the fragments of green glass would make quite a delightful pattern, if the whole mess didn't make Aaron feel so inadequate. He drops the tea towel amongst the disarray and starts sweeping the wine and glass into the centre. Soft streaks of wine colour the fabric with each slow deliberate motion as Aaron collects everything into a single pile and scoops it into a dustpan. The plastic handle bends under the weight of the wine as Aaron rushes to the bin, and with a quick flick he dumps the wine, tea towel and all, into the trash can. Aaron dismisses the towel as a lost cause and grabs a fresh one to polish the floor.

Once the floor is clean again, and the second tea towel disposed of, Aaron returns to the cellar to replace the blown light bulb. It hangs, naked and isolated, from the centre of the ceiling, the bottles on all sides flickering as they reflect the hallway light in mocking contrast. Aaron unscrews the globe and carries it out into the kitchen light, peering at faded letters to determine the voltage. He opens the top cupboard above the fridge and pulls out a box of new globes. A crackle of harsh laughter erupts from the dining room. *They must be enjoying that wine*, Aaron thinks. *I must get them more before the laughter changes.* He rifles through the box with increased haste to find a suitable replacement globe. With an 'Ah-ha' as he finds one with the perfect match, Aaron returns to the cellar and begins screwing the new globe in. A sudden light blasts his eyes. He squeezes his eyelids shut and turns away from the globe's radiance as tears seep out into the fresh light. *Not an energy saver, then.*

Aaron forces himself to blink his eyes open into the searing light. After a few tries he can see his surroundings, the globe fully screwed in and on all sides racks of wine bottles reflecting the light. He presses a handkerchief fished from his breast pocket to his eyes to dab away the remaining hot tears from his cheek and reaches back into the box for more of the shiraz he dropped. This time he grips the bottles extra tightly as he guards himself from the door.

Aaron makes it out to the kitchen safely and decants the two bottles ready for presentation to the guests.

'The idea of religion has always fascinated me,' Samuel pipes, his cheeks flushing a warm red. 'But what doesn't make sense to me is how the deity chooses its prophet in our world. There's no quality control. There's no guarantee that each word was written down correctly and that's not even touching on the topic of the sanity of the person writing it.'

'That position is a little too literal,' Randall chides.

'I think so as well,' David adds in his commanding tone. *He's ready to preach*, Aaron thinks as he sits back at the table. 'Religious texts are always overused and destroy the benefits of religion. A lot of keeping the masses happy is about pandering to their feelings.'

'What are those?' Aubrey jokes.

'Something you threw overboard when you voted conservative,' Jennifer teases.

'Prove it!' Aubrey winks.

'Anyway,' David continues, 'it's all about keeping the masses happy. A happier populous equals more spending and less hostility. Religion offers one potential means to effectively do that, if it's used right. It has been proven to work over thousands of years.'

'Damn that dastardly education for getting in the way,' Samuels says.

'True, religion is great for the less educated to find a place for themselves. We can't be too harsh on religion,' David smiles across at Aaron. Aaron shivers. The look sits sincere and strange in Aaron's mind. 'Without religion we wouldn't have our way of life and the breeder's immoral ways would be rife. Imagine it, uncontrolled, without any morals.' The guests cringe simultaneously.

'I suppose that is true,' Aubrey says. She glances at her watch. 'Oh gosh. Time has really gotten away from us. I have a six o'clock flight tomorrow morning. We should be heading off.'

'Us too,' Randall adds. 'I have a full day of patients tomorrow.'

Aubrey pushes her chair back and quickly grabs the back of Jennifer's to pull it out for her.

'Thank you,' Jennifer whispers with a smile.

Aubrey pushes the chairs back in before grabbing the goblet and downing the half cup of wine left in a single gulp.

'Delicious, Aaron,' she says through purple teeth. 'You always delight us with your skills as a host.'

'Yes, thank you Aaron,' the others add.

David escorts them out to the front door, leaving Aaron to tidy the mess on the table. *They hardly touched the new bottles*, he sighs, noticing the two almost full decanters on the table. Aaron reaches for one and fills his goblet. He downs half the goblet's contents in the first swig, enjoying the end of social protocols for the evening. The tart shiraz sucks on his cheeks. The quick rush of alcohol distracts him from his closing duties as host. His muscles relax into a calmer demeanour. The rigidity in his spine smooths to a natural bend.

Aaron begins his work at the table, scraping and stacking the plates. The noise of knives on plates covers the sound of the door shutting and David returning to his seat. Aaron looks up when he notices the chair at the head of the table drag out and David plonk himself into it. David loosens his tie and top button. Stale cologne wafts out from under the shirt as he sags into the seat.

'Another successful dinner party, I think,' David mutters, pouring himself another round of wine. 'I should have nights off more often so that I can do things like that.'

'It is nice having people over,' Aaron answers, eyes focussed on clearing the table. Most of the tableware has made it to the dishwasher, leaving just the candles and their drinks on the table.

'Sit down Aaron, we need to talk,' David commands. Aaron sits down without hesitation. 'I think it's time we consider having children.'

'What do you mean?' Aaron asks blankly.

'Children, family. My career is where I need it to be and I think it's time we consider having children. My income is clearly enough to live off and you're home a lot so you'll be able to raise them. Of course, if I get another promotion we can hire you some help around the home, but you're organised enough to keep it under control. What are your thoughts?'

'Well. Um—I haven't really thought about children. I didn't think we would ever be one of those couples.'

'I think we can be. It will create a lot of great opportunities for us. Open some doors at the bank. They look kindly on working parents in the executive offices.'

'There's a lot to organise for it. Birth contracts take a lot of time,' Aaron thinks aloud.

'I've already spoken to the lawyers, they can have one done by the end of the week.'

'Okay. That's quick. But there are so many other questions. What arrangements do we want?'

'Obviously we won't do shared parenting with a female couple. It's too much hard work and commitment to keep it functioning for twenty years. Besides, there's a chance I could be transferred. Being sole parents makes it easier.'

'So we would…' Aaron explores, puzzled.

'Rent a womb from a breeder,' David states matter-of-factly. 'They're happy to take any money they can get and there are some who are happy to pop out children regularly if they get cash for it.'

'Wait, but how does that work? Won't that jeopardise our parental rights?'

'No, our rights will be fine,' David answers. 'We'll both appear on the birth certificate as the parents as per normal. No-one will know that we got it from a breeder, not that anyone asks anyway.'

'Um. I'm not sure. It's a lot of work.'

'Well, think about it,' David pulls out his phone. 'I have a meeting with the lawyers next week and an appointment tomorrow to have my sperm collected and tested. So no sex tonight, so I can provide a proper sample.'

'Your sperm?'

'Of course I should be the father, it's my career under the spotlight,' David mumbles off as he glares intently at the screen on his phone. A sense of urgency creases across his brow, and he scratches on his cheek in frustration. Aaron looks on knowingly as David scrolls down on the phone's screen.

'I have to go into the office,' he says. 'Timothy just messaged. The CEO has decided he's visiting tomorrow instead of next week, so now we have to collate a week's worth of data before the morning meeting.'

'That's okay,' Aaron recites. 'I'll just be tidying up.'

'Thanks,' David says shoving his chair back. The sudden movement drags noisily on the tiles. David walks over to the coat hanger and swings his jacket on. 'Oh, and start thinking about the child. I will need your signature before I see the lawyers next week.'

Aaron nods solemnly at David's back as he struts out of the room and out of the apartment. Aaron hears the door lock and silence fall over the room, leaving him to ponder over a child being thrust into his life. He plays with the goblet between his fingers, letting the glass drag heavily across the tablecloth. The folds in the fabric ripple out towards the edge of the table. Aaron plays the images in his mind as if it were water shivering out on an azure sea, but this escape fails to provide a clear route away from his thoughts. He tries to drag his mind back to the idea of a baby bopping around the apartment. The immaculate leather couch turns to smears of vomit and faeces. The sharp glass corners on the coffee table shatter in a broken mess on the floor. Screams wail down the hallway.

Aaron jumps up from his seat to retract his mind from the horror. He quickly distracts himself by removing the wine and the last of the goblets from the table. He rushes to fold the tablecloth, revealing the solid redwood underneath. He lazily flicks the crumbs into the sink and throws the tablecloth into the laundry basket, then returns to survey the tidiness of the living spaces. The rooms have returned to their usual state as if untouched by the sudden intrusion of guests. Aaron brushes himself off, satisfied with the condition of the apartment.

An sudden wave of exhaustion flushes over Aaron as he heads to his bedroom. The automatic directions of his relaxing muscles guides him into the master bedroom. The king-size bed looms in the centre of the room with a red and gold patterned cover lying crisply on top. Aaron strips down to his underwear and places his folded clothes on a seat next to the teak dresser. His skin cries out in pleasure as he slides into his silk pyjamas. A weight rises from his chest as he eases under the sheets. From his comfortable position he can see through the walk-in robe and to the vast space that is the ensuite.

Why children? he thinks. *Why now? We've never spoken about kids before.* Aaron shakes his head to divert himself from his concerns. He reaches over to his bedside table and pulls a novel out from the top drawer. The tattered cover feels flimsy in his hand. The cheap romance novel is imprinted in his imagination. Undiscouraged by the number of times he has read the book before, Aaron opens it and loses himself in the terrible writing. Each misspelled word and fragmented phrase read blissfully in his mind as a diversion from the perfection he has found in his real life. *Maybe that's why I'm afraid. I don't want change.* He shakes his head again to concentrate on the discoloured paper.

The hero of the novel, a military man, is swept off his feet by the exotic carpenter Diego. Aaron laughs at the concept of the novel. He has read many similar books while waiting for David to come to bed yet this one shines through as a clear favourite. The impossible plot line, the useless air of hopeful dreaming, encapsulate him in a manner he can't achieve with other romance novels. He chuckles to himself at the thought of the names: Diego and Mike. An impossible love between the boring, rigid man and the intriguing stranger.

Aaron starts reading from the dog-eared page and nestles further into the bed ready for the dreamy sex scene pumped to an explosive level with steamy descriptions. *It doesn't sound even close to reality. It's too silly. It's nothing like anything David and I do*, Aaron snickers to himself.

2.

AARON ROLLS OVER and stretches his arm across an empty bed. He sleepily squeezes the sheets knowing there wouldn't be anyone next to him. *Wishful thinking.* His eyes blink to clear the sleepy veil. A gentle morning glow is already spreading across the room. From the bed Aaron can see the reflective shine of the early sun on the buildings around them. He reaches for his phone, the screen flashes awake to tell him it's still early. Aaron groans. *I'm not going back to sleep now*, he thinks.

Aaron slides out of bed and straightens the sheets so that they again look untouched and perfect. Stumbling, he makes his way to the shower to splash himself alert. Sunlight streams through broad windows, illuminating the twin basins, the free-standing bath, the open shower, and the sprawl of tiles between them. The artificial flowers look gorgeously real under the fresh sunlight.

Aaron strips and steps into the shower. The rush of water pummels him awake. The massaging torrent touches him intimately. He begins to rub himself in hastened motions. He moves through the steps of cleaning, each area of flesh receiving sparse attention before he finishes with a quick rinse.

Outside the shower he pats himself down ready for his beauty treatment. The bottles of all-natural cleansers and gentle moisturisers queue in ranks like soldiers inside his basin cupboard. Aaron manoeuvres through the production line of cleansers, pressing upwards as he washes and moisturises his cheeks and forehead. The routine proceeds as usual, leaving Aaron's mind blank and unoccupied, anticipating the coffee promised at the end of his ritual.

Next to him the second sink sits dry. A single razor and toothbrush sit in a cup on the sink, both looking like they've never been used. *We may as well use work's money*, Aaron thinks, knowing that David's bathroom at work sees a regular rotation of fresh razors and toothbrushes at the bank's expense.

Aaron shakes his head and walks out the bathroom to find track pants and a gym shirt to spend his morning in. A click resonates from the kitchen. A growing hiss follows, signalling to Aaron that his prized coffee machine is heating up for the day. Music begins playing from back in the bedroom. Aaron follows its rising, nauseating tune to his phone and silences it. *The day can begin now*, he thinks, walking out to the kitchen.

Aaron surveys the pristine kitchen surrounding him. Small pots of fresh herbs grow under an artificial sunlight cage in the corner. The coffee machine puffs its final belch of steam as it reaches optimum temperature. Its stainless steel matches the rest of the appliances. Aaron walks over and begins his final preparation before he finds housework to consume his day. The grinder sparks alight as soon as he touches the switch. The blissful waft of roasted beans wanders through the air. Aaron greedily inhales the fresh smell of the coffee.

The instant rush of caffeine triggers his mind. *So is that why David hasn't wanted sex for a while?* Aaron ponders. *He's been waiting to test his sperm. Children! Why does he want children suddenly? Does that mean he'll want sex tonight if he comes home? Of course, stupid, he's having a stressful meeting today.* Desire washes over Aaron. He has an important task to prepare for now. Eagerness teases him, knowing he needs to be ready for his husband when he comes home.

An idea appears in Aaron's mind, and titillates him as he thinks it over. He works through the potential problems, the timing required, the unknown state of David's schedule. *The appointment would need to be in the afternoon, leaving his after work drinks time free.* Aaron smiles, committed to the idea. He sips on his coffee and runs through the timing and preparation needed for his plan. Having himself ready would be easy. He could only hope that David would be available and willing.

A moment of concern strikes Aaron. He hasn't visited David at work for years and doesn't call anymore, especially when David is coming home late. Aaron picks his teeth with his thumb nail as he thinks anxiously. The click of his nail quickly irritates him. He places both hands on his coffee mug and starts attacking the ceramic with tiny agitated taps of his fingers.

It will be fine, Aaron thinks. *I'll take him food. His favourite food. Pie and a crispy pork belly salad. He can't say no to that, and then we take it from there. It will be romantic, just like when we were dating.* A confident smile returns to Aaron. The pride in his work shines in his eyes.

Aaron downs the last of the coffee and starts his work in the kitchen. He pulls his baking equipment out from under the bench. *First the trial run and then the proper pastry*, he confirms to himself. He pulls the pork pieces out of the freezer to thaw while he begins on the pie, which he can eat for lunch to test the quality.

The day passes in a buzz of activity and passion. Aaron's kitchen remains clean despite the quantity of ingredients passing over the bench and stove. On a rack the final pie sits to cool to a transportable temperature. Aaron fiddles with the salad, which sits in a container ready to go. He sprinkles the crispy pork bits on top of the dressed salad and seals the lid.

Against the reflective door of the refrigerator he checks his own presentation. Satisfied there are no flour or sauce splashes on his skin he leaves the kitchen for the wardrobe. Inside the selections hang evenly spaced before him. He can see each potential option without moving a single fibre. He eyes off a handstitched suit hanging near the centre. The lower neckline and tight shirt always get him looks. He delicately holds the bottom of the jacket and swings the suit out for him to see from a new angle. Happy with his choice he whips off his house clothes and slides into the welcoming fabric of the suit. The mirror shows a gratifying sight for Aaron. He can see the small sprout of chest hair and the full shape of his toned legs against the material of the pants.

Aaron gathers himself and heads downstairs with the food to hail a taxi. Traffic on the main road outside never ceases to flow. Outside he spots three taxis cruising slowly in front of the apartment buildings. Their dawdling pace drags them slowly near the pavement and out of the main traffic flow. Aaron signals the first one and jumps in the back as soon as it pulls up.

'To the Central Bank Building please,' he states to the driver.

'Right away, sir,' the middle-aged driver replies.

The aroma of freshly baked pie fills the taxi. Aaron smiles to himself. A small thrill of surprising David at work sends flutters to his heart. He still hasn't decided on what to do with the children idea. He smiles to himself again. *None of that matters. Tonight is about us and some quality time.*

Aaron looks forwards and sees the afternoon traffic backing up in front of them. The short distance to the bank could be easily walked, Aaron knew this, but didn't want to risk it with the food. A shadow on the driver's face calls Aaron's attention. He stares at the rear vision mirror directly at the distracted driver. A red and purple bruise presses angrily against the driver's cheek. A dark red mark forms a fresh scab on his lip.

'Excuse me, are you okay?' Aaron asks instantly at the sight of injury.

'Huh, sorry what?' The driver feigns. 'Oh yeah, that's nothing to worry about.'

'It looks new,' Aaron insists. A flush of worry consumes him. 'Are you sure you're okay? A doctor really should look at something like that to make sure you're fit to drive.'

'It's nothing. I'm fine.'

'I think you should pull over, I can take another taxi.'

'NO! Please don't,' the driver implores. 'I'm fine. Please don't get out. I need the work. I can't lose another job. If I go to the doctor they will say I can't drive and I will lose my job. Please, I have a family.'

'What? Why would they fire you? How did it happen?' Aaron pauses. 'You're a breeder!' Aaron accuses. He shrinks into himself, embarrassed. 'Oh my gods, I'm so sorry. I didn't mean to say that. You're a hetero. I mean, you're queer. I'm sorry I don't want to offend I just don't know the correct term anymore.'

'That's okay. You don't need to apologise,' the driver dismisses Aaron's concerns. 'I just can't lose anymore fares. My boss will fire me just for who I am if he could.'

'But what about you?' Aaron composes himself. 'That doesn't look too good,' he motions towards the bruise.

'It's nothing. I'm used to it. I've received worse. This is the worst breeder beaters can do in daylight. Night is another story.'

The driver's blasé nature startles Aaron, yet a strange feeling mingles in with his concern.

'You're fine being beaten?' Aaron asks.

'No, of course not,' the driver shrugs, pulling into the right lane. 'But I'm one of the lucky ones. I have a job and I don't cruise at night so I know my family is safe. Here we are.'

Aaron gives him a sympathetic glance while handing over a few notes.

'Keep the change,' Aaron says.

'No, I can't really.' Aaron ignores the driver and climbs out of the car. 'I really can't.'

'You must need it more than I do,' Aaron fakes offence. The driver drops his eyes to the passenger seat.

'Thank you sir,' he says. The windows wind up and the driver pulls back out into the traffic.

Aaron turns away from the road and confronts the massive structure in front of him. The dated building still stands proudly amongst its modern neighbours. A continuing presence of legacy grips onto the outside structure of the building. From memory Aaron knows the inside is much newer than the exterior presents.

'Good evening, may I help you,' a porter greets Aaron the moment he steps over the threshold.

'Yes please,' Aaron returns the courtesy. 'I'm here with a delivery for Mr Jones on the twelfth floor. My name is Aaron. You will no doubt get his assistant Timothy, who knows what to do.'

'Very good.' The porter retrieves a phone from his belt and presses the memorised extension. 'Good evening. I have an Aaron to see Mr Jones. Yes. Yes. Very good. Thank you.' He returns to Aaron. 'I'll buzz you up.'

Aaron nods and follows the porter towards the nearest staff elevator. Aaron recognises the procedure. He waits three feet back from the elevator for further instruction. The porter takes the lead and presses for an elevator. After the ding of the elevator's arrival, its doors open and the porter swipes his card in front of the sensor inside the carriage.

'If you're here past six you will need to ask the security at reception to check and buzz you out of the building,' the porter instructs as he presses David's floor number.

'Thank you,' Aaron repeats.

Aaron rises and drops eagerly on his toes. In the reflection of the elevator he can see the perfect lines and bumps on his suit. The green bag of food hangs next to him as a memento of his mission. The elevator rises slowly. Aaron's body twitches from the blood flushing through him excitedly. A tingling sensation runs over his skin. Aaron taps impatiently, waiting for the old wheeze of the elevator to tell him he has arrived.

Aaron steps out of the door and spots Timothy waiting

for him to one side. Timothy's eyes run a slow, scolding inspection down Aaron. Aaron notes the tightness of Timothy's business shirt. The buttons press against the sculpted thin layer of muscle under the fabric. His pants are hoisted tight to show off an obvious bulge under the fly. Timothy clears his throat.

'Mr Jones is in an incredibly important meeting right now,' Timothy imitates sincerity. 'Is there anything I can help you with?'

'Yes, you can fetch David for me,' Aaron says drily.

'I'm afraid he is very busy. I'm not sure he can step out right now.' Aaron spots a flash of hatred cross Timothy's face. The corner of Timothy's lip curls in a slight twitch. 'Unless there's anything else I can do for you, pass on a message or something, I think it's best if you leave. We are very busy.'

'You're a bank, of course you're busy,' Aaron keeps his voice neutral. 'David's a very intelligent man, as you know, he most certainly can manage to see me for a moment without it impacting on his work.'

Timothy glares at Aaron. The twitch in his lip flickers intensely.

'Fine,' he surrenders. Timothy struts out of the room.

Aaron stands confidently on the spot. The dry movement of the air conditioning hugs around him and pulls at his skin. The smell of pie continues to seep from the bag next to him. Aaron feels the steam reaching up to his knuckles from the bag. David rounds the corner with a snap of his head and stares down Aaron.

'What?' he whispers his demand.

'I bought you some dinner,' Aaron holds up the bag proudly. 'I made one of your favourites.'

'You didn't need to come in for that,' David rubs his eyebrows. 'Timothy has already taken care of dinner for us.'

'I didn't just bring you dinner,' Aaron ignores the mention of Timothy's name. 'I thought since you had your test today we could duck into your office and spend a little time together.' Aaron holds his spare arm out to highlight the effort put into his trim appearance. David stares blankly at Aaron.

'We're very busy. The CEO has instigated a new modelling system for my department, which he wants operational by the end of the year,' David continues. 'You can leave the food though. We will probably get hungry again later. I should be home after that though, if everything runs as planned,' David grabs the bag and turns ready to resume his work.

'David,' Aaron calls after him. David stops and looks over his shoulder. Words freeze inside Aaron's throat. A muddled assortment of thoughts blocks his ability to speak. Timothy steps out from the corner and glares down at Aaron, his hands gripping onto several folders to emulate importance. 'Never mind,' he finishes and turns to leave the building.

The ride down the elevator drags slowly. Aaron hunches towards the floor, his head hanging in defeat. *I'm such an idiot*, Aaron smacks his forehead. The ding of the door opening wakes Aaron from his self-loathing. Outside the porter smiles at him.

'Good timing,' he chimes. 'We were just about to lock up for the night. No need to buzz you out.'

Aaron forces out a smile of thanks and heads swiftly to the door. The evening air cools Aaron's skin. He folds his arms to hug himself. Disappointment shivers through him, much like the cold. He looks down the street as the lights flickering to life paint the night in bleak colours.

Aaron starts walking away from the bank. His feet take

him roughly in the direction of home, each resolute step back towards the apartment is counteracted by another, hesitant and dragging. The whoosh of cars and people eager to get home pass unnoticed by Aaron. He traps his thoughts, forcing a blankness to hide the rush of self-doubt from his brimming mind.

A sandwich board stops Aaron in his path with a hard slap against his leg. Aaron pats the chalk dust off his pant leg as he reads the smudged text. *Oh look, it's happy hour still,* he thinks to himself, *I could do worse.* Aaron pushes open the pub door and enters the dimly lit room. The sticky-sour smell of spilt beer fills his nostrils. Two bartenders move swiftly behind the hardwood bar, smiling at the workers unwinding their drinks. *The day's over for them as well then,* Aaron thinks.

Aaron walks slowly up to the bar and sits on a cushioned stool. Nearby a female couple snuggle behind two glasses of sparkling wine. A group of men are deep in debate around their beers. Older businessmen lean importantly on the bar as if still at work negotiating deals.

'What will it be?' the young bartender asks. Aaron reads the name Cameron on his badge.

'Something strong will do,' Aaron says non-committedly.

'Rough day?' Cameron inquires.

'Anti-climactic.' A small smile sneaks into the corner of Aaron's mouth.

'I think I have just the thing. Are you partial to tequila?'

'Dangerously so,' Aaron smirks.

Cameron smiles and starts pouring ice, tequila and liquor from a bottle that Aaron doesn't recognise into a tumbler. Cameron garnishes the drink with a slice of lime and pushes it across the bar.

'There you go mate. Make that one five bucks.' Aaron hands over the cash. 'Cheers. Let me know if you need anything else.'

Aaron eyes Cameron as he walks away. A confident sway shifts through Cameron's hips and the sharp muscular lines of his back lift Aaron a little out his depression. He takes a sip on his drink. The harsh zap of tequila warms his lips the moment they meet. The burn is soothed by a sugary cleanse in the aftertaste. Aaron's eyes widen at the sudden buzz flowing through him.

'I said it was just the thing,' Cameron yells from the other end of the bar.

Aaron raises his glass to toast the bartender and takes another sip. The intoxicating whirl of the first few fingers loosens the thoughts he suppressed when leaving the bank. *It could have worked,* Aaron thinks. *It's just a matter of timing. Maybe next time. Maybe I should book in with David. That would mean dealing with Timothy.* He spins the glass on its base, watching the circles of condensation form on the bar and be dragged away with the next turn. *I just have to be patient. He'll notice eventually.*

'It really was a tough day, huh?' Cameron interrupts his thoughts. 'Would you like another?' He nods at the empty glass in Aaron's hand.

'Gods, wow,' Aaron says, realising he has already downed the entire glass. 'Sure.'

'Mind if I join you? The rush for happy hour is almost over and I'm about to clock off?'

Aaron looks into Cameron's eyes, where he finds a playful glint among the blue. The youth in Cameron's face is almost hidden by his finely groomed stubble.

'Why not?' Aaron responds.

Cameron whips out a second glass and mixes together two more drinks. He hands one to Aaron and sips on the other.

'So, what do you do?' Cameron asks.

'I'm a homemaker.'

'Homemaker? You look too young to be married. I can't imagine myself getting married until I'm much older, and I find the right guy.'

'I'm sure there's a right guy out there for you,' Aaron takes a sip of his drink. *Why is he talking to me? Is he just being friendly?* 'Are you here full-time?'

'Nah, this is one of many jobs for me. I can't stay in the one place all the time or I start getting bored and depressed. I'm always on the move from job to job. Keeps it fresh. If you ever want to step out from your husbandly duties, I'm sure I could hook you up with extra work, a little something to pass the time.'

'What makes you think I want a job?' Aaron stares curiously at Cameron. Cameron doesn't flinch as he takes a sip of his drink.

'Playing homemaker can't be your only work, unless you've got children on the go.' Aaron cringes at the mention of children and swallows half the glass to remove the painful thoughts. 'Oh, I'm sorry. I should know by now bringing up the topic of children affects everyone differently.'

'Yeah, and the effects kick in even before you've started,' Aaron grumbles.

'Just starting out, hey?'

'In theory. It was kind of thrust upon me,' Aaron loosens some more. 'This might be my last decent drink before the long ride begins and I have to devote all my time and energy to a child.'

'Better make it a long drink then,' Cameron says, topping them up again. 'How does something like that get dumped on you?'

'My husband is very determined. He knows what he wants, and then just makes it happen. That's one of the reasons I married him. Oh crap!'

'What?' Cameron straightens up at Aaron's exclamation.

'I need to get home. I haven't cooked dinner or cleaned anything yet, in case David comes home,' Aaron sighs. His body feels heavy as he forces himself back into his rigid routine. *I can't rely on just the pie*, the voice in his head hums.

'So, David is it? Tell him I said hi,' Cameron holds his hand out for Aaron's glass. Aaron pours the last of it down his throat, the chill of the ice cools his lips. 'And if you're ever nearby again and just want to chat I'm either here, or working in the Spring Street Art Gallery, or over at the Glenwood Bookshop Café, or if it's late or a weekend I'm probably on shift at the DD Club.'

'The DD Club?' Aaron asks standing, readying himself to leave.

'Oh, you really are married,' Cameron teases. 'The Driller's Dungeon Club. It's a themed bar and club catering to most kinked tastes,' Cameron winks. Aaron smiles back, to hide his confusion while taking in one last frame of Cameron's vibrant and intriguing features. His solid build stands proudly behind the bar as Aaron heads to the door and paces home.

Aaron is quick to make it back home. The door echoes through the empty apartment as Aaron closes it behind him. *That's just to be expected*. Despite knowing David won't be home until late, Aaron prepares dinner. *Another dinner*. The routine has kept the relationship together and means

David remains free to take networking opportunities any-where, including home for food. The food prep is dull, but the tedium evaporates, continuous replays of Cameron's smile through Aaron's mind. Aaron smiles too, reflecting on their playful conversation, and the invitation to talk again sparks a strange sense of curiosity. Aaron never gets to go out without David anymore, and just getting a drink alone was strange. *It was fun*, Aaron pauses in his thoughts. A wide grin stretches across his lips. Unseen wrinkles curl up around his beaming eyes. *It was fun*.

Later that evening, dinner in the fridge and the house clean, Aaron finds himself in bed staring at the same page of his novel. Having managed to open the book, he sits blankly glaring at the one page. His finger runs gently back and forth along one edge in absentminded distraction as his mind drifts further and further from the romance sprawled before him. The thought of laughing and cooking with Cameron plays in his mind. Cameron smiles as Aaron holds a tray of food in front of him.

A sudden crash from the front door startles Aaron from his fantasies. He recognises the heavy steps smacking onto the tiles. David's custom-made shoes echo through the apartment with each tired step.

'Good evening,' Aaron says as David enters the bedroom.

David groans a response and sits down on the edge of the bed. He unties his shoes and pushes them, socks and all, onto the floor. He stands slowly and removes the rest of his clothes, letting them all flop into a mess on the ground. Aaron watches carefully as David turns to face him, their eyes meeting in a stare. A sense of familiarity floats in the air between them. A flash shimmers in David's eyes.

David slides off his underwear and stares down at Aaron.

He holds the branded elastic for a moment before adding it to the pile of clothes on the floor. David stands naked at the end of the bed. Aaron gazes at his husband's nude form. The slow growth of David's belly over several years has lead to a solid bump at his stomach, while his nipples point ever-further towards the ground. Between his legs his penis stands erect.

Aaron pushes his pyjama pants off and folds them onto the bedside table. David smirks greedily and slides under the quilt next to Aaron. Aaron prepares to please his husband. He rolls over onto his side and bends his buttocks outwards for David. He wriggles into a warm embrace against his pillow and waits. He can feel the bed shake as David adds moisture to his penis and shuffles closer to Aaron. David presses his belly against Aaron's back. Moist heat seeps into Aaron's skin. The coolness of the lubricant makes Aaron shiver, shortly followed by the expected sting of penetration. He bites into the pillow to stop himself from moving away from his husband and the pain. David pushes his erection harder into Aaron in a few steady movements. As quickly as it began, a final thrust signals the end of their lovemaking. David sighs a final shiver and retracts his penis from Aaron.

'Good night,' David says as he switches the light off and rolls over onto his side of the bed.

'Good night,' Aaron responds.

Aaron lays still, not wanting to disturb David as he falls asleep. Within minutes David's heavy breathing becomes shuddering snores. Aaron takes the opportunity to slide out of bed and freshen up the tenderness left by David. Aaron retrieves a moist towelette from the stash hidden in the bottom drawer of the bathroom and wipes himself clean. A strange familiarity comforts Aaron. The routine of their intimacy has returned. *Normality*, Aaron sighs. He flushes his wipes and sneaks back into bed next to David. The rhythm of David's snoring soothes Aaron as he dozes off into his own dreams.

3.

'WHAT DOES THAT MEAN?' David shouts. The sound of David's frustration jolts Aaron awake. 'Right, so there's nothing I can do to change it?'

Aaron rubs his eyes and stretches himself out of bed. Aaron's shoulder pops as he extends his arm, a smile of relief flashing across his face as his muscles relax. He lifts himself off the mattress, remakes the bed and turns his attention to the mess on the floor. David's clothes remain on the carpet where he dumped them the night before, his underwear clumped on top. Aaron straightens his own pyjamas before reaching down and scrunching the dirty clothes together to put in the laundry basket. A heavy scent of air freshener and fragrance blossoms from David's clothes. The usual aroma of the ground coffee in the kitchen fails to penetrate the thick scent of office odours. He passes through the wardrobe, tidying David's mess as he moves.

A crash echoes from the living room. Aaron hears David curse angrily, then his swearing fades to mutters. Aaron rushes to dispose of the washing and duck out to the living room. He finds David bent over, scooping up his broken phone.

'Is everything okay in here?' Aaron asks.

'No, the bloody thing's destroyed again,' David's words disappear into mumbles.

'Careful, don't cut yourself. I'll grab the dustpan.'

'Don't bother. I've got all of it. It didn't completely shatter.'

Aaron remains standing at the edge of the room. His eyes follow David's movements, waiting for any instruction.

'I heard back from the reproductive clinic,' David discloses eventually, his voice subdued, 'the semen analysis indicates my sperm count is too low and my motility too poor to ever hope of fathering children.'

Aaron's jaw drops in shock and disbelief at the news. A wave of pity surges over him as the many implications break the surface of his thoughts, and the resignation on David's face adds an eddy of uncertainty and dismay. Aaron shivers through the churning wash of emotions but keeps his arms to his side, knowing how important is was to remain neutral, lest David's reaction escalate.

David rubs his forehead, pushing up thick folds of skin under the pressure of his fingers.

'We just can't have a family. Godsdamnit! I won't be able to build the working parent credentials I'll need to become an upper-level executive.'

'But what about my sperm?' Aaron whispers.

David's eyes shoot up and glare at Aaron. Aaron falls silent and instinctively wraps himself in his own arms.

'What about yours?' David's voice rises. 'We're talking about mine! I'm never going to be a father.' Aaron opens his mouth but resists speaking further. 'If I can't have my own kids I don't want any. What kind of banker can't produce his own offspring?! That bloody clinic is good for nothing.'

'We could still have children together,' Aaron suggests, throwing aside his own misgivings about having a family in favour of David's wishes, 'I'm sure there's some way that you can become a father.'

'Are you stupid or just deaf? I can't have children. Any children we have now won't be mine. Why the hell would I want to be a father to someone else's kid?' Aaron swallows down the hurt that swells against his throat. 'Now I'm going to get old, die and leave no legacy. My bloodline stops with me.' David throws his arms up in defeat. 'I need to get out and clear my head. I'm going to the office early. Work will get my mind off this nonsense.'

David storms from the room. Aaron hears the crash of the bin lid, signalling the phone's complete demise. *He'll have another phone at work*, Aaron reminds himself to soothe his anxiety. He slowly walks to the kitchen and hones in on the coffee machine. His eyes focus intently down on the shine of the steel while his ears follow the noises of David preparing to leave. A rough bashing of cupboard doors marks David's movements through the apartment.

The coffee machine hisses through the last drops of espresso. Aaron removes the mug and pours the frothed milk into the coffee. His usual precision latte art plops into a random lump of white at the top of the mug. Aaron ignores the overloaded froth and sips on the edge of the coffee.

'I'll be late home,' David grunts from the front door. A final thud and silence falls throughout the apartment.

Aaron's shoulders slump at the sound of the door locking. The stiffness that had clamped around his spine gently loosens. But even as his body relaxes, pained thoughts rush through his mind. *Why couldn't we use my sperm? What's wrong with me?* His eyes glaze over as he disappears into his own head. *Why does it matter who the biological father is? We'll both still be dads to any children we have.*

Aaron's agonised rumination persists until memories of a calming smile flash across his eyes. Cameron's intrigue and playfulness buzz in Aaron's thoughts. His relaxed nature infects Aaron with a restful mindset, and thoughts of the seemingly impossible family evaporate. *Will I find him at the café or the gallery?* Aaron wonders for a second time before doubt bursts in his mind. Aaron shakes his head to chase out the dreamy thoughts of Cameron, guilt rushing to take its place. Aaron's back spasms once more into a series of knots on his spine. He groans through the ache.

Aaron sets down his mug as his eyes are drawn out the kitchen window to the buzz of activity that hums below him. The city swells into its daily enterprise. The musing continues. *The café or the gallery?* The doubt falls away at the thought of stepping out of the house by himself to see Cameron. A surge of adrenaline twitches through his fingers. The decision is made. He places his half-drunk coffee on the sink and hurries into the bedroom.

Café or gallery, café or gallery? Aaron pauses in the middle of the wardrobe with his clothes presented before him. *Smart casual*, he decides, walking to his collared shirts and pants.

Aaron's chest lightens as he collects his keys and wallet and heads out of the apartment. He notices that a skip has found its way into his step, and excitement fills him with an unfamiliar warmth. *I'll be back to clean before David gets home*, he confirms to himself.

Café or gallery? he repeats to himself. *It has to be one of them. I didn't finish get to my coffee, so café first. If he's not there at least I'll get a coffee.* Aaron nods as he steps into the elevator and pushes the button for the ground floor. *Glenwood Bookshop Café*, Aaron remembers. He recalls purchasing a romance novel from there, but doesn't remember ever seeing Cameron.

The trek to the shop is a twenty minute stroll, but under influence of the thrilling sense of anticipation Aaron makes it within sight of the bookshop's sign at a speedy gallop. The curving letters of the sign hover bright and yellow across the top of the shop window. An antique planter box underneath it provides a cottage feel to the store. Aaron's chest rises, his smile lifting with the airiness inside him.

'I knew you couldn't resist me.' Aaron hears as he closes on the bookshop. 'It was only a matter of time.' Aaron spins around to be greeted by Cameron's widening grin. A sense of calm settles over Aaron the moment he spots the cheekiness in Cameron's eyes.

'It's hard to go anywhere without seeing you, you're everywhere,' Aaron responds timidly. He can feel a small blush heat his cheeks.

'Well, you've found me,' Cameron takes Aaron by the crook of the arm and leads him towards the bookshop. 'And you beat me to work. It's early still so I suppose I could make a coffee for us both so we can chat before I have to actually do any work.'

'Sounds horrible,' Aaron jokes. 'The work thing, not us having coffee together. That sounds nice. I mean lovely. Sorry, I'm muddling my words.' Aaron pauses to collect his thoughts. His cheeks glow a deeper shade of red.

'So coffee it is?' Cameron says as he opens the shop door.

Cameron steps aside to let Aaron enter first. The fresh smell of coffee and baked goods makes the saliva spill into Aaron's mouth. The coffee machine whirs and hums behind a counter near the door. The true depth of the shop is hidden by the narrow façade out front. Five rows of shelves run parallel to each other and disappear into the shadows beyond Aaron's vision. Plush armchairs surround small wooden tables throughout the entire store. The random collection of furniture doesn't have any matching items amongst them. A small cluster of early customers huddle on one of the couches and quietly chat amongst themselves. Small lattes sit between them, the steam slowly dying away.

'I forgot how nice this place is,' Aaron says.

'It is pretty cute, isn't it? It can get a bit dusty and stuffy around the shelves sometimes.' Cameron steps behind the counter and stands with an air of faux professionalism. 'How can I help you today, sir?' he says with a deadpan face. 'Might I suggest the croissant? Baked fresh this morning.' The butler's voice drops away. 'Well I think this morning. Who knows? What I do know is they've been in the freezer for months before we whack them in the oven here. So latte for you?'

'Yes please,' Aaron smiles.

'Take a seat anywhere. I won't be long.'

Aaron turns to the room. He picks a two-seater green lounge on the far side from the coffee counter. The cushion embraces him as he lowers himself into it, and Aaron allows himself to fully relax as he sinks into the couch's soft fabric. From the seat he can see someone walk casually amongst the bookshelves, grabbing books out and moving them to a new place without reading the blurbs. Aaron guesses it is one of the staff and follows them as they glance over the titles, her finger running along the binders as she reads. In Aaron's mind an odd sense of intimacy appears between the woman and the books as she touches along the spines.

'Here we are,' Cameron announces as he places two lattes down and sits next to Aaron. 'That's Cheryl,' he adds, 'she runs the shop. No-one knows more about the books in here than she does. Her knowledge of where to find everything is insane.'

'What's she doing at the moment? It looks very personal.'

'They're like her babies,' Cameron says casually. 'She takes care of them and keeps everything in order. It makes my job so much easier because I can find a book without looking for long. Where the computer says a book is, it is. So, what brings you here today?'

The sudden change in conversation startles Aaron. He hadn't actually thought of a good reason other than to see Cameron. *Is it too weird to say it was just for him?*

'I—um—I needed to get out,' Aaron stutters.

'Is being a homemaker starting to exhaust you?' Cameron winks.

'Actually yes,' Aaron admits. His shoulders slump back into the sofa. 'No, I mean—I don't know.'

'Well, you do look more relaxed. Does that mean the family planning is going well?'

Cameron takes a quick sip of his latte. Aaron feels his face crunch into a frown. He shakes his head and reaches for his own coffee to break his thought process. Cameron watches on, a smirk twitching his left cheek.

'I can't be sure whether or not you're happy with the idea of children,' Cameron says over the top of his glass.

'I'm confused,' Aaron confesses, 'David found out he can't have children so now it looks like we aren't going to have any.'

'What about you? Can you have kids?'

'I don't know. I suggested that to David but he wants our children to be his own genetic offspring. But now that he can't have kids he doesn't want any. It's all happening too fast. A couple of nights ago he announced we were having children and now it's all off again and I'm just so confused. At first I didn't want children but as soon as David said he couldn't have biological ones I offered help so that we could become parents. I'm not sure what I want.' Cameron looks upon Aaron with a ponderous stare. His lips don't move other than to sip his coffee. Aaron matches his eyes. 'I think I just needed someone to talk to and something different to do for the day.'

'Aww,' Cameron straightens up, his full smile glowing at Aaron. 'And I'm the one you thought of when you needed to talk to someone. You don't even know me. That's either sweet or desperate.' Cameron jokingly pokes Aaron in the arm. The gentle touch leaves a hot circle on Aaron's flesh, firing off a wave of tiny prickles.

'I suppose I don't know you other than as the guy from the bar.'

'People do more with people they know less.'

'What does that mean?' Aaron's brow furrows.

'Well—you know,' Cameron prods. Aaron doesn't respond. 'I'm sure you've had your share of hook-ups before getting married.' Aaron shakes his head. 'Seriously? You've only been with David?'

'Yes, we were high school sweethearts. I've never wanted anyone else. I sort of had a traditional upbringing.'

'That's sweet. And it's all gone to plan for you two?'

'Up until now, yes. Very much so. Everything David has planned for his career has worked out. We've had everything we could ever need or want. These difficulties around having a family are a setback but I'm sure we will work through it.' Aaron feels his eyes droop at the thought of plans not working out for David. He forces a smile onto his face. 'So, enough about me. What's up with you? Who are you? Other than a free spirit with too many jobs on the go, of course.'

'Not enough I say,' Cameron laughs. 'Well, where to start. I'm Cameron. Leo. Twenty-one. Single. I've lived here my whole life, still live at home with my mums. But it's a huge house, I have my own place out back with a kitchenette and bathroom so I'm pretty much independent of them.'

'That's nice that you can still be at home. I can't imagine living at home with my dads now. We would drive each other mad.'

'It's fine for the moment until my brother comes home. He's on tour with the army. We have to share the small flat. Let's just say we don't always do well when we are constantly within each other's proximity.'

'Gosh, is he away often then?'

'Yeah, about six months of the year. He actually gets home tomorrow, which is why, just by pure coincidence of course, that I have accepted every party invite and shift at work I possibly can for the next few months.'

'But when will you be home?'

'As little as possible. Only when I need somewhere to sleep and wash.'

Cameron's carefree attitude infects Aaron with a sudden calmness. The freedom in Cameron's life entices Aaron with a sense of endless possibilities.

'What do you want to do in the long term?' Aaron asks.

'No idea,' Cameron shrugs. 'I've always been told to do whatever I want and be anything I want, as long as it involves marriage, so I decided to work and to save for travels. I wouldn't mind getting overseas sometime soon. I'll see if I can get a work visa while I'm there.'

'And then what?'

Cameron shrugs again. 'That's way too far into the future to worry about. My plans could change many times before then. How could anyone plan that far in advance?'

David does, Aaron holds himself back from saying it out loud.

'Excuse me,' Cheryl interrupts in a calm whisper. 'Cameron, could you please get the muffins out ready for the rush? The regulars are about to start coming through.'

'Sure thing, Cheryl,' Cameron nods. Cheryl turns and disappears back into the shelves. 'I guess that brings our date to a close,' Cameron smiles and swigs the last of his coffee. 'It's been great chatting. Where are you off to now?'

Aaron pauses, coffee near his chin. His options tick through his head easily. *Go home and prepare for David I guess.*

'Just off home,' Aaron says. 'Nothing planned yet.'

'See, you're getting there,' Cameron slaps him on the shoulder. 'Before you know it you will be jet-setting across the globe.' Cameron stands up and pauses for a moment. A look of contemplation flickers across his eyes. 'Do you know how to make coffee?'

'What? Me?' Aaron stutters.

'Yes you. Who else have I been talking to since getting here?'

'Yeah I know how to make coffee. Why?'

'Proper coffee, not the watery filtered stuff?'

'Yes. Espresso coffee. I have a machine and grinder at home I use all the time.'

'Sweet. Hold on.' Cameron turns and calls down the shelves. 'Cheryl?'

'Yes,' she answers in a neutral tone from behind the books.

'This is my friend Aaron.'

'Twenty-six, Virgo,' Aaron whispers.

'Twenty-six, Virgo,' Cameron continues. 'He makes coffee. Can I put him to work?'

'Sure,' Cheryl says without thought. 'But for tips only though. I can barely afford to keep you, Cameron.'

Cameron turns back down to Aaron. 'So it's settled then. You're working with me this morning.' Aaron's mouth opens but he can't muster a sound of protest. 'Don't worry, it's only a three-hour shift and I've spent most of it sitting down so far. You'll be fine. Come on.'

Cameron grabs Aaron's hand. The warmth of his touch burns against the cold sweat on Aaron's palm. Cameron leads him behind the counter and throws an apron at him.

'Here, chuck this on,' he says as he ties his own around his waist. 'I'll turn you into a shop boy before the day is over.'

'I've never done any of this before,' Aaron finally manages to protest. 'I've never had to work. What if I get something wrong?'

'You're starting to sound way too cute. Never had a job,' Cameron chuckles. 'It's never too late to get yourself one. Have you never had to worry about money?'

'No. Never. I've always had allowances either from my dads or David,' Aaron says, his hands behind his back perfecting the bow on the apron strings. 'I've kept everything in order around the house so that David can concentrate on work. A lot of his work used to be done at home but since his first decent promotion a couple of years back he's been working out of a nice office in the city.'

Cameron opens his mouth ready to keep talking but is cut off by the sound of the door opening. His smile shifts seamlessly from Aaron straight to the middle-aged lady bedecked in pants suit and loaded with briefcases.

'Morning Sharon,' Cameron says.

'Morning love,' Sharon answers. Cameron's infectious smile leaps across to the door and appears on Sharon's face. The stress around her eyes seems to evaporate the moment she sees Cameron.

'The usual is it?'

'Yes, and a chocolate croissant please, I feel like I might crash without a sugar hit.'

'Have a seat, it will be right over.'

A hint of concern appears in her eyes. She points between Cameron and Aaron.

'Are you training a replacement?' she asks.

'Not today,' Cameron says. Sharon's smile returns. 'He's a friend of mine I'm putting to work for the day. You get to be the first taster. Be gentle.'

'You know I will,' Sharon says playfully as she turns to take a seat on one of the couches.

'Do you know everyone?' Aaron asks quietly.

'Pretty much everyone who comes in here,' Cameron answers. 'Most of our regulars are in here every day or so. We need a double shot long black. Can you handle that?'

Aaron nods and turns to the coffee machine. The sleek device before him seems to be simply a larger version of his machine at home. The steamer nozzle is slightly longer and the switches light up but otherwise Aaron recognises the controls before him.

He takes his time brewing the coffee, knowing Cameron is watching behind him. The coffee dribbles out of the handle in a creamy trickle to leave a thick layer of light brown crema on the top of the long black.

'Not bad,' Cameron says.

Aaron turns to present the coffee on a saucer. Cameron leans casually on the counter, his left hip sticking into the air. He straightens up at the sight of the coffee and relieves Aaron of it.

'Won't be long,' he says, stepping away from the counter and towards Sharon with the coffee in one hand and croissant in another.

The sudden breeze of fresh air calls Aaron's attention back to the door. A semi-hunched figure in gym clothes creaks their way to the counter.

'Morning Cameron. I need coffee,' she croaks, her fingers digging through her purse for change.

Aaron recognises the blonde-tipped hair and small pearl earrings. The rest of her face remains hidden under the shadow of her hair.

'Aubrey?' he whispers.

'Huh, yeah,' Aubrey glances up. She blinks away the tired haze that coats her eyes as if confused about where she is. Her eyes light up suddenly. 'Oh Aaron. I didn't recognise you outside your apartment. I didn't know you worked here.' Her back stiffens and returns to the confident posture Aaron remembers from their dinner parties.

'I don't actually. I'm just here with—'

'Morning Aubrey. Big night?' Cameron cuts in as he returns to the counter.

'Um—yeah, kind of,' Aubrey glances between Cameron and Aaron, her eyes darting back and forth, gleaning as much information as she can find. 'I had a late night at work and then my PT kicked my butt this morning. I'll be feeling it all day.'

'Have you met Aaron already?'

'Oh yes, I go way back with his husband.' Aubrey turns back to Aaron. 'It's so strange seeing you out and about. I think I've only ever seen you at your house or at work functions.' Cameron laughs playfully. Aubrey turns back to Cameron. 'This guy makes the meanest pork roast I've ever had. I've tried following his recipe but it never comes out the same.'

'I didn't know that. The secrets you keep from people, Aaron,' Cameron says. 'So, latte then?'

'Yes please. The biggest you've got. It was lovely seeing you Aaron. Say hi to David for me,' Aubrey says. She drops change onto the counter and walks over to a small chair with a newspaper on it.

'Here, use this one,' Cameron says holding a giant disposable cup. 'It's such a small city when you think about it.'

Too true, Aaron thinks. Seeing Aubrey startles Aaron's mind. Confusion and doubt run rampant, pressing heavily against his chest. *How boring am I if people don't even remember seeing me out of my own kitchen?* Lost in thought, the warmth of the cup and fresh smell of ground coffee beans fail to register as Aaron goes through the motions of making the latte. Suddenly, he arrives at a decision.

'I need to go,' Aaron says with a start.

'What? Why?' Cameron asks.

'I—um—just remembered something I need to get done.' Aaron starts to remove his apron.

'Okay. I'm sure you do,' Cameron winks and nods towards Aubrey. 'Well here's my number.' Cameron takes Aaron's hand and gently prints a mobile number on to the back. 'If you're free tomorrow give me a call and we can go to the welcome home party tomorrow for my brother and his army mates. Mum says I have to make an effort, so I agreed to this one because, I have to admit, it's usually fun and there's heaps of free drinks and food. You'll enjoy it.'

'Sure, thanks.'

Aaron drops the apron on the counter and walks hurriedly towards the door. The sudden fresh air snatches him back from his fluster. Each step away from the bookshop and Aubrey soothes his nerves. *Why did I do that?* He looks down at the number on his hand. A little 'x' sits at the end of the phone number. He ponders to himself as he makes his way home. *It was just weird. Nothing to be worried about*, he tells himself. *I will run into people David knows outside of the apartment. I do have a life*. Doubt increases. *At least I think I do*. The weight of self-consciousness anchors his stomach, causing a wave of nausea to wash over him. *I do have a life?*

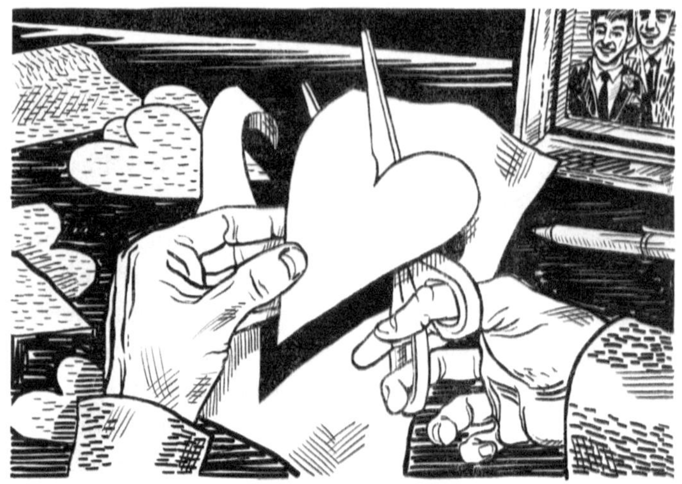

4.

THE LINGERING SCENT of coffee follows Aaron through the front door as he enters the apartment. The oiliness of the bookshop café clings to his clothes and hair as little reminders of his time with Cameron. Aaron eases the door shut and heads straight into the bathroom. He strips out of his clothes and places them into the washing basket.

Steam from the shower opens his pores the moment he steps into the large cubical. The hot water massages his naked skin. *Do I have a life?* Aaron repeats to himself. He stands still under the water letting the liquid trickle down the lines of his body. His hand rises to press against the warmth of his chest. Beneath the thickness he feels his heart beat. The thuds are calm and consistent. *At least physical life.* Aaron moved his hand down his abdomen. The bumps of his muscles press firm against the touch of his fingers. He follows them down to a tuff of hair rising from his groin as his hand passes over the pubic bone.

A twitch wakes him from his daydreaming. His hands snap out of their slow movements and resume the familiar automatic motions of washing himself. The soap runs across his skin to quickly clean it. As soon as his ritual is complete he switches off the tap and steps out of the shower.

As Aaron becomes immersed in the routine of drying another thought catches him, and he turns his head back to the shower with a cautious expression. *What happened there?* he thinks. *I was enjoying that.* He places a hand back onto his chest and feels around the shape of the muscles. A firmness pushes back against the touch of his fingers. Aaron presses harder, triggering a pleasurable ache to spasm across his chest. He reaches across to the other side with his hand and rubs his finger deep into the skin. He groans through the shuddering of each muscle.

Aaron shuts his eyes to focus his attention on the feeling in his muscles. He massages harder and harder. A tingling sensation fires across his right shoulder. He traces the prickling against his skin around until it stops at his neck. His entire hand fits around the back of his neck. His thumb and forefinger squeeze towards each other. The pressure builds in the flesh across his neck. His mind goes black through the intensity of his own touch. It urges his fingers to grip tighter into his neck.

Caught in this new pleasure, Aaron's feet slip out from under him on the wet tiles. He reaches out instinctively, his fingers latching onto the metal of the towel rack and gripping tightly. His body swings heavily down and sharp pain fires through his hip and arm as they hit the wall and floor.

In a daze, Aaron pulls himself into a sitting position on the floor and waits for his whirling vision to clear. His naked buttocks complain about the bite of the cold tiles while his legs refuse to move from their position sprawled in front of him. Above him Aaron hears a creaking, which reverberates into the back of his skull. Aaron tries to pull himself upright again, but with a final squeal the towel rack snaps clear of the wall. Aaron drops back onto the floor, the now useless metal bar in his right hand dumping its load of towels into a lumpy heap on the floor.

As Aaron takes in the scene before him, a feeling of weightlessness swells within his chest. He doesn't struggle against the urge as laughter bursts out uncontrollably. His chest spasms with each wave of giggles, the pain dissipating through the mirth. He lies back onto the tiles and rolls through the laughter, broken towel rack still in hand. His breathing becomes heavier as the laughter echoes through its final heaves. Aaron drops the rack next to him with a chilling clang. *I'm so stupid*, his mind continues to chuckle.

Aaron glances across to the fresh holes in the wall. Disappointment quickly fills him. A wave of regret floods through him as he eyes the damage he has caused to his home. Cracks radiate from the hole in the tiles like small veins striking along the wall. Intrigue sparks in Aaron. The disfiguration on the otherwise neat hole draws his gaze, the exposed wall creating a raw sensation. Aaron sits up and touches the hole with the tip of his finger. The crumbs stick to his skin and rub coarsely.

A muffled clicking sound startles Aaron back to reality. The front door. Aaron jumps off the ground and pushes the towel rack up against the wall. He snatches a towel off the floor to cover himself. The door thuds shut and is followed by determined footsteps marching around the apartment. The footsteps get louder as they get closer. Aaron straightens himself up and moves out into the bedroom. David twists around and glares at Aaron. The intense stare quickly fades as David's attention fixates on something on Aaron's body.

David's eyes widen with a hint of caring.

'Are you okay?' he asks, pointing to Aaron's side.

Aaron looks down. A red bruise rises tenderly to the surface on top of his hip. He waves his hand as if to dismiss it.

'Yeah, I'm fine,' Aaron says. 'I just slipped in the bathroom and broke the towel rack. It looks worse than it is.'

'You broke the towel rack?!' The look of care evaporates from David's face. 'That's just great. Another thing to add to a shit day.'

'No, no, it's all fine. It's just the screws that need fixing. I will take care of it,' Aaron says.

David stares down at Aaron as if waiting for something else to go wrong. Aaron feels flustered. Without a dismissal he can only wait in the spotlight of David's attention. *He hasn't done this for a while*, Aaron thinks. *He never gives me this much attention for something so small.*

'Is there something you're looking for?' Aaron probes.

'I left a report I had to study here,' David says, his gaze not shifting from Aaron. His eyes move between Aaron's bruise and his face as if trying to piece together a mystery. A small thrill tingles up Aaron's spine at the attention. 'I'll probably be late again tonight,' David finally says.

David detaches his glare and stomps over to his side of the bed. He looks down on the short stack of papers on the bedside table to read the title before placing them inside his briefcase. Without another word or glance he exits the bedroom and heads straight for the front door. Aaron remains standing on the spot, trapped in his own thoughts. *Intrigue seems to get his attention. He spent longer than normal looking at me. I need to give him something to figure out.*

The lure of a new mission entices Aaron into action. He quickly dresses and rushes about tidying the apartment to his required standard, all the while his mind races for ideas to challenge David. *I could place a trail of chocolates*, Aaron shakes his head. *No, the chocolate would get everywhere. Maybe I could hide all his left shoes and leave clues to find them.* Aaron's face drops. He stands over the kitchen sink mindlessly polishing the last of the surfaces while he concentrates on ideas to bait David into looking at him the same way he used to.

Aaron's eyes spark alight. An idea blossoms in his head and grows into a plan. *Romantic. Sweet. Another chance to communicate.* A broad smile stretches Aaron's face into hard creases. He nods to himself as he tests the idea. *It should work*, he confirms.

He tosses the cloth into the sink and strides from the room. He heads to the study and straight behind the solid wooden desk. Stationery lines the edges of the desk, untouched in years. He drags a stack of notepaper from under the photo of him and David to the centre of the desk. He sets to work with pen and scissors, cutting the paper into a selection of large heart-shaped pieces. On each bit of paper he scrawls a note and carefully folds it in half, or screws it up in rejection and throws it away. The bin soon overflows with rejected ideas. Aaron ignores the growing mess to focus on getting the clues written in time.

Once all the notes are written Aaron charges around the house, placing them all in their correct order. He looks outside to see that darkness has taken the city again. The sun has been set for hours, meaning David could be home again soon.

In the kitchen Aaron quickly tosses together a basic pasta and leaves it in the oven. From the kitchen cupboard he collects an assortment of candles and takes them into the guestroom. The scent of burning candles quickly fills the room. *Now it's just me left to hide and the scavenger hunt can begin*, he smiles to himself.

Aaron ducks from the room and quickly returns in a high-cut silk dressing gown. Air teases up his legs and over every inch of skin not covered by his underwear. Aaron shuts the guestroom door and climbs onto the bed ready to wait however long it takes for David to come home. He opens the romance novel in his hand and begins to stare aimlessly at the same page as last night. Excitement rushes through him. The anticipation tickles through his body in shivers of adrenaline. He keeps swallowing to stop his mouth drying out from the nervous thrill that is driving him.

Shortly after eleven Aaron hears the door ease open and shut again. The footsteps in the hall halt a few steps from the door. *He's reading the first one*, Aaron's whole body begins to quiver. He shuts the book and slides it into the empty drawer next to the bed. He moves the pillows to lift him higher. A cold draft brushes further up his leg as he pushes the gown suggestively to one side. He swallows and breathes deeply to cool his nerves.

The steps resume, moving determinedly towards the guestroom door. Confusion washes away Aaron's nerves. The door snaps open. Light flickers off David's darkened face. David stands in the doorway holding a love heart clue in his hand. Aaron lays motionless, waiting to David to make the first move.

'I don't have time for this crap,' David hisses. He waves the scrap of paper in the air. 'I need to concentrate on work. More so than ever thanks to that useless bloody clinic.'

'But, I just thought—' Aaron lifts himself off the pillows. His legs instinctively curl under him.

'Thought nothing. Do you want me to succeed or not?' Aaron's head twitches as a nod. 'Good. Now let me get on with work. All of these,' he waves the heart in the air again, 'better be gone by tomorrow and the house back to normal. We're hosting a dinner party. You'll need to cook for me and four guests.'

David turns and slams the door, the small paper heart thrown out of his hand in the process. The scrunched paper drops to the floor without a sound. Aaron sits in silence. His face remains stunned in a blank stare. Around him the candles continue to flicker with the agitated air.

The hours tick by without Aaron moving. The candles fizzle out their last breaths of life. Aaron curls onto his side, eyes open. *Something's changed, this isn't right*, he keeps repeating in his head. Darkness grows around him, consuming him in a deep embrace. Soon the cycling of his thoughts exhausts him, forcing him into a fitful sleep on the guest bed.

Aaron wakes the next day to a harsh light burning through the guestroom window. The direct blast of the sun fills the room with heat. Sweat spills over his skin and coats him in a soggy cocoon. Aaron rolls over and lifts himself off the quilt. His legs wobble and flop to the floor.

'Gah, why did I sleep here?' Aaron says.

I suppose I should make myself breakfast, Aaron hisses to himself while massaging the lines across his forehead.

Aaron stomps out of the room into the unwelcoming silence blanketing the rest of the apartment. A tomb-like breath wheezes through the hallway as Aaron makes his way to the kitchen, sucking the warmth from his skin. The sight of cups in the sink snatches Aaron's attention. *Dinner party tonight,* he remembers. As he reaches out to start washing the mugs a smear of blue on his hand catches his attention.

The series of digits are no longer precise but still clear on his skin. *Cameron's number. The party*, Aaron remembers.

His body sparks alight with a dreamy anticipation. Aaron pulls out his phone and dials the number. Each ring of the dial tone sends shivers through Aaron. He prepares to hang up on the twelfth ring when a quiet click sounds through the earpiece.

'Hello,' Aaron recognises Cameron's voice immediately. The infectious smile spreads across his face.

'Hi Cameron, it's me calling,' Aaron says.

'Hello me. How are you? I'm assuming me is Aaron,' Cameron mocks.

'Oh, yes, sorry I forgot you don't know my number.'

'I do now. Now I just need to know where you live and my insidious plan to take over your life will come to fruition.'

'Well, it's in the Great Wall Building.' Aaron pauses. 'I get it now, you were making a joke about taking over my life. I'm a bit slow this morning.'

'This morning? Don't you mean afternoon? Did you have a big night last night?'

Aaron looks around the room in confusion. He spots the clock on the wall and mutters.

'I must have lost track of time,' he says. 'I'm a bit out of routine at the moment.'

'While you're out of whack are you coming to the party tonight?'

'That's what I was calling you about. I would love to come but don't know where I'm going, or when.'

'Don't fret. You can come with me. I'll pick you up out the front of your building in an hour.'

'In an hour,' Aaron's heart begins to race. 'Isn't that a bit early?'

'Kind of, but our mums want us to have a chance to say hey before the festivities begin.'

'Your mums are going?'

'Yeah, but they won't stay too long. They just want to see their darling boys together. They do it every time Jake comes home from overseas. At least this time it will be in public and you'll be there to dampen their obsessing. So, see you in an hour?'

'Definitely, I'll be out the front. Do I need to bring anything?'

'Just yourself and a sense of humour. Some of the meatheads can be a bit testy when they first return from overseas. Half of them will be drunk from pre-drinks.'

They hang up, leaving Aaron in silent contemplation. His heart is still fluttering at the thought of going to a party without David. *What if someone I know is there?* he frets. A lump grows in his chest. His heart heaves with the sudden rise of doubt. *I'll just smile*, Aaron nods to himself, calming his nerves. *It can't be that bad that I'm welcoming troops home.*

Aaron darts about getting ready. His party attire hangs unworn in the wardrobe. He retrieves an outfit and squeezes into it, the tight fabric stretching along his skin. A strange façade flickers in the mirror next to him. He pauses and stares deeply into the reflective surface. His image looks back at him. The clothes sit comfortably on him. The tension usually in his shoulders is replaced by a relaxed posture. His face perks up in an eager grin. Lightness runs through his body. He finishes getting ready and rushes downstairs to wait for Cameron. He glances at his watch and realises Cameron should be there at any moment.

'Well hello there,' Cameron says from across the lobby. His confident voice echoes off the cold stone walls.

Aaron looks up to see Cameron dressed casually. His shirt hangs out of his jeans, hiding all but a tiny glint of silver belt buckle. His hair sits up in rough spikes as if he deliberately messed his hair to dress down.

'You look hot,' Cameron says in a matter-of-fact tone.

'Oh, um,' Aaron blushes and stutters, 'you look nice as well.'

'Cheers, but I know that's a lie.' Cameron holds his arms out to show off the lack of tidiness in his dress. 'I know no matter how I dress my mums will always fix something, so I left them something to fix. In the end I should look how I normally do. Well, my hair will be combed down a bit more.'

'Such a generous son,' Aaron laughs. 'Do they that every time?'

'Every. Single. Time. You'll see. I once left a black smear on my cheek to see how far I could take it. It worked. They fussed about cleaning it off as if I was still five.'

Cameron links into Aaron's arm and begins leading him to the door.

'So, I was thinking we take a taxi so neither of us has to drive. Believe me, we'll need a few drinks to get through this one,' Cameron says.

'Is it really that bad?' Aaron asks. Cameron smirks and winks at Aaron.

Once in the taxi Cameron dives straight into the list of warnings about his family, and so the drive through peak hour traffic flies by for Aaron. Cameron's hands flap about with each passionate tale as he details how different he is from his brother, and yet all Aaron could find was similarities. They both take on too much work in order to save enough money to see the world. Neither of them wants to leave home for the sake of free accommodation. Both abandoned their success at school to take on jobs just for the cash.

Aaron smiles through the entire trip. Cameron's urge to list his family's faults gives Aaron new insight into who Cameron is, and Aaron just nods while taking in every detail Cameron reveals.

The taxi slows out the front of the Mellors Hotel. Light radiates from the large glass frontage. The pretence of gaudy opulence exudes from the building's huge chandelier illuminating the massive lobby and the excessively formal dress of its staff. Small clusters of people dressed in military uniform and semi-formal attire mingle around the entrance chatting.

'It looks like we aren't the only early birds,' Cameron says as he holds open the car door for Aaron. 'There they are,' Cameron points across the pavement to a woman in a black dress waving at them. A second woman wearing a pantsuit stands in conversation with a young man in uniform. A single medal gleams from his chest as he talks.

Cameron waves back and shuts the taxi door. As he leads Aaron across to his family he turns his head slightly to whisper.

'Jake looks like he's in a bit of a mood,' Cameron says over his shoulder.

As they move closer Aaron starts to fall behind Cameron, his throat getting drier with each step.

'Hello darling,' Cameron's mum swings her arms out to pull him into a tight embrace.

'Hi mum,' Cameron responds. 'This is my friend Aaron, twenty-six, Virgo. Aaron this are my mums Denise, forty-three, Leo, and Susan, forty-three, Libra.'

Susan releases Cameron and throws her arms out to take Aaron in a fierce hug.

'Pleasure to meet you,' Susan says.

Denise follows in a quieter fashion. She shakes Aaron's hand warmly and releases him quickly for the next introduction.

'This is my brother Jake, twenty-three, Leo,' Cameron adds.

Jake holds out his hand and firmly grasps Aaron's. Aaron smiles to hide the cringe of pain from the rough handshake.

'Lovely to meet you all,' Aaron says.

The politeness dissipates instantly into an air of familiarity.

'Look at how nicely your friend Aaron is dressed, Cameron,' Susan says. 'I'm surprised you haven't learnt a thing or two.'

Cameron catches Aaron's gaze with a roll of his eyes as his mums start fussing over his presentation. They move quickly to slick back down his hair and tuck in his shirt, and only release him from their onslaught when they are satisfied with their work.

'We should go inside,' Jake announces confidently.

Aaron focusses in on Jake. The family resemblance between Jake and Cameron was instantly clear to him. The same blue eyes, which Susan also shares, gaze around the immediate area as if scanning for a threat. The muscular lines under his jacket press proudly against the military brass. Jake's face resembles the intrigue of Cameron's smile yet holds an austerity that distinguishes him.

They all follow Jake as he leads the group into the hotel lobby. The chill of the air conditioner smacks into their faces as they cross the threshold. Aaron hugs himself with his arms to stop his body heat being leached away. Jake moves across the lobby towards double doors where two men in tuxedos stand at attention holding trays of sparkling wine.

'Good evening,' they greet robotically.

'Yes please,' Cameron says snatching two flutes. He hands one to Aaron. 'You may need a few to warm up. It can be a tough crowd.'

'Cheers,' Aaron says, accepting the chilled glass into his fingers.

'Don't be silly, Cameron. They're harmless,' Denise says.

'Mostly harmless,' Cameron clarifies. 'What I was implying is that some of them are a bit thick. You don't need to have brains to be in the army and I reckon half of them have their wits beaten out of them in the training process,' Cameron continues to tease.

Denise instinctively steps between Cameron and Jake. Jake glares at Cameron, appearing half-confused as if he didn't quite hear what had been said.

'Your brother has a very important role, he has to be smart for that,' Denise defends. 'You saw the practise exams he bought home. They were huge.'

'It's not that important. He's a glorified groundskeeper who has access to automatic weapons,' Cameron says while staring down his brother.

'So Aaron, are you and Cameron just friends or is there something he's not telling us?' Susan asks. A sly grin sneaks across her face. Cameron rolls his eyes and takes a long swig of his champagne.

'We're just friends,' Aaron blushes. He looks over Cameron's shoulder to see Jake quietly step away.

'He's married, mum,' Cameron cuts in.

'I guessed that with the ring but I still like to ask. You could have put it there and not told us.'

'Susan,' Denise shakes her head. 'Our boys are both still young. Things are different these days. You can be forty and not married. It was completely different when we were young. We were married with Jake on the way when we were both twenty.'

'I know, I know. I just want to make sure my boys find someone to keep them happy.'

Aaron's phone vibrates to life in his pocket.

'Excuse me for a moment,' he says.

'Take your time,' Cameron answers. 'I think my mums are about to start their usual probing. I should just send them a highlights letter,' Cameron smiles to himself and turns back to his family.

The phone buzzes incessantly, demanding attention. Aaron steps away from the group and whips his phone out of his pocket while Cameron and his mums continue to walk deeper into the function hall. Aaron's finger moves across the screen ready to answer. David's name flashes up on the display. Aaron's finger hovers over the answer button. *He's probably wondering where dinner is*, Aaron thinks. Maybe I should have left some cooked food out.

The phone continues to vibrate in Aaron's hand. The sense of urgency fades as his hand adjusts to its constant movements. David's name continues to flash for a second before the screen falls black and the phone stops ringing. Aaron stares down at the phone. His mind sits as blank as the phone screen, unable to decide what to do.

Before Aaron can take action the phone shrills to life again with David's name rampant on the screen. A flash of anger flickers across Aaron's mind. In instinctive movements he flicks the phone to silent and shoves it back into his pocket. A strange swell of determination balloons inside his chest. He lifts the flute to celebrate the weird strength he feels and gulps down the last of his drink in one hit.

'You look like you need another,' Jake grumbles next to him.

'I think I do,' Aaron forces out while holding back the fizzing inside his nose. 'Where did everyone else run off to?'

'Our mums have lined up a date for Cameron,' Jake nods across the heads in the crowd towards the buffet table. 'They'll probably be a while.'

Aaron follows Jake's nod to spot Cameron smiling politely at a clean-shaven man in uniform. The cropped hair and straight pressed jacket look as fresh as the man's face. Aaron watches Denise and Susan step casually away from the conversation leaving Cameron with a new friend.

'That's Andrew, he's just back from his first tour. Mum asked for a name so I gave them his because he's new. I wanted to be sure I picked someone I haven't set them on before. Poor guy.' Aaron flashes a confused look at Jake., who shrugs. 'He'll get over it.' The serious tone of Jake's voice soothes Aaron's concerns about Jake's brashness towards Cameron. 'So, would you like a drink? I can escort you to the bar,' Jake offers, a note of authority hangs in his voice.

'Yes please,' Aaron responds.

Jake accompanies Aaron across the room to the bar and finds a couple of high stools for them at a small table before disappearing towards the bar. He promptly returns with two more champagnes and passes one across the table to Aaron. Amongst the sternness in Jake's face Aaron spots a softness he recognises from Cameron. Aaron relaxes into the seat with the wine as if he has known Jake for years. The giddy excitement and thrill of Cameron's presence dissipates around his brother, who's quiet self-assurance begins to fill Aaron with a sense of security and belonging. The sensation of being grounded and secure lures Aaron's attention.

'I'm sorry Cameron dragged you along to this,' Jake starts. 'Despite all the booze it's a fairly rigid affair.'

'Don't be sorry. It is definitely better than the night at home I had planned. There's only so much conversation with bankers I can take before I start feeling like I could vomit at any moment.'

'I know that feeling. Six months on base with the same people. There's only so much to talk about before they're back where they started.'

'Some people don't have anything exciting in their lives to talk about. Congratulations you managed to write a report that is beneath your pay grade,' Aaron toasts sarcastically. Jake watches on with a smirk as Aaron downs half the glass of wine and straightens up for the rest of his rant. 'I don't think I can take another dinner party where the primary topic of discussion is how to get people to spend more money so that they can feel confident with the economy.'

'Spoken like someone who has never had to worry about money,' Jake baits.

'I suppose. I've never really had to worry about spending or budgets. David takes care of all that. I just make sure everything in the apartment works.'

'You two look like you're hitting it off,' Denise pounces into the conversation. She and Susan squeeze seats up to the table. 'Cameron's set with Andrew. He sounds like a lovely gentleman. You're really good at spotting them.' Jake rolls his eyes.

'Now to get you sorted,' Susan says, ignoring Jake's obvious disinterest. 'Aaron, what is it you do?'

'Mum, we've established that he's married. Just keep that in mind before starting the interrogation,' Jake recites.

'I know, I know,' Susan waves her hand to dismiss Jake's

objections. 'But what about that lovely lad who was standing next to Andrew when we interrupted. He was very polite.'

'Despite our rudeness,' Denise adds.

'You mean Richard?' Jake asks. 'The blond one with the scar across his forehead.'

'Yes, that's the one. It must have been a nasty cut to get a scar like that. What about him? Army men marry each other all the time.'

'I'm not his type mum.'

'How can you be sure? Have you asked him? I'm sure you would look good together.'

'I'm not his type,' Jake lifts his head to deliberately catches his mother's eyes. 'And because he is a good soldier we don't ask him about it.'

Susan stares blankly between her son and wife. Denise twitches her head as if to signal Susan to an obvious answer. Susan's face snaps from confused and into a loud gasp.

'He's a—' she nods.

'Have you finished trying to set us up for the evening, mum?' Susan glances around the room, her eyes hunting out any possible suitors. 'Mum?' Jake directs to Denise.

'Susan darling. Sweetie,' Denise says in a gentle tone. 'I think tonight we should just enjoy the fact that Jake is home again safely. You can matchmake next week after he's settled in again.'

Susan sighs. The energy of the hunt continues to twitch through her body as she shuffles uncomfortably on her seat.

'So, Aaron. We should probably do a proper introduction. Cameron hasn't told us much about you, I'm sure,' Denise's chin rises as she begins to talk with an air of social grace. 'As Cameron already said I'm Denise, forty-three and Leo. This is my wife Susan, forty-four last week and

Libra. And this is my son Jake, who has just returned from six months on the eastern front with the army. He's twenty-three and also a Leo.'

Aaron nods his greeting around the room.

'I'm Aaron. Twenty-six and Virgo. For the past five years I have been married to my partner David Jones. We met in high school.'

'See you can marry young still,' Susan shrills. Her energy for matchmaking launches again at the fresh evidence of young marriage. 'No children?'

'Not yet,' Aaron says neutrally. 'Work makes it a little complicated at the moment. David's an executive banker.'

'I'm sure he must work ridiculous hours,' Denise interjects to lead the conversation away from partnerships. 'Same as Jake here. At home it looks like he does nothing all day but we know when he's away on duty he's lucky to get three hours sleep each night.'

'Why's that?' Aaron throws in, happy the conversation has moved on. 'What's happening around the base to keep you up all night?'

'Technically it's within an active warzone,' Jake's chest puffs. His medal bounces from the sudden movement. 'One of my team's roles was to make sure the base is ready to jump to action at any time of day. We have to maintain the area so that patrolling troops are clear to come and go as required, and they have to come and go at all hours so we have to be ready.'

'Knowing that, we don't push him around at home,' Denise says. 'Except to be tidy, which isn't too much to ask from a military man. It's the complete opposite for Cameron. He's a slob around the house. He still has the same insane work ethic as Jake though. I've lost track of how many hours he works. He must get it from the donor because I don't think either myself or Denise has ever been that extreme with our work.'

'There are huge differences between Cameron and I,' Jake defends. 'I work to protect the country. He works for himself. I have a sense of duty. He's just into money.'

'And challenges. Each of his jobs is different,' Aaron slips in. 'This serving the country idea seems a bit strange to me,' he adds ignorantly. Denise and Susan shrink backwards.

'Why's that?' Jake asks. The calmness in his tone brings his mothers back into the light.

'I don't know,' Aaron shrugs. 'It feels a lot like propaganda.'

'I'm going to get us some drinks,' Denise snaps up from her chair. 'Would anyone like something?'

'Can you see if you can just get a bottle of champagne?' Jake suggests. 'Saves us having to get up every ten minutes. And I think a few shots are in order for all of us.' Denise turns her head up at Jake. 'It's just to celebrate my safe return.'

'That's probably a good idea,' Susan slips out of her seat. 'I'll help you carry it.' The mums rush to the bar as if on a new mission.

'Did I say something wrong?' Aaron asks.

'Not to me. You'll have to excuse them. They're old fashioned. I've changed since someone first questioned me on the ideas of propaganda. And that wasn't really the issue anyway. He was another date courtesy of mum's handiwork and he was an arsehole who just happened to offer me a reason to get angry. Let's just say he promptly left the building and I haven't seen him since.'

'Wow, they really do want to see you married.'

'Yeah, like I said, they're old-fashioned,' Jake pauses to

have a drink. 'Are you really uncomfortable about the duty to the country concept?'

'A little. I have to admit. I don't know that much about it but every time someone talks about it can't help but think back to the Old War footage we were shown at school. Entire nations convinced to support something we now consider evil. How do we know that what we're doing won't be treated the same in a few decades' time?'

'Good point,' Jake raises his eyebrow. 'First of all you used 'we'. You're suckered in without knowing it,' he laughs. He shakes his head as his smug giggles die down. 'Things have changed since the Old Wars. We don't always like what we do and what we really don't like we don't have to do. The army is more open to criticism and scrutiny than it used to be. At one march protestors threw flour because of some dodgy bread deal, which barely involved anyone in the armed forces. It may have looked like they were arrested on TV— which they were for a bit just until the march was over—but after they were invited to the official dinners with a couple of commanders. They got to vent their frustration directly to the hierarchy, and I don't think they've ever protested like that since, they just go straight to whoever's in charge to air their concerns.' Jake flashes a glance around the room. 'Looks like mum and mum are taking their time,' he flicks his head towards the bar. Aaron spots them in deep conversation with a couple of soldiers. The glint in Susan's eyes tells him she's in her element. Across the room he spots Cameron laughing with Andrew still, his arm resting on Andrew's shoulder. 'Conversation is getting a bit deep here. I think we should take it elsewhere with a nice bottle of vodka. I haven't had a good drink in ages.'

Before Aaron can object Jake ducks off to the bar and

returns triumphantly with a bottle of vodka in one hand and two glasses of ice in the other.

'Shall we?' He offers the nook of his elbow with confidence, which Aaron accepts. 'The other side of the bar is a lounge, which apparently no-one has taken to yet.' Aaron looks questioningly at Jake. Jake shrugs. 'Apparently you civilians have this idea that you can't question anyone in the army. I asked for a bottle of vodka and a quiet space and the poor bartender offloaded it as if he would rather shit himself than reject me.'

Jake chuckles quietly as he leads them through a carpeted door and into a plush lounge area. The intimate space sits vacant around them. The waitress behind the bar snaps to attention as they enter the room. She jumps off her seat and slips the magazine she was reading under the bar. A practised smile eases across her face while her hands clench together behind her back to show she is ready for them.

The thick carpet melds around each of their steps as Jake leads them to a corner booth and serves up the first round of vodka. Aaron finds himself gushing with conversation the moment he sits into the leather cushion and takes his first sip of the crisp vodka. The serious tone of the earlier conversation evaporates with the second glass. Aaron finds himself in a field of untested thoughts. He sits back and nods as Jake details the routine of the army base and his squad. The similarities between Aaron's life of routine and seeming excitement of the army become more apparent as Jake speaks more about taking orders from others, a similarity that adds another level to Aaron's sense of comfort with Jake.

Jake holds the vodka bottle upside down and watches the last drop fall into his glass. Aaron lounges back into the seat with a haze fogging his vision. Through his stillness he senses a light vibration again from his pocket. His instincts tick behind his eyes in protest of his lack of moment. He stretches forward and picks up his glass. He sips at the now iceless drink while his phone shivers for attention in his pocket.

'It looks like it's going nicely out here,' Cameron's voice snaps Aaron out of his dazed state. Andrew swings behind, his uniform crumpled and medal hanging from his pants. 'I'm just checking in,' Cameron continues with a confident tone. 'Will you be alright to get home?' He looks straight down at Aaron. Aaron nods lazily. 'Good then. I think I can trust you with my brother. I'm off to play war with this tipsy fellow here. Until next time.' Cameron leans in and pecks Aaron on his cheek.

Cameron glares at Jake, turns and saunters from the room, his hand latched onto the eager Andrew.

'I don't know what that was about,' Aaron says once Cameron leaves the room.

Jake's hand slips heavily onto Aaron's upper thigh. Aaron holds still at the sudden warmth against his skin. He turns to see what Jake is doing when a pair of lips press roughly against his own. He swallows back a gasp for air and relaxes into the soft texture of the lips. The solid pressure against his mouth eases into a slow massaging movement. Vodka numbs Aaron's ability to protest. He sits still, waiting for a tongue to slap its way against his teeth. It doesn't come. Jake's lips continue to move against Aaron's. Sharp whiskers press and contract from his skin with each motion. Aaron surrenders to the tenderness and moves his mouth back against Jake's. Jake throws his arms around Aaron and presses their chests together.

A sharp pinching in Aaron's chest shocks him back to reality. The drunken wash of vodka shimmers across his vision. He pushes Jake away from him and slumps back against the seat.

'What? What's wrong?' Jake asks, his arms and face still in position ready to kiss.

'Nothing, I just can't,' Aaron slurs. 'I think I need to go.'

'Don't worry about it. You're married. I'm in the army. It's not like we can do anything serious. Who knows where we'll both be in a month's time.'

'No—it's just—I can't. Not tonight.' Aaron stumbles to standing. 'Goodnight. It was lovely meeting you,' he adds before dragging himself out the door to hail a taxi.

5.

AARON WAKES THE next day consumed by a sense of gloom. His head creaks from the remnants of last night's vodka extravaganza. The room around him blurs in a sticky haze. He spots a series of white lumps around the bed, the stubs of spent candles from his attempt at romance the other night. *The guestroom*, he remembers. He groans as he pushes himself up into a seated position. Something metallic presses sharply into his hip as he moves uncomfortably. He extracts his belt buckle from beneath his pelvis and threads the leather back through it. Waves of nausea rock his stomach with each clumsy movement.

'Where were you?' A shadow growls from the door. Aaron blinks his vision clear to see David standing in the doorway with his arms crossed. 'The dinner party was a total farce. You made me look like a complete fool last night. What do you have to say for yourself?'

'I'm sure it was fine,' Aaron croaks.

'It most certainly was not!' David bellows. He stomps further into the room so that he towers over Aaron. who shrinks back against the pillows. 'There was nothing ready. You were nowhere to be found. You didn't answer your phone. And these—' he throws a scrunched up assortment of love heart notes on the bed, 'were scattered through the apartment like a trail of shame. Do you know what my colleagues think of me now?'

'That you're sweet?'

'No! You complete idiot! All the hard work I put in and you treat me like this. Without me we would have nothing. You'd be nothing! If you don't stay in line or I could miss out on the next promotion. Is that what you want? Do you want me to fail? Now that I won't have the status as a working parent we need to work harder than ever, and this is what you do to me?'

'It's not a big deal. I just went out. I'm sure dinner was fine. There's always takeaway,' Aaron grumbles as he rubs his eyes to hide his rising frustration. His head reels in protest at the unnecessary movements.

'You are so stupid! You have no idea how much work I do. How much I bring to all this?' He swings his arms around as if showing the apartment to Aaron for the first time.

'What about me?' Aaron bursts out. David steps back. Shock flashes across his face at the snap in Aaron's voice.

'What about you?' He regains some confidence. 'I heard about you playing shop. Aubrey mentioned bumping into you and some so-called friend. Who is he?'

'He's a friend,' Aaron fires back.

'No he's not. Not if I don't know him. You better not see him again or get any ideas about being some shop tart when this place is a mess. We're supposed to be a team, remember. You potter around all day, doing gods know what. And now you think you can go play shop in a café. I actually work.' *Ah, so that's what this is about,* Aaron keeps himself silent. *You don't think I do any work.* Determination rests behind his eyes, but remains patient knowing David can't listen when he's grandstanding. 'What? Do you have no response to that? I knew you wouldn't, you're a useless piece of shit. I'm going to work. This apartment had better be spotless again when I get home. I'll forgive this one incident but it better not happen again. Is that understood?' Aaron tilts his head forwards in a slight nod. 'Understood?' David's voice echoes down the hallway behind.

'Yes,' Aaron concedes sullenly.

'Good. Go clean yourself, you look terrible.'

David slams the guestroom door and marches from the house, his shoes stomping on the tiles with each step. The thud as the front door slams shut reverberates throughout the apartment. Aaron curls into himself and cradles his aching head. He closes his eyes and tries to rock himself into unconsciousness in a vain attempt to dull the headache rampaging against his skull. Then a more effective remedy appears in his mind as the memory of the kiss with Jake spontaneously blossoms into his consciousness. The tenderness in Jake's tipsy touch reignites a passion and sense of safety. Aaron's chin itches from the scrape of Jake's stubble He relishes the irritation as a part of the exquisite experience, and uncurls himself onto the bed. A fresh sense of ease seeps through his muscles at the recollection of Jake's touch.

I need to get out of here. Aaron's eyes snap open. He ignores the lingering hangover and quickly surveys the mess around the apartment. A plan of action comes to him swiftly. He chuckles to himself at how simple it is.

Aaron opens the guestroom wardrobe, the shelves empty except for winter sheets and spare blankets.. Aaron lazily throws the lumpy remnants of the candles into the back of the closet with a dull thud. The wax are closely followed by scraps of paper and the used sheets. Aaron slams the door shut, and he instantly regrets the noise as the fresh headache resurges inside his skull. He grips his hair and cringes through the deep throbbing.

Aaron ventures from the guestroom in search of pain relief. The smell of burnt fat chokes the apartment. Aaron traces the scent to the kitchen and discovers a cascade of dishes strewn across the bench. Aaron moans in dismay at the sight of his kitchen. He hastily loads the plates—food scraps and all—straight into the dishwasher and eases the door shut. He cringes again in anticipation of a loud click that would aggravate his headache further, but the latch eases shut almost soundlessly.

His sigh of relief is intruded by the doorbell's ringing peal. Aaron moans and latches onto his ears.

'Yes?' he groans through the receiver once the buzzing stops.

'It's me. Let me up. I need to pee,' Cameron's perky voice chirps through the speaker.

Aaron buzzes him in. He leans on the wall pressing his ear to the door, waiting to hear the elevator. A muffled ding signals Aaron. He jerks the door open before Cameron can get close enough to knock.

'Well, hello. You're eager,' Cameron smiles. He eyes Aaron over quickly. 'But you look like hell. What did my brother do to you?'

'He gave me a sound education in the adverse effects of vodka,' Aaron mutters back.

'Where's your toilet, I've been busting since Andrew's house.'

Aaron nods down the hallway. Cameron skips awkwardly towards the bathroom. Aaron drags himself back into the kitchen and glares at the coffee machine, willing it to magically produce coffee without effort or noise. He blocks his ears as he flicks on the grinder in a futile attempt at self-preservation. The aroma tingles in Aaron's nose, and his brain perks up in anticipation.

'Phew, that was a close one,' Cameron says as he struts into the kitchen. 'I should have planned my escape from Andrew's a little better. But I get to see you so it all worked out.'

'Coffee?' Aaron offers. He can feel colour seep back into his face.

'Yes please.' Cameron leans against the counter while Aaron steams their milk. 'Nice place you've got. You really take care of it.'

'Oh, it's a shameful mess this morning. David wasn't too happy that I was out last night instead of cooking for his dinner party. That's to be expected though.' Aaron hands a warm mug of coffee across to Cameron. He hugs it in both hands.

'You can't be here all the time. You need a life. So, you and Jake, huh? What happened there?'

'Um—I don't really know. You and your brother are so completely different. We ended up having a debate about nationalism.' *And then he kissed me*, Aaron remembers. He hides a simmering grin.

'Gods, that would have been intense. How'd he take it?'

'Quite well, I think.' Aaron feels his heart skip a beat

at the memory of Jake's hand on his thigh. A shiver rushes down to his leg. Aaron shakes it off. 'You seemed to hit it off with Andrew. Your mums will be happy.'

'Not really,' Cameron dismisses. 'He was fun. I might go back there for sex again but nothing serious. There's only so much biceps for brains I can handle. They take a lot of work.' Aaron's mouth falls open. 'What is it? Is something wrong?'

'No—just—I,' Aaron stutters. 'I knew you were direct but didn't realise you spoke like that. It's—it's—'

'Crass?' Cameron suggests. Aaron nods. 'It's just sex and that's nothing. I haven't even gone into detail yet.'

'No, that's fine,' Aaron says, 'I don't need explicit details, thanks.'

'But that's the fun bit. You're missing out. You can get all the juicy gossip, like how good they are in bed, how big they are. All the good stuff.'

'How big they are?' Aaron stares perplexed. Cameron watches back, waiting for Aaron to continue speaking. Aaron freezes on the spot unsure of what is expected.

'Yes,' Cameron breaks the silence. 'How big they are.'

'What does that mean? I saw Andrew last night. I know how tall he is.'

'Oh, you're serious!' Cameron bursts into a fit of laughter. He slides his mug onto the counter so he can hold himself upright. 'I thought you were messing with me. You're too cute. I'm talking about how big their cock is.' Aaron grimaces. The sound of *that* word hits him like a personal insult. Cameron composes himself. 'Are you okay?'

'It's just that word. I haven't heard anyone use it since school. I've never liked it,' Aaron answers coldly.

'You know it's just a word, right? What word would you use?'

'If I had to, I would say penis.'

'Now that sounds really weird to me. Do you use that word when you're in bed with David?'

'No,' Aaron suddenly feels reserved. 'We don't really talk about it.'

'You have sex though? Surely?' Cameron prods.

'Sometimes. When David is home and wants it. He's just always too busy.'

'Well then just do it with someone else. Are you allowed to?'

'What?' Aaron straightens up.

'Sorry, I didn't mean to offend you. It's just that some married people have lovers on the side. I used to sleep with a businessman who was in an open relationship because he didn't get to see his husband as much as he would like but still wanted to take care of his sexual needs. It was fun for about a year until his husband wanted to get involved as well.'

'What, you mean like polygamy?' Aaron's shoulders relax as his curiosity increases.

'No, nothing like that. Although sometimes couples could do that I suppose. It would depend on what works for them, I suppose. I think it's okay as long as everyone is happy.'

Cameron is cut off by his phone ringing in his pocket. He excuses himself to leave Aaron alone with his thoughts. *As long as they're happy*, echoes in his mind. *Am I happy?* A wave of sadness spills through him. *Last night I was happy but right now I'm not*, he all but confirms his doubts. The thought of stepping outside and spending the day outside the apartment inflates him with confidence when compared to the idea of sitting inside alone all day finding menial tasks to pass the time.

'That was Mum,' Cameron says, stepping back in the

kitchen. 'Apparently tonight there's a dinner at home. Jake will be there and no doubt she'll find a way to invite Andrew. Would you like to come as well? They said I could bring anyone.'

'Sure,' Aaron smiles, now that plans for him to leave the apartment existed. Seeing Jake again is also a happy circumstance. The desire to dress up and go out again overpowers his hangover self-pity. 'What time?'

'Aim for seven. If Andrew is there I'll try and make an early escape for work.' Cameron finishes his coffee and places the mug in the dishwasher. He laughs at the state of the machine. 'I guess David really can't cope without you,' he chuckles.

'I guess not,' Aaron says shyly.

'I'll message you the address. I've got to go in to work for a couple of hours. Thanks for the toilet and the coffee,' Cameron waves as he ducks out into the hallway and towards the door. 'Don't feel the need to dress up like last night. It's just a family dinner.' Cameron smiles and leaves Aaron alone in the apartment.

The excitement of going out again powers Aaron through the afternoon. He showers and changes the second Cameron leaves the apartment. He paces the living room waiting for the time to leave, and has to change his shirt as the pacing turns the fabric into a sweaty gym rag. He snatches every bit of paper he spots on the floor and throws them into the guestroom wardrobe, confident David would never open it. He nods at the clock once satisfied it's no longer too early to leave. He grabs a bottle of wine from the cellar and rushes out the door. *David won't be home for dinner*, he reminds himself in the elevator. *No point wasting nice food*. All of Aaron's body except his leg remains still. His right knee jiggles on the spot, shaking his entire leg. The shoe taps quietly on the carpeted floor of the taxi. Waves of happiness and excitement gush through him as he emerges from the taxi in front of the address Cameron messaged him.

The quaint little house sits squashed in a row of identical two-storey buildings. The walls, the entire house, seem to breathe as Aaron watches. The curtains flicker in the light with each breath of air the house takes. Aaron races up the stone path to the door and pushes the doorbell.

Susan opens the solid wooden door.

'Aaron,' she reaches out and hugs him. 'You shouldn't have,' she says, eyeing off the bottle of wine. 'Come in. We're all in the dining room. Andrew popped in a bit earlier for some afternoon tea so he's going to join us for dinner,' she adds casually.

She steps aside to let Aaron in and directs him down the hallway once the door is locked shut. Carpet covers every inch of floor. The thick wool hugs Aaron's shoes with each step. Aaron glances around the walls to take in the many family photos covering the stained wallpaper.

The hallway opens into a small dining room. Heads lift to see who has arrived.

'We're so glad you could make it,' Denise says from next to Andrew.

Aaron catches an exhausted eye roll from Cameron who looks as if he has been tied to the other chair next to Andrew. Jake stands and shakes Aaron's hand with a firm grip.

'Good to see you again,' he says, signalling to the seat next to him.

'A drink anyone?' Susan offers.

'Yes please, whatever is open is fine,' Aaron says politely.

'It will all be open in a second,' Susan pats his shoulder.

'Red, white, in between, or bubbles?' she asks.

'Bubbles would be lovely thank you.' Aaron's stomach grumbles in protest at the idea of him drinking more alcohol.

Through the window Aaron spots a small building in the backyard with a single light on. The simple structure looks like an oversized play house. *That must be Cameron and Jake's house*, Aaron thinks.

The conversation continues as a natural extension of the previous night. Denise gushes over Andrew while Susan serves a hearty roast around them. The sweet smell of roasted vegetables and fat trails into the room behind each plate. Aaron cautiously nibbles away at his meat.

'Are you sure you don't need a hand with anything?' Aaron asks for the third time.

'No, not at all. You just sit here and relax.'

Aaron's leg twitches nervously. The impulse to serve makes it hard to sit still. He pours water and passes the wine to calm his instincts.

'Are you usually the one serving at home, Aaron dear?' Denise finally asks, leaving Andrew be for a moment.

'Yes, I am,' Aaron answers. He can feel heat rise to his cheeks, either from the wine or the question. 'It's weird, in a nice way, to just sit and enjoy the food.'

'I know that feeling,' Susan says, winking at Denise. 'That's why I like going out for dinner when we can.'

'So what do you do with yourself other than cook at home?' Denise cuts in. 'Any plans for children?'

Aaron shudders.

'Not at the moment,' he says calmly. 'Maybe one day but I'm not sure I want to be a parent.'

'Really? But it is so rewarding,' Denise nods to her two boys. 'It has always been privilege to have such amazing sons even if sometimes they quibble or stay away from home for months on end. Especially these days when it's getting harder to have children, with the new government regulations. I suppose even more so for men. All we had to do was find a donor.'

'It wasn't just that,' Susan adds. 'It takes a lot of time and uncertainty when trying to get pregnant. And a lot of time with swollen limbs. My feet still haven't recovered from these two,' she gestures at Jake and Cameron.

'I blame Cameron,' Jake jokes. 'He was the last one out.'

Aaron's eyes widen as he listens to their banter.

'Come off it,' Cameron rebuts, 'everything that happened to mum's body started with you. I just had to make do with your mistakes.'

'Cameron,' Denise scolds. Aaron spots Susan hiding a smirk to feign disapproval.

'Children are a full-time job,' Aaron steers the conversation away from Susan's body. 'David and I don't know where we will be living in the next year or so. I'd rather be settled in one house permanently first.'

'Sounds very smart,' Denise yawns. 'I think it's time for us old girls to leave you boys alone. I'm sure you don't want us cramping your style,' she winks at Cameron. Cameron rolls his eyes behind her back before shrugging at Aaron.

Denise leads Susan out of the room leaving the four men in silence. Jake spins his wine glass on its base. The glass grips on the worn tablecloth and twists a circle of wrinkles into the fabric.

'Sorry about them,' Cameron breaks the silence. 'I think that's where I get my forwardness from. They seem to only have marriage and kids on their brains. At least this one gets to escape for most of the year.' He nods to Jake.

'You could too. All you need to do is join the military,' Jake says dryly.

'Right. Well, I'd love to stay,' Cameron says loudly. 'But I need to get to work.'

'You're working tonight?' Jake asks.

'Yes, some of us need to work all year round.'

'I can walk you there if you like,' Andrew offers, and eager look in his face.

'Sure, if you want,' Cameron says.

'And you're going dressed like that?' Jake asks.

'Why not? I work at a club. It doesn't matter what I wear.' Cameron turns to Aaron. 'I'm glad you could make it tonight. I hope you had a good time. Would you like to come with us?' Andrew's face drops. The whites of his eyes bulges and shimmers in the light.

'Not this time,' Aaron says. 'I think I need a quieter one than last night.'

'No worries. I'll leave you in Jake's semi-capable hands. Have a good one.'

Cameron struts out towards the door with Andrew snapping at his heels. The door shuts leaving a warm silence between Jake and Aaron. Aaron sits upright and sips on the remainder of his wine. He glances down at Jake who looks deep in thought.

'Sorry about last night,' Jake finally mutters. 'I didn't mean to make you feel weird. I just thought we had a connection.' His eyes fixate on the tablecloth.

'That's alright,' Aaron says, keeping his gaze level. 'I'm sorry I rushed off so quickly. I realised I needed to get home.'

'Oh, okay,' Jake perks up. 'So, do you want to escape the prying eyes of my mums? We could watch a movie out the back.' He points towards the back door.

'Sure, sounds fun.'

Jake stands without hesitation and leads Aaron outside. Brisk air catches them as they make the short walk across the path and to the detached house. Mustiness wafts out from the darkness as Jake opens the door. A glow from under one of the inside doors casts shadows towards the entranceway.

'Cameron seems to never switch his light off,' Jake explains as he turns the lights on.

Aaron blinks his view clear to see the small space around him. Plush sofas take up half the room and face a large flat screen television. Next to him a single bench, sink and fridge mark the only signs of a kitchen. An extra door stands next to Cameron's bedroom.

'Would you like a beer?' Jake offers. Aaron nods. 'Cool, have a seat anywhere. I'll crank up the hard drive.'

Aaron sinks into one side of the couch. Dust puffs up into his nostrils as he sits down. Aaron twitches his nose to clear it off the musty odour assaulting his senses. The tickling in his sinuses is quickly doubled by a second onslaught of dust as Jake drops heavily next to him.

'Here you go,' Jake says handing Aaron a cold beer. He picks up the remote next to him. 'So what do you feel like watching? I have loads of action movies and comedies.'

'Anything really? I'm not sure what has come out recently,' Aaron says.

Aaron takes a sip of beer. The icy temperature catches him by surprise, and he chokes on his mouthful, spitting out what he isn't able to swallow. He covers his mouth, feeling mortified with embarrassment.

'Sorry, the fridge is always close to freezing,' Jake remarks at Aaron's gasp for air. 'And that's even with it set on low.'

Jake places his hand on Aaron's back and rubs in a slow circular motion. The touch is warm and soothing, and Aaron's skin begins to release the tension from the cold inside him. He presses his shoulder blades back, pushing himself into Jake's fingers. Aaron loses himself in the pleasurable feeling as Jake expands his hand and pushes deeper. Aaron shuts his eyes, feeling himself sway and surrender into Jake's control, the sharp cold of the bottle in his hand all but forgotten.

Hot lips smack onto Aaron's. Aaron flinches in surprise but soon melts into Jake's mouth massaging against his. Jake's hand continues to rub on his back in motion with the kissing. Jake's stubble is rough on Aaron's mouth. The rush of each kiss quickly intensifies. Jake's tongue pokes around Aaron's lips. Aaron opens ready to accommodate a lashing tongue in his mouth, but Jake remains playful, teasing him, and retreats with each movement to focus on Aaron's lips.

Aaron feels the power in Jake's arms as he manoeuvres Aaron onto his back, his legs left dangling to intertwine with Jake's. A hard lump below Jake's waist presses against Aaron's leg. Aaron gasps and the beer slips from his hand, spilling onto the carpet.

'Is everything okay?' Jake retracts his lips. Aaron nods timidly, feeling his own pulse rise. 'Are you sure?'

Aaron pauses, knowing where his next answer will lead. His thoughts flash to his life and home with David. The memory of the loneliness of the apartment creates a hollow pit in his stomach. The spite in the last words David spoke to him in the morning hurt and sadden him. Aaron matches Jake's eyes as he realises that all he wants right now, is to be comforted.

'Yes, this is fine,' Aaron says shyly.

Jake smiles and leans back from Aaron. His hands drag his shirt over the top of his head. A dark mat of chest hair grows like a shadow hanging on Jake's pecs. Aaron glances over the solid build of Jake's body. Jake's movements are powerful and deliberate as he lowers himself back onto Aaron and they resume kissing tenderly. Aaron surrenders to the pressure on top of him. He slides a hand around Jake's back and follows the line of his spine with the tips of his fingers.

Aaron's hips begin to rock as Jake unfastens his belt. Rough knuckles dig into Aaron's groin. Aaron raises his hips obligingly, and Jake follows through, sliding Aaron's jeans down over his smooth toned legs, underwear and all, to leave his lower half exposed. As the jeans fall to the floor, Jake sits back, gazing down on Aaron.

'Don't stop,' Aaron whispers.

'I just needed a moment,' Jake reassures him, 'to take in how stunning you are.'

Then, with a renewed sense of urgency Jake kicks hastily at his own pants.

In his enthusiasm, Jake's jeans catch at the ankle as he peels them off. He stands, a little awkwardly, to complete the process. Then, fully aware of Aaron eyes on him, Jake slowly removes his underwear to expose his erect penis. Aaron smiles through his nervousness. He rolls over to present himself. His face drags across the dusty cushions as he lowers his face and raises his arse into the air.

'What are you doing?' Jake asks, placing a hand on Aaron's shoulder.

'I thought this is what you wanted,' Aaron mumbles into the sofa, confused.

Jake pulls Aaron back around to face him.

'I would love to fuck you. Oh gods, how I would love to do that,' Jake says softly. 'But we don't need to straight away.'

Aaron's brow creases. He allows Jake to lower him onto

his back and unbutton his shirt. A dimple forms in Jake's left cheek along with a mischievous grin. Aaron watches like a statue, waiting for Jake to move. Jake kisses Aaron lightly on the lips. Small kisses continue around Aaron's neck and trail down his chest. Moisture traces the path of Jake's lips down Aaron's body. Aaron shuts his eyes as Jake's tongue tickles around his stomach to his hip. Jake pauses there for a moment, shifting position. Aaron squints over his chin to see what's happening. Before he can get a good view Jake takes Aaron's cock into his mouth. His body stiffens and toes curl, the sensation completely foreign to him. Unable to stop himself, Aaron moans loudly, and pulls at Jake's shoulders, unsure how long he can cope with this intensity. Jake continues at his task, unfazed. Pressure builds deep within Aaron's groin, along with a euphoria within his chest and tingling on his face. These new sensations combine into one overwhelming feeling as Aaron's body suddenly convulses. A rush of heat and pleasure fires through his entire body out from his penis. Then Aaron subsides back into the cushions.

Jake retracts and smiles proudly at Aaron.

'What—what, was that?' Aaron gasps.

Jake lifts himself up to kiss Aaron again. Aaron's lips move limply in response.

'What was what?' Jake grins.

'The thing you just did with your mouth.'

'Have you never had a blowjob before?' Jake stares, perplexedly.

'Is that what a blowjob is?' Aaron's head sits heavily against the seat cushion.

'Oh, I'm so sorry that you've lived your whole life without ever having a blowjob. How does that happen to a person?'

'I don't know,' Aaron shrugs. He feels his sight fade into

blissful blankness. 'I don't think I've ever done that. I haven't really spoken about it before.'

'Seriously?' Jake collapses onto the couch grinning. Aaron feels the point of Jake's softening penis against his leg.

'Yeah. I've only ever been with David. We've always stuck to our routine,' Aaron mumbles. A thought triggers inside Aaron's head. 'Oh crap, David,' Aaron snaps, suddenly alert.

His fingers reach determinedly for the buttons on his shirt. Jake leans away from Aaron to let the flurry of activity occur unhindered.

'Are you worried David will find out what we just did?' Jake asks.

'No. I just need to get home,' Aaron stutters. His pulls his jeans on and grabs at his shoes on the floor.

'Okay. But just to be clear. I don't know David and have no intention of telling anyone about this. It's easier that way,' Jake says casually from the couch.

'Thank you,' Aaron breathes heavily. He pats himself down, feeling for any missing bumps. He counts the contents of his pocket and nods once, satisfied. 'It was nice seeing you again Jake.' Aaron turns ready for the door.

'Wait,' Jake calls.

Aaron spins around to see Jake strutting towards him, comfortably with his nakedness. He reaches Aaron and wraps his arms completely around him. Aaron surrenders to the biceps squeezing against his shoulder. Jake releases slightly to look Aaron in the face. He pushes his face forward. Their lips meet again. Their chests heave into each other's with a deep embrace. Jake pulls away leaving Aaron swaying on the spot. A saltiness lingers on Aaron's teeth.

'Can I see you again?' Jake asks. Aaron nods automatically. 'Tomorrow maybe? I'll be here. Just let me know.'

Jake reaches down and pulls Aaron's phone out of his pocket. He taps confidently onto the screen.

'This is my number,' Jake says as he hands the phone back. 'Feel free to call me whenever.'

Aaron continues to nod as he accepts his phone back and slips it in his pocket. His head continues its blissful daze as he moves towards the street. A buzz hums in the back of Aaron's head. The tingling makes his head move lightly in all directions. He starts his trek back to the apartment, a soft smirk stuck on his face.

6.

THE RUSH OF excitement that sustains on his trip home evaporates the moment he steps into the apartment. The stillness is disrupted only by the hum of the refrigerator. Aware now that life could be so much more, Aaron realises how soulless the apartment feels. It leaches his energy with each step further inside. His feet drag heavily across the tiles to the kitchen. Aaron flicks the lights on as he meanders through the work of preparing a token meal, or perhaps simply the mess of one, to make David think he has been home all night. The artificial yellow glow of the lights around the apartment stains the walls with an obnoxious glare. Aaron strains to think of cooking ideas. Inspiration fails him. He stares blankly at the cold food in the fridge.

Aaron's mind wanders. The memory of Jake's body against his, its warmth, pulsates through him. Each remembered touch of Jake's fingers is so vivid it's as though Jake were still pressing into him. Aaron feels a flush return to his cheeks.

Aaron spots a bag of tomatoes in the fridge. *Pasta it is*, he nods, dragging the heavy plastic bag out and onto the counter. Aaron zones himself into the routine of a simple dish. The aroma of chilli and tomato quickly consumes the apartment. Aaron's thoughts rest comfortably under the circulating memory of his time with Jake. He loses himself reliving each shudder of pleasure and every scrape of a whisker on his lip.

Aaron loads the pasta onto two plates resigned to the certainty that they would be binned tomorrow. The scent of the food lingers on Aaron's hands as he heads to bed. He flops semi-clothed onto the quilt, then his eyes glaze over as he stumbles to sleep.

Aaron wakes early the next morning alone in the bed. He rubs his eyes as he surveys the room. *David must have slept at work again*, he concludes from the undisturbed room. Loneliness washes over him. He plonks back against the pillow and stares at the white ceiling. The smell of pasta no longer heralds a home-cooked meal but stale leftovers. He grabs his phone from the bed side table and unlocks the screen. A strange number flashes back at him. *Jake's number.* Aaron shoots upright. His heart races. Blood fills his muscles to the point of bursting. *I forgot to save it. He said he's free today.*

Aaron hits dial on his phone and presses the receiver to his ear, waiting eagerly.

'Hello,' a voice groans.

'Hi Jake,' Aaron says, perky before he thinks to restrain it.

'Aaron?'

'Yes, it's me.' Aaron calms himself. 'I'm sorry. I didn't realise it was so early. Are you still in bed?'

'Yeah. In bed still. I guess I'm awake now. What's up?'

'Well,' Aaron pauses. He feels a stutter ready to roll across his tongue. He holds it back. 'I was just ringing to see what you're up to today.'

'Nothing planned yet. Did you have anything in mind?'

'Not really. Were you in the mood for anything in particular? I'm open to suggestions.'

'Would you like to come over? We can hang out.'

'Sure,' Aaron sucks in a deep breath through his open smile. 'That would be lovely.'

'Cool. We can take it from there. I just need to shower and then feel free to come along. Head straight out the back. There won't be anyone home in the main house.'

'Will do. Seeya soon.'

Aaron hangs up. A squeal rises and halts in his throat. Excitement charges energy. He kicks himself out of bed and charges into the shower.

The taxi ride to Jake's house feels impossibly slow. The tedious conversation from the driver about numerous aspects of the weather grates against Aaron's patience. His foot taps impatiently on the car floor. His tense calves press against his skinny jeans as his leg jiggles restlessly. A single drop of sweat releases itself from the back of his head and tickles his neck. When the taxi pulls up at Jake's house Aaron hurriedly hands over cash and leaps out of the car. He finds the side gate that he used the night before. The latch creaks louder than he remembers. Aaron dislodges some flakes of paint in his rush to push open the gate.

Aaron reaches and taps on Jake's door before the rest of his body has come to a complete stop. He readjusts himself, finding his clothes pulled out of place in the final stretch to the door. Midway through pulling his shirt down the door opens. Jake stands behind it in a pair of briefs. His expansive chest glistens under fresh droplets of water. Aaron traces one as it follows the line of his stomach and disappears into the fabric of his underwear.

'I'm so sorry. I fell back asleep. I only just got out the shower,' Jake says.

Aaron loses focus. A burning twitches in his lips. He dives forwards, finding Jake's lips on his charge. They smack together and stumble back into the room with a muffled thud. Jake steadies himself to shut the door before surrendering completely to Aaron. Jake lowers himself directly onto the floor. Aaron follows him down. Aaron's thoughts muddle as he lands on top of Jake. Aaron gasps between hard kisses and presses his hands into the crumb-filled carpet to remove some weight off Jake's body. A recognisable firmness presses into Aaron's leg.

Aaron pushes himself off Jake and rapidly strips naked, then lays himself back down on the still wet chest. The naked torsos rubbing together creates a suction between their chests, and Jake giggles at the sound of the gushing air. Aaron ignores the snickers to concentrate on his task. He follows the example of Jake's the previous night to trace his tongue down to Jake's cock and then take it into his mouth, moving the briefs to one side. Eager to please, Aaron swallows the entire shaft at the first thrust. But, unprepared for what this would demand of him, he chokes and gags. Aaron persists, his enthusiasm undiminished despite the tears that stream down his face as he tries to emulate the pleasure Jake had given him.

Jake groans. His fingers dig into the back of Aaron's head. how to read those signs. Jake is enjoying his efforts. Aaron continues his motion. His own muscles begin to tense. His movements become shallow. He can feel his skin ready to explode. Jake makes his final cry. Cum spurts into Aaron's mouth. And then again, and again. Aaron swallows it hurriedly, intrigued by its heat and salty-sweet taste.

Aaron lifts his watering eyes to match the dazed look on Jake's face.

'Wow, I was not expecting that,' Jake sighs, 'especially not from someone who didn't know what a blowjob was until last night.'

'To be fair, I wasn't planning it either,' Aaron admits. 'I only decided to when I saw you standing like that in the doorway.'

Aaron slides up next to Jake and kisses him lightly on his lips.

'Not that I'm not enjoying this,' Jake says. 'But should we move to my bed. It will be far more comfortable.'

'Certainly, which room is it again?' Aaron nods towards the two bedroom doors.

'The one of the left.' Jake looks down at his foot. 'We might want to clean that up first.'

Aaron follows Jake's line of sight to a wet mark on the floor. The goopy liquid is thick and glistens white as it stretches across the carpet and onto Jake's ankle.

'What's that? I thought I got all of it.' Aaron says shyly.

'You got mine. You came as well.'

'I what?'

'Please say you know what came means,' Jake grins.

'I—yes I know what that means. I just didn't realise I had.'

'It sounds like you have a lot to learn.'

Jake takes Aaron's hand and finds a towel for them both. Aaron cleans the carpet before Jake leads them into the bedroom to sprawl comfortably onto the patchwork quilt.

Aaron snuggles up against Jake's arms. The heady scent of fresh sweat heats onto Aaron's neck is so pungent he can feel it physically. He presses his body against Jake's as if ready to be consumed by him.

'Was that the first time you've ever sucked someone's cock?' Jake says.

'What?' Aaron cringes.

'Your first blowjob. Y'know, putting a cock in your mouth.'

'Oh yes. Never done it before.'

'You were amazing,' Jake pulls him in tighter. 'So, why did you cringe just then, when I asked you?'

'Oh nothing. It's just that word.'

'Cock?'

'Yes,' Aaron feels less of a cringe this time. 'It's just not a word I hear often.'

'Don't you and David talk in bed? I hear it all the time. What do you guys call it?'

'Nothing really. We don't really talk during sex. Or about sex. It's just a penis.'

'Just penis,' Jake teases, 'not cock, dick, prick, sergeant at arms, knob—'

'No, none of them,' Aaron cuts Jake off. 'We just don't talk about it.'

'What? At all? But how do you have sex then? Just lay still and take it?' Aaron glares up at Jake. Jake's arm loosens on Aaron's shoulder. 'Seriously?' Aaron shrugs glumly. 'But what about your other boyfriends? Surely you did more with them.'

'No, I haven't slept with anyone but David, until now. We met in high school and have been together since. We first kissed after few dates but didn't sleep together until our wedding night. David's a bit traditional that way. I didn't mind waiting. Since being married we've only done one thing in bed.'

'Well— as you say, until now. We haven't slept together yet. That was just a bit of oral. Sex is something different.'

'Isn't that sex as well?' Aaron pushes himself up onto his elbow. His eyes look curiously down at Jake.

'Not for me. That's just a bit of fun. Sex is actually fuck-ing.'

'Ugh, so crass. I'm still not sure I even know what you mean.'

'Come on. You know. Penetration.' Aaron stares blankly. 'Anal intercourse. That's man sex. To me anyway. If I counted everything else as sex I would have had a lot more partners than I admit to now.'

'Gosh, how many people have you been with?'

'A lot when I was younger. Less now. I can't play around too much when I'm on duty. A barracks is too small. Word gets around too easily for my liking. I can hear guys going at it in the bunks all the time. Girls too.' Jake notices Aaron's eyes widen. 'You do know other people have sex all the time right?' Jake pokes Aaron in his ribs. Aaron nods, trying not to giggle at the tickling. 'I suppose you don't talk about it that much.'

'Never really. I've spent a lot of time alone in the apart-ment since David got his latest promotion. I think I once spent a week without seeing another person.'

'What the hell? How is that possible?' Jake pushes him-self up against his pillow. Aaron resettles his head against Jake's chest.

'I order groceries online and they get delivered. It just pops up outside. I guess I didn't have any need to leave the apartment. I just wait for David to come home. I'm always there when he needs.'

'That's sad. Are you a bit insane?'

'I don't think so. Why would you say that?'

'You see a lot of things on active duty. I've seen what happens to people that get kept in isolation before on duty. In jail they use it as a punishment. Isolation is a punishment for people who are already in jail. It's not natural to be so alone. Didn't you long for anyone?'

'Just David. He's all I've ever needed. All this new stuff feels a bit overwhelming for me.' Aaron shakes his head. The bizarreness of the situation tugs at his thoughts. 'You still haven't told me how many people you've been with.'

'To summarise,' Jake clears his throat. His shoulders broaden like he's reporting to an officer. 'One high school boyfriend, short but fun, and two since then. One was serious. That one was way too intense. I had to end it because it was draining. We loved each other but seemed to be destroying each other in the relationship.'

'I can understand that. Destruction isn't what a relationship is about. You should be there for each other.'

'Like you and David? You're always there for him. Where is he?'

'He's working to support me,' Aaron rebuts. A flash of defensiveness hardens his gaze. He lowers his eyes to prevent Jake from seeing it. 'Together we have everything we've ever wanted. A secure house. Plenty of money.'

'No life for you though,' Jake says with a smirk. 'Do you want to go to come with me to Cameron's club tonight? That dungeon place?' Aaron gapes, not daring to answer. 'Look, I've been there before. Between the two of us I think we can keep you safe. It's not as scary as the name implies. I'll tell

Cameron we bumped into each in the street and we felt like doing something.'

Aaron opens his mouth to protest. Any number of excuses to avoid going to a club run across his mind, but none stand up to scrutiny. *There's already food in the fridge. The house is clean. I could just be out stocking the wine cellar. Doesn't doesn't know when I do that.*

'Okay, I'll go,' Aaron nods.

'Great,' Jake answers. 'It doesn't open until later so we've got plenty of time to kill. So, would you like to sleep together?'

Aaron doesn't answer immediately. He holds his head back as if contemplating the options before leaning in to kiss Jake tenderly on the lips. Jake strips off his underwear and throws them onto the floor. Here in the daylight, without any sense of urgency or reason to hurry, Aaron feels comfortable to take his time. He allows himself a moment to examine Jake's body in detail. Aaron wants to see past the impressive muscles and learn what stories this body has to tell. Aaron traces his fingers lightly over Jake's square handsome jaw down past a scar on his neck. The scar isn't big, but it isn't small either, and Aaron wonders if it came from a battle wound, or a childhood accident, or something else. As Aaron's hand gently cups the pleasing swell of Jake's pectoral muscles, and luxuriates in the thick hair that covers them, he notices a slight enlargement of the left nipple. He suspects the it's the remnant of an old piercing. Evidence of a rebellious youth, perhaps? So you weren't always a straight-laced military man, Aaron muses. As Aaron nuzzles his face into Jakes belly, he is pleased to observe that the muscle is solid but not ripped, that Jake was the kind of man who valued his fitness over looking good, that he earned his impressive body through hard work rather than bought it from a gym. And all through his ponderings Aaron remained acutely aware of the insistent swelling between Jake's legs that progresses with Aaron's exploration of his body. Aaron takes the opportunity to now glance down at Jake's penis—no—his cock, still motivated by curiosity. A single dark vein runs to the tip of the foreskin throbs from the pressure of the blood inside. The light tan colour of the foreskin no longer covers the entire erection, now the red-purple helmet-shaped protrudes, already glistening with a tiny dewy drop. Aaron thinks of it as a sock for the head of the penis, it's strange up close, the first foreskin he's ever seen in person. Dark tuffs of hair twist around the base of the shaft and coat the testicles. Aaron reaches down and strokes carefully on the edges of the hair. Jake purrs in response to the touch of each hair around his testicles. Aaron presses deeper, caressing the scrotum. The wrinkled skin smooths under his fingers. Jake continues to groan with the touch. Aaron's finger fingers become more inquisitive and pinch gently at the scrotum.

'Whoa, slow down,' Jake snaps out of his whimper. 'Save the kink for later. Let's just be gentle for now.'

'Okay, sure thing,' Aaron answers, somewhat confused.

Aaron pulls himself away from Jake to ready himself on his knees. Jake's eyes follow down Aaron's lean back to the rounded bumps of his butt. The back of his hand traces around to the back of Aaron's leg.

'Why don't you go first?' Jake suggests.

'What?' Aaron straightens. The suggestion startles him out his pose. 'What do you mean by that?'

Jake chuckles and pushes Aaron onto his back. Aaron lays still, the back of his head pressed against the pillow.

'Do you want to fuck me first? Here, I'll show you,' Jake teases.

Jake reaches over to a drawer and pulls out a small packet and bottle of lubricant. He tears open the foil with his fingers. Inside is a floppy circle of rubber. Jake fiddles for a moment before grabbing the shaft of Aaron's cock and rolling it onto his erection. Jake rolls his fingers down it until satisfied it is smooth. He squirts lubricant onto Aaron's penis. The chill of the liquid shudders through Aaron's groin.

Jake stretches a leg across Aaron to ready himself. His face creases in silent pain at the point of insertion. Jake calms his breaths as he wills his muscles to relax. Aaron feels a warmth engulf his penis that grips more tightly with each of Jake's movements. Jake takes control, riding slowly up and down on Aaron. He alternates his rhythms, grinding in circular motions on Aaron's hips. Aaron's body tenses and tingles as his shaft eases in and out of Jake. Jake massages his palms into Aaron's chest, teasing his nipples with gentle movements. His strong hands hold ever more tightly onto Aaron as he quickens the pace. Jake maintains his enthusiastic energetic approach and leads them both to quick climax. Their bodies shudder through the last of their ejaculations.

'Now, for my least favourite part,' Jake shuts his eyes and pushes himself off Aaron's penis.

Muscles inside of Jake eject Aaron's penis with ease. The stranger pleasure shivers through Aaron's now sensitive shaft. Around his penis the condom hangs limply with a light shadow smeared over it. Jake whips tissues out of a drawer and skilfully removes the condom without losing a single drip.

Aaron's eyes become heavy. His head sinks back into the pillow. Jake adjusts himself to lie next to Aaron.

'This is strange,' Aaron confesses.

'Huh, how so?' Jake snuggles into his pillow.

'Sex with someone other than David. Aren't I supposed to feel guilty?'

'It's just sex. Are you planning on leaving David?'

'No, I've never wanted to be anywhere but with David. So I thought anyway. This seems different. This is fun but I don't feel like I've done anything wrong. David's never home much these days. It's like we're just together because it works, which it does, technically speaking.'

'So what's the problem?' Jake mutters as his eyes start to droop.

'I thought I would feel bad. I don't feel anything bad about what we are doing here. I don't have any guilt. Is that wrong?'

'Not in my books.' Jake throws an arm around Aaron and pulls him in tight. 'Don't stress about not stressing. Just relax. Enjoy the moment. We can head off to the club later and have some more fun.'

Aaron releases the tension in his muscles. His skin presses against Jake's fresh sweat. He hears Jake's breathing become regular and gentle. He decides to shut is own eyes to ease into a dreamless sleep.

The last shadows of daylight are flickering through the window when Aaron wakes up. The sheets are cold against his skin. He lifts himself up and notices he is alone in the bed. In the distance he can hear the muffled sound of water running. His eyes light up eagerly at the thought of Jake in the shower. He shoves the sheets off and tiptoes out of the room. The splashing gets louder as he crosses the living room. His hand pauses on the doorhandle before silent pressing down on the metal grip.

Aaron eases the door open. Steam fills the small bathroom. Aaron can see Jake's naked body moving amongst the mist. The hairs on his chest are slicked down. A fine film of soap shimmers across Jake's skin.

'Would you care to join me?'

Aaron jumps at the sound of Jake's voice. Jake continues to splash water across himself as if nothing was said.

'Um, what?' Aaron straightens up.

'Care you join me? You're already naked. You may as well jump in here.'

Aaron shrugs. He feels his penis twitch at the thought of showering with Jake. He shuts the bathroom door behind him. Jake pushes the shower screen open and stands waiting, one hip dropped seductively. Aaron carefully steps onto the wet tiles. Water splatters across his body. His chest quickly becomes wet and slick. Jake leans into him. His soapy skin glides across Aaron's. Their chest hairs slide past each other easily. Their kiss comes naturally to them. The unspoken comfort guides Aaron into a soft embrace. Jake erection taps on Aaron's leg within moments of their lips connecting.

'Is it my turn then?' Jake whispers.

Aaron nods. He kisses Jake a final time before turning around. A blast of cold air rushes into the shower when Jake opens it to retrieve a condom. Aaron curls his fingers around the top of the shower frame and spreads his legs. Jake teases his cock around Aaron's entrance before slowly pressuring it inside. Aaron's muscles surrender to Jake's commands. Aaron's cheek presses against the shower screen, wiping condensation off the glass with each thrust. The jolts behind him vary in intensity. Aaron can feel his cock swell with his own ecstasy.

Their voices echo each other in orgasm. Jake puffs. His

head drops onto Aaron's shoulder. Aaron remains still. His legs continue to twitch from his climax even as Jake pulls out of him. A hand traces down Aaron's back and slips between his buttocks. Aaron's eyes snap open wide. The tenderness of Jake's touch feels foreign to him. He cleans Aaron from behind, soothing the soreness of Jake's penetration.

They rinse themselves off and dress ready to leave for the nightclub. Jake throws on a torn shirt and loose leather pants. He slides his feet into his military grade boots. Once the shoes are tied he stands tall, his shoulders broad and ready to march. The semi-trashy attire teases Aaron. The slits in the fabric allow only glimpses of the body he still wishes to study intimately. Jake's trash casual is a start contrast to Aaron's sleek attire.

Aaron barely thinks anything of Jake's fashion choices until they park near the venue. Tatty, loose clothing, kept in line by suspenders is a frequent theme among many people walking in the same direction. The people converge on a single point, making their numbers look exaggerated. A blank wall stands before them. Dirt streaks down the side of the walls. The downtrodden warehouse stains the street that is otherwise rows of apartments and office buildings. It sits deep in the shadows of the taller buildings.

'Where are we going?' Aaron asks.

'In there,' Jake nods towards the warehouse.

'That's a club? I can't see an entrance.'

'It's around the side. It's an old delivery entrance that brings you in halfway up the building.' He points to the general flow of the crowd down a side alley. 'Just to get our story straight. I think we should say that you called by to say hi to Cameron. I was the only one home so I said I'd come here with you. How does that sound?'

'I think that should work. He won't ask too many questions will he?'

'Nah he shouldn't. And if he does just ask him about Andrew. I'm sure that will shut him up.'

Jake and Aaron turn around the corner of the building. A rusted looking ramp leads up to a double door in the middle of the wall. Blue paint marks 'DD' above the door. A queue slowly moves through the doors and into a darkness that no light from outside seems to be able to penetrate. Aaron and Jake make their way to the entrance where they are ushered in by two bulky security guards without hassle. Aaron strains his eyes to adjust to the darkness. Jake places a hand on his back and walks Aaron away from the door. A clink of metal grates against the bottom of Aaron's shoe. He looks down. The level he finds himself on consists only of a series of metal platforms separated by empty air.

As Aaron's eyes adjust to the gloom he can make out the expansive layout engulfing them. Just beyond the entrance several large metal platforms sprawl out, connected by a series of bridges. Several people lean over the edge gazing at a scene below. Aaron looks for the spectacle that holds their attention, and finds a seething dance floor, packed solid with gyrating punters in various states of undress. Aaron looks up into the shadowy rafters above them to find a third level of bridges leading to dark spaces veiled in plastic to prevent curious eyes peering in.

'Over there,' Jake points across to the bar on the opposite wall of their level. Cameron stands behind it casually chatting to a man sitting at one end.

Jake drops his hand off Aaron's back as they approach.

'Well, fancy seeing you here,' Cameron straightens upon seeing Jake. 'Have you been sent to spy on me?'

'You wish you were that interesting,' Jake retorts.

'And I'm very surprised at to see you here,' Cameron glints at Aaron. 'And delighted. How did you know where to find me?'

Aaron opens his mouth to answer but is beaten by Jake.

'He came by our house but no-one else was home. I thought I'd show him where you work.'

'How sweet of you,' Cameron jibes. 'So drinks then? You might need a stiff one before I give you the tour. It will be an eye-opener for you.'

'Wait, what?' Aaron answers, startled.

'You'll see. We have a lot of married couples come through here so maybe you'll surprise us all and enjoy it just as much as they do.'

Cameron doesn't wait for an order. He starts mixing layers of alcohol into glasses of ice. He tops it off with cola from the soda fountain and pushes them across the bar.

'This one's on me,' he whispers.

'How sweet of you,' Jake rolls his eyes. He takes his drink and begins sipping.

Aaron looks down at the glass for a moment. The single lime wedge is buoyed by bubbles. It looks completely innocuous.

'What is it?' Aaron asks.

'It's just a Long Island Ice Tea. It's one hell of a way to kick off the night.'

Aaron sips on his drink. The sweet cola taste hits his mouth first, then he waits with the straw hanging from his lip for the burn of spirit to follow.

'How much alcohol is in this?' Aaron asks.

'Loads. Doesn't taste like it though. That's the point,' Cameron says.

Aaron shifts his attention to the commotion below.

'What is this place? I've never heard of it except from you.'

'Well,' Cameron pauses. His jaws moves side to side, his eyes peer upwards waiting for words to form. 'It's a specialised club that caters for fetishes. I don't think I can say any more than that. If you hold on, I think I can sneak off to give you a tour now. Making punters feel welcome is part of my job description anyway. Give me a second.'

Cameron heads off to the other end of the bar and whispers to another worker, who nods in response.

'Are you sure you're ready for this Jake?' Cameron teases as he steps out from behind the bar. 'I can hold your hand if you need.' Jake glares in response. 'Right, let's get this tour on the go. As you can see the entire venue spreads over three levels. Bar and hangout spaces are on this level. This is where I work most of the time.' He points down to the strobe-lit chaos beneath them. 'That's the pit. Sometimes people are stuck raving for days down there. We have to force-feed them food and water just to get them out the door. There's not much but sweat and music down there. It can be fun if that's your kind of thing.'

They reach a staircase on the opposite wall from the entrance. Cameron pauses to allow a couple of men to climb the stairs before his little tour group.

'Before we head up I'm just going to say that this is the interesting part of the club,' Cameron instructs. 'You might see some things you don't agree with but keep your mind open and your mouth shut. We're all consenting adults here and we do not judge other's for what they're into.'

Cameron takes the lead up the stairs. Jake follows behind, his steps heavy as if wanting to slow his ascent. The steps level out onto a small platform. Aaron senses the emptiness below him. His feet grow unsteady. He sips on his drink to distract himself from the wide gap that falls down to the pit. Cameron continues walking towards a blacked out room in front of them.

'These used to be the offices,' he explains. 'Before the windows were removed they were great for watching over the entire building.'

Cameron pushes the layer of plastic at the door to one side. He holds it for Aaron and Jake to pass. Inside another plastic sheet hangs before them. Shadows move like puppetry in the room beyond. Cameron pushes through the sheet and immediately steps to the side to find a corner to watch from.

A strong smell of dust and leather is the first thing Aaron senses as he enters the room. back down his shock at the second thing he notices and stands in the corner with Cameron. Jake continues in with a nonplussed look on his face.

A man swings from the ceiling in the middle of the room. Leather straps hold him with his body facing down at the grotty linoleum. He bites down on a red ball strapped in his mouth. His body droops naked except for a black G-string and support straps. A second man sits in the corner, a black apron covering his bare chest, tight black mask hiding every facial feature. Around the room men and women dressed in black watch on eagerly. Some arms twitch as if resisting the urge to get involved.

The knee-high boots of the masked man tap menacingly on the floor as he paces in front of a series of implements precisely mounted on the wall. His hand hovers momentarily over each tool as he passes—a swat, a chain, a pinwheel, a whip. Finally he selects a small black club that wobbles as it's lifted from the wall. The hanging man nods, begging enthusiastically.

The masked man rubs his thumb and forefinger along the shaft of the rubber club. He swiftly marches over to the hanging man and beats the club down onto the back of the man's leg. The hanging man cries out, his shriek muffled by the red ball. Aaron grabs onto Jake's arm, his nails digging into the fabric of the shirt and the glass slipping from his hand.

Glass shatters across the floor. Everyone in the room snaps their head around at Aaron. The glare of the masked man is livid. Cameron opens his mouth ready to coordinate the clean-up, but before he can speak the masked man is already standing before Aaron, towering over him. Aaron feels Jake's muscles tense beneath his fingers, but Jake remains still. The man tilts his head assessing Aaron. Aaron stares back, too startled to do anything else.

The man leans in towards Aaron.

'What a good idea,' he smirks.

The masked man squats and surveys the glass on the floor. He picks up a large, pointed shard and holds it between him and Aaron. They both focus on the wet glass. He turns back to the hanging man, facing Aaron from the opposite side to ensure Aaron had a clear view. The hanging man groans and nods his head excitedly as the sharp edge of the shard is held to the top of the his back. Silence hushes over the room as he slowly moves the glass along the man's spine. At first the touch is light, barely enough pressure to scratch the surface. The man in the apron glances up at Aaron. His arm tenses. The glass moves deeper the further it travels, a dark stain in its wake. The hanging man begins to moan. His body convulses in exquisite pain. The spectators gape in awe and pleasure. The hanging man's moans intensify. The shudders increase. The masked man halts his progress at the lower back and then steps back. The glass shard remains upright in the hanging man's skin. The top point sparkles in the dull light. The hanging man sighs through the last of his orgasm. His body twitches through its final moments of ecstasy.

Aaron marvels at the tableau dangling before him as his eyes absorb every detail. A guiding hand pushes against Aaron's back as Cameron leads him from the room.

'I wasn't expecting that,' Cameron starts. He glances around. 'Didn't Jake follow us out? Doesn't matter. He can take care of himself.'

'Excuse me,' a man in a latex shirt scuttles across the platform towards them. 'Excuse me.'

'Yes?' Cameron looks across at the man.

'Would you by chance happen to be Mickey Dukes?' he asks. His eyes widen excitedly.

'Not now,' Cameron hushes.

'I'm so sorry to intrude. I just wanted to say I love your work. I think I have at least five of your—'

'Not now,' Cameron forces. 'Please leave. This isn't the time.'

The man drops his eyes and hangs his head as he wanders down the stairs, deflated.

'What was that about?' Aaron says blankly.

'Never mind. Are you okay? That was Dungeon's light kink room.' He nods at the room behind them. 'I wasn't expecting that.'

'Yeah I'm fine,' Aaron answer blandly. 'I've never seen anything like that before. I didn't realise people did that.'

'Well, that's nothing. The Driller Room is something unto itself. I'm not even sure it's legal. That's why I told you not to judge. People like different things. Are you sure you're okay?'

Aaron nods. The plastic sheet flaps behind them.

'Here, this is your job,' Jake mutters, his hand full of glass fragments.

'What the hell? Piss off.' Cameron throws his hands up in protest. 'Why would you do that? Just leave it in there. Have you seen the boots on those people, they can step on anything and not feel it.'

'Well, what am I supposed to do with a handful of glass?'

'If you're super keen you could see if that guy in there wants more glass stabbed into him, or you could just chuck it in the bin behind you.'

Jake looks behind him for the alleged bin. He pushes the lid back and throws the glass inside.

'So, what are we doing?' Jake says, wiping his hands on his pants.

'I need to get back to work,' Cameron responds. 'I'll see you guys later. You can take care of him can't you?' Jake continues to shake his head. 'Right, and if Mum asks. Andrew isn't right for me. He's a nice lad but I can't date anyone who is military.'

'Fair enough,' Jake mumbles.

Cameron waves and saunters down the stairs to the second level. Jake moves closer to Aaron, following Cameron with his eyes until he is completely out of sight.

'Now you know where he works,' Jake says.

'It explains a lot. I can see why you two are so open about sex if you see this kind of thing regularly.'

'I don't. I can't speak for Cameron. I have no idea what he does when I'm away. All I know is he always has a lot of money spare, so must get a lot of work.'

'He said he's saving for overseas.'

'It don't really care.' Jake shrugs. 'So, do you want to kick this place?' Jake winks.

'I would love to,' Aaron croaks, suddenly flushed with desire. 'But I do need to get home. I have a husband remember.'

'That's okay. I know I'm just the side-candy.' Jake pokes Aaron in the ribs. 'Can I at least find you a taxi?'

'Sure. That's a very gentlemanly thing to do.'

Jake escorts Aaron outside and into the fresh air. Jake throws his arm up and hails the first taxi he sees.

'I'm assuming you can pay for your own cab,' Jake says.

'Oh right, so that's the chivalry stops?' Aaron smiles. 'Of course I can. David gives me an allowance.'

'Alright then. So goodnight. Will I see you tomorrow?' Jake steps closer to Aaron.

'I think you might,' Aaron's eyes glow with mischievousness. 'Should I call beforehand or just sneak in?'

'You should probably call,' Jake nods. 'I don't know what Cameron's schedule is. I don't want him walking in on anything untoward,' he smirks.

'Fair enough. So until tomorrow.'

Aaron sneaks forward. He quickly pecks a kiss Jake on the cheek and ducks away into the taxi. Aaron watches Jake touch the skin of his cheek as he settles in the car.

7.

THERE IS NO sign of David when Aaron returns home. The lights still left on from when Aaron rushed out that morning, seem both stark and gloomy at the same time. Aaron curses at the sound of the refrigerator humming in the background. The solitary buzz in the apartment irritates him.

The image of the man being scratched with glass lingers behind Aaron's eyes. Even in his imagination he doesn't try to blink the image away. The laceration on the man's skin rises line a wave across his flesh. Aaron runs his fingernail down the back of his arm, wincing at the pain as the sharp nail traverses his skin. He presses deeper, his knuckle bending under the pressure, until his skin prickles. Aaron retracts his finger and inspects the damage. A fine red line marks his skin under his sparse arm hair and it feels slightly warm but there is no sign of blood or damage to the skin despite the now-dissipating pain. *How did that guy cope?* Aaron thinks. He watches the redness fade.

Aaron shrugs off the pain and heads to the kitchen. He pulls the leftover pasta out of the fridge. His hands stick to the cold plates. He wrinkles his nose at the congealed lumps as he scrapes the pasta into the bin and shoves the plates into the sink.

He returns to the fridge and stares blankly at the empty shelves. The two spaces allocated for prepared dinners stand out like a beacon of Aaron's indolence. He flounders through cooking a fresh meal, the recipe driven by laziness as he shoves the remaining ingredients from the fridge into the frypan. He allows the random bits of chicken and bacon to sizzle until they're tough and dry before he switches off the heat. Aaron pulls out two large bowls. The ceramic clatters on the marble bench top as he places them down. He retrieves salad leaves and a jar of dressing from the fridge. He aimlessly tosses the meat into the bowls along with salad leaves and tomatoes, and splashes on the first dressing he comes across. The hodge-podge of food is probably edible, but Aaron fails to care through his apathy.

Aaron shoves the bowls in the fridge and groans. A vague list of chores recites itself automatically in the back of Aaron's mind. His shoulders drop at the thought of unfinished duties. *Damn David. It's not like he's really here*, Aaron moans to himself. He heads to the bedroom and tears the sheets off the bed. He replaces them with fresh ones from the wardrobe. He adds the bathroom towels to the heap on the floor. Soon the pile is bigger than a single load of the washing machine. Aaron stands in the middle of the room gazing over his work. The mundane assortment of sheets and towels fix a solid knot of boredom in his stomach. Resigned, he bundles the washing into his arms.

Aaron takes the bundle to the guestroom. He pushes the

dirty laundry to the back of the wardrobe. Aaron slams the door and leaves for his own bedroom. He quickly washes ready to climb into bed, acting as if he hadn't left the confines of the apartment.

Aaron's romance novel lies open against his chest. The deep voice and chiselled skin of Diego embarking on an erotic getaway fails to capture his imagination. *Is that normal?* Aaron's retraces his memory to the hanging man. *Do people really enjoy that? Why would they do that to themselves? How do they even work out they like it? It can't feel right. It's nothing like being with Jake. That feels incredible. Have they forgotten what pleasure is? I've only just felt it, how could they lose it? Unless it was all a show. Maybe they were faking it. How am I supposed to know whether it's real or fake? I don't know them.*

Aaron falls asleep with the image of the hanging man imprinted in his dreams. The surreal scene plays on rotation. Aaron stands as an observer, an outsider to his dreams, a distant thought lingering outside the reality of the beatings against the hanging man. The masked man walks straight through Aaron, his arm reaching for a glass bottle behind him. Aaron watches glass shatter everywhere as the man brings the bottle down across the head of the hanging man. The hanging man screams in pleasure. The noise of his groans quakes through the room around Aaron. He feels the floor give way to nothingness.

'Then I jumped awake,' Aaron says the next day as he recounts the dream to Jake.

'What a messed up dream. Maybe we shouldn't have gone to Cameron's club,' Jake strokes Aaron's naked back.

'No, I'm glad I went. I think I'm just confused about how I feel knowing people enjoy pain like that.'

The sweat on Aaron's skin is almost dry. Their vigorous

sex ended with Aaron riding on Jake's cock like a carousel pony. Their bodies are learning each other. Aaron feels Jake's rhythm pulsate through him. Holding onto Jake's chest through the afterglow no longer seems like pressing down on a stranger.

'It's not a place for everyone,' Jake says. 'I knew it would be a little confronting for a first-timer but I never expected anything like that.'

'It was interesting,' Aaron rolls onto his back and stares dreamily at the grotty ceiling. 'I think it makes them happy otherwise they wouldn't do it. I keep trying to compare it to what I feel and whether or not I'm happy.'

'Are you happy?'

'I think so. I'm definitely not seeking a beating to find happiness,' Aaron smiles. 'I think I'm happier away from home though. The apartment bores me now. Even when I first met Cameron it was fun just being somewhere new.'

'So it's not just me and the awesome sex?' Jake teases.

'Well there's that too. That makes me very happy. Touching is also new to me. Touching like this. Lying together naked and being able to explore each other. With David I don't even know if he has a birth mark. There are parts on his body I don't think I've even seen or it's been that long that I don't remember what he's hiding under his clothes. Since the whole baby thing I haven't really seen him except when he wants something. I keep making food and presenting the apartment how he wants but I'm not sure he's coming home.'

'Maybe he's having an affair as well,' Jake suggests.

'Probably with that possessive snot Timothy,' Aaron mutters.

'Oh, there is someone?'

'It's just his personal assistant. He's obviously into David or he wouldn't agree to work such ridiculous hours.'

'Does that bother you?'

'What? The PA or the affair? Timothy has never been nice to me, the prick, but I don't think I care actually about David having an affair.' Aaron's eyebrows crease. 'I wouldn't be surprised if he has been. It would explain why he only comes home when he needs to put a show on for guests or for a change of clothes. It takes the heat off me a bit, especially if someone finds out about this.'

'It would be a complete accident if someone finds out about this. I'm leaving in a couple months and you won't hear from me while I'm on duty so it won't look obvious. If anyone was suspicious of anything, they'd only think we had a one night stand.'

'What's that?'

'Come on?' Jake's eyes widen. 'After all the new words you've learnt you're trying to tell me that you don't know what a one night stand is?'

'I think I might. You know I've never really spoken about sexual things. My dads were certainly too awkward to talk to me about sex and David's upbringing was just as conservative. Is it a sexual position? I only know the ones I've done with you plus the matrimonial position I do with David.'

'No, it's more of an approach to sex. It's where you have sex with someone once and never speak to them again.'

'That's horrible. Do people actually do that?' Aaron pauses and shrugs. 'I suppose I didn't know people enjoyed pain until last night.'

'Yep, you don't even have to know their name beforehand. Sometimes you might just look at each other and go for it.'

'Have you done that?'

'I tried to once at a beat,' Jake spots the confused expression on Aaron's face. 'To be honest I didn't know what it was either when I first heard of it. It's a place where people go specifically for anonymous, public sex. It's what people used before the internet. A park or a beach or something like that with plenty of hiding places. The trouble is most of them are loaded with breeders. The one time I tried it was mostly women coming up to me. I didn't know what to do. I wasn't expecting that. I thought it was a public sex place, not—that. In the end I didn't have sex but I got to see enough. Not my thing.'

'I don't think I would be into that either. It sounds way too public for my liking.'

'What do you think you would be into?' Jake strokes the back of his finger down Aaron's side. 'I guess you would have to choose from what we've done together.'

'I like everything we've done together. I like kissing. Gentle kissing. I don't like the way David forces his tongue on me when we kiss. Other than that I think I just like the skin contact.'

'What about watching sex? Not like what we saw last night, obviously. But something more vanilla. There's plenty of porn.'

'Porn? I don't know. I've never seen any.'

'But you do know there word, at least,' Jake pokes Aaron's rib. 'That's a first.' He jabs again, tickling Aaron.

Aaron giggles and grabs hold of Jake's finger. He wrestles the finger away from his skin. The muscles in Jake's arm barely tense and Aaron can tell he isn't using his full strength. In one swift move Jake rolls himself between Aaron's legs, pinning Aaron's arms behind his head.

'That's unfair,' Aaron puffs. 'You're much stronger than me.'

Someone knocks heavily at the door.

'Who's that?' Aaron asks.

'I don't know,' Jake shrugs. 'Anyone who actually comes back here has a key. Well, except you.'

'Jake, I know you're in there,' a man calls out.

'Oh fuck me. Not now,' Jake curses, releasing Aaron.

'Jake, let me in,' the person continues to knock.

'What is it? Are you okay?' Aaron curls up to try and peer out the gap in the window.

'Just stay here. Don't leave the room,' Jake says as he struggles with his pants. 'It's my ex, Kyle.' He pulls a wrinkled shirt over his head. 'I'll get rid of him quickly. he doesn't see you. I don't want him to make a scene.'

Aaron nods as Jake shuts the door behind him, leaving him alone in the musty room.

'What are you doing here?' Jake asks.

'I came here to see you,' Kyle answers, his voice clearer now the front door is open. 'You didn't tell me that you were back from duty. I only found out when I bumped into Susan at the supermarket.'

'You shouldn't be here Kyle. We've been over this,' Jake voice levels out into a steady calm.

'Aren't you going to invite me in? It's been ages. We should really catch up.'

'No,' Jake orders. His voice deeper is than Aaron recognises. 'You need to leave.'

'Gods, why? Just let me in. Wait. Is there someone in there with you?'

The hairs on Aaron's neck stand up. Blood rushes to his feet.

'You need to leave because I don't want to see you. You need to leave now. I don't want to have to call the police again.'

'Gods damn it, fine. I'll leave. You don't need to be such a prig about it. I'll see you around.'

The door lock clicks back into place. Aaron's muscles relax. Cold sweat coats his skin. Jake walks back into the room. He strips naked and flops back onto the bed, defeated.

'Sorry about that,' Jake says. 'I didn't think he would try coming over again.'

'What did he do?' Aaron rubs his fingers through Jake's hair.

'He's the intense ex I told you about. We loved each other but it was destructive. When I wouldn't let him in last time he scratched 'cunt' onto the front door and he repeatedly drove past the house really slowly. I had to get the police to visit him to make him stop.'

'Cunt? Is that another word I should know about?'

'It's not a nice word and my mums really don't like it. It has too many bad connotations.'

'Cunt doesn't sound that bad,' Aaron adds. 'It actually sounds cute.'

'Ugh, I can't stand how innocent you are,' Jake presses his finger on the top of Aaron's nose. 'I bet you don't even know what cunt means.'

'No,' Aaron sighs. 'But I still think it sounds cute.'

'It's an offensive word for vagina. It's as if the words cock and arsehole had a baby and decided to call it motherfucker, and then hooked up with breeder and had a baby of its own.'

'That's a lot of babies. Wait, and what's the final word-baby?'

'Cunt.'

'So cunt is the ultimate swear word that just means vagina?' Aaron asks. Jake nods. 'That doesn't sound like much of a swear word.'

'That doesn't sound like you. You're the man who cringed when I said cock for the first time around you,' Jake teases.

'Yeah, but I knew what cock meant, which is gets me thinking.'

'I hope that's not contagious.'

'You dick,' Aaron pokes his tongue out and shoves his finger into Jake's ribs. 'See I can swear.'

'I know that. You've already said cunt five times.'

'Because I didn't know what it meant. Is that where all the power is in swear words? It's all about what we think of them.' Aaron sinks further back into the bed. 'Think about how much more I could have achieved if I just had cunt behind me.'

'You're out of control now. I should call the police. I don't know this Aaron. You've gone all philosophical, next you'll get me to join the church.'

'Don't be silly. I'm not religious like my dads, just apparently very traditional. I kind of knew that before but it's much clearer now. I should have gone to university.'

'Why?' Jake laughs.

'Because I think I need to learn more. Didn't you go to university?'

'No,' Jake shakes his head slowly. 'I went into the army. I did army training. You know I'm in the army right?'

'Of course I know that,' Aaron playfully slaps him on the chest. 'But you still had an education. I feel so stupid around everyone.'

'You shouldn't feel stupid around Cameron. He's a special one.'

'Play nice,' Aaron prods. 'If it wasn't for him I wouldn't have met you.'

'True, I guess I can allow some credit. Every now and

then. But I don't think you need to go to university. I think you just need to get away from your home more. I know you love David but staying in that apartment alone all that time doesn't let you experience much.'

'I know you're right,' Aaron concedes. 'I should just be out of the apartment more. It's fun out here. So much more air.' He smirks.

Aaron leans in for a deep kiss. He throws himself on top of Jake, grinding his buttocks across Jake's crotch. He slides back and forth against Jake's cock until it's hard once again. Jake lays back patiently as Aaron fumbles a condom onto his erection and positions himself over top. Aaron sighs as Jake's penis enters him. Aaron experiments with the control he has from this position, twisting his hips in circles on top of Jake.

'Do you like that?' Aaron says, his hands massaging into Jake's chest. Jake nods. 'Do you really like it?'

'Of course I do,' Jake moans.

'Tell me what you like about it.' Jake stares confused at Aaron. 'We don't talk during sex. I thought it might be interesting to try. I could say cunt a few times, if that helps.'

'I'm sure you could. What do you want me to say?'

'Do you want me to fuck your cock harder?' Aaron tries to purr.

'Whoa, that's intense,' Jake teases through his heavy breathing. 'Dirty talk isn't my thing. How about this? Can you feel your stomach muscles move with each rise and fall?' Aaron nods. 'Below that and just above your cock is another muscle. Try tensing that.'

Aaron concentrates on his movements. He feels his stomach tighten and his sphincter grip harder onto Jake's shaft. Jake's head presses hard against the pillow. His face contorts and pales. Aaron recognises the twitching of Jake's jaw. The sight of Jake climaxing prompts Aaron to his own orgasm, and cum sprays across Jake's torso. Aaron stays on top, feeling the erection soften inside of him.

'I would ask where you learnt that but I already know the answer,' Jake pants.

Jake screws his face up as his penis is ejected from Aaron. He reaches for the damp towel next to the bed and wipes the mess off both of them.

'I think I agree with you. Dirty talk didn't seem to add much to it for me,' Aaron muses.

'You should watch porn. That's all they do. Way too much dirty talk. It doesn't sound right.'

Aaron plonks himself back next to Jake. Outside he sees the light start to fade.

'I think I should head off,' he says.

'Really, why so early?' Jake asks.

'I have a feeling David will be home tonight. He hasn't been around the last couple of nights. I don't think he has a week's worth of shirts in his office.'

'Are you going to leave a little something for me to remember you by?' Jake grins. His places the back of his hand to his forehead pretending to faint.

'You're right out of a novel,' Aaron teases.

Aaron looks around the room. The piles of clothes on the floor offer no inspiration. On the bedside table Aaron spots a small flower with a twisted wire stem tossed amongst a pile of coins and pens. Aaron ponders over the small object. Aaron grins as he picks the flower up and readies to hand it to Jake. Jake watches on while Aaron bends the wire stem into a flatter curve. He slides the flower into Jake's pubic hair. The wire slips under the rough curls just above his penis. Aaron manipulates the metal until the forget-me-not is secured.

'There you are, a token of my affection,' Aaron says.

'Why thank you,' Jake answers sarcastically. 'What made you think of that?'

'I don't know. It just came to me.'

Aaron kisses Jake one last time before dressing and sneaking out the door. The lights are still off in the main house when Aaron struts out the side gate to the road. He walks to the end of the street before hailing a taxi to make the trek back to his apartment. On the way home he ducks into a small market to gather a couple bags of extra groceries to cover his tracks if David has beaten him home.

'What do you mean cancelled?' Aaron hears David shout the moment he opens the front door. The shopping bags knock heavily as he struggles with the door. 'That just isn't good enough.'

Aaron tiptoes towards the kitchen. *He must be on his phone*, Aaron decides when he can't hear anyone else in the apartment. He hauls the grocery bags onto the kitchen bench ready to unpack them. David catches sight of Aaron from the dining room. Aaron catches an intense glare as David locks onto a fresh target. David hangs up his phone and charges into the kitchen. His mouth opens for a lecture when he spots the bags of food on the bench. He lowers his finger. The anger in his eyes dissipates.

'Is everything okay?' Aaron asks calmly.

'Yes, everything is fine,' David grumbles. 'Bad day at work. I expected you to be home but you weren't. I didn't think you would be out shopping.'

'Neither did I,' Aaron prepares his lies. 'But there was a screw up with the usual delivery so a lot of things I needed were missing. I had to duck to the market before I could start cooking. I'm sorry but dinner will be a little late now.'

Aaron hides his surprise at his own ability to lie. Once he started talking the words began to flow out of him with steady conviction. Aaron feels that his statement is true even though he knows it is an outright lie.

'That's okay,' David says, his shoulders slumping as he calms down more. 'Are there any leftovers? I need to stock up and head back to the office. I told Timothy I was just grabbing some fresh clothes anyway. I've left him preparing the quarterly statements ready for the board meeting tomorrow. Of course, there was an error so I'll spend the night double-checking figures again.'

'Yeah there's some salad in the fridge.'

'Great! Can you put that into a container for me? I might take all of it. It will save us ordering dinner in again.' A hint of determination returns to David's eyes. 'Before I forget, I have to cut your allowance.' Aaron turns away to hide the obvious eye rolling. *Of course you have to cut mine but you won't touch yours. Anything I need doesn't affect you.* 'I was just talking our credit cards over with the bank and our main saver has been temporarily frozen. I don't know when we will get access back to it. Apparently there's been some erratic spending and the anti-theft mechanisms of the bank shut it down automatically.' Aaron freezes. Aaron knows his spending has increased so he could get around town. 'I checked over it, there's nothing unexpected. The usual cab fares might be a little more than normal. Maybe a couple double charges here and there but that money will be returned to us.'

Aaron hands David the plastic containers of food. His mind races at the thought of David not returning home that night. A sense of freedom passes through him as the usual expectation that David could return at any moment evaporates.

'David,' Aaron says softly. 'I've been thinking. Is there any chance I can get your schedules for the day?' David opens his mouth to protest. His shoulders drop back ready for a corporate speech. 'I don't need any information about exactly what you are doing.' David relaxes a little. 'More just your movements. It's all so I can make sure that all your clothes are ready when you need them and the food is still hot and fresh rather than reheated.'

'You don't need to know where I am. You've been doing fine for years.'

Aaron's heart smacks hard against his chest. He swallows to remove the speed of the beating.

'It's to help cut down my spending,' Aaron says. David's ears visibly perk up. 'If I know when you'll be home I can plan the correct amount of groceries. It will cut down on how much we spend on food. It will taste a lot nicer as well.'

'Very well, if it makes things cheaper,' David says. 'I'll have Timothy message through my daily schedule at the beginning of the day.'

David grabs the plastic containers and a bag Aaron assumes is loaded with clothes.

'Thank you,' Aaron says. 'Have a good night,' he calls to David's back.

David doesn't answer. The lock clicks in place behind him. Aaron skips around the kitchen, as he puts away the remaining groceries, success beaming on his face and delight tearing in his eyes. *Is this what being happy feels like?* The freedom of knowing when to be home for David reduces the risk of being with Jake. *I can spend all the time I want away now, without getting caught.*

Aaron dances his way through dinner preparations. He fries himself some celebratory chicken. The smoke from the oil permeates the entire apartment. Aaron snacks on the crispy bits of chicken until he feels bloated and satisfied. The stench of oil seeps deep into his pores. The layer of grease and dirt makes Aaron smile. Aaron continues his new sense of freedom in the bathroom. He fills the tub with steaming water and bath salts.

The boost in Aaron's esteem swells his confidence. Aaron ducks out to the cellar while the water is pouring into the bath. He opens the chilly room and glances over the shadows stacked against the wall. *David would never know*, he reassures himself. *David never knows what we have.* He reaches for the premium section and selects one covered with dust. He removes the bottle from the bottom shelf. The rack still looks full in the inky darkness. He brushes off the dust and eyes the label. *1998 Syrah. A good year I think.* He takes the bottle and along with a glass back into the bathroom.

Aaron strips down and tosses his clothes into the washing basket. He turns off the water and dips his toe into the water. Heat prickles through the skin of his foot at a pleasing temperature, and he lowers himself completely into the water until only his head sits just above the water level. The stem of the wine glass disappears into the bubbles as he sips the extravagant shiraz.

The first two glasses are quickly emptied. The blackcurrant smoothness of the wine flows easily across Aaron's tongue. He tilts his head back, letting the last drop of the glass trickle in, adding to the tipsiness Aaron feels. He places the glass on the floor and eases back completely into the bath. He shuts his eyes, letting his skin soften and melt into the water.

Aaron touches his chest. He presses into the muscle to force it to release into complete relaxation. His skin feels smooth under his finger. The pressure of his finger comforts him. The soap coating his skin rubs slickly under his hand. Aaron starts rubbing across his stomach. His muscles rise and quiver as he explores his body. Small tuffs of hair move effortlessly in the weightlessness of the water. His mind begins to wander. His body draws deep breaths as if he is with Jake in bed ready to have sex. He follows his hand further down his body. The small bushel of pubic hair scratches against his skin. Aaron moves his other hand down to cup his floating testicles. Pictures of Jake naked on top of him rush through his mind. He massages his scrotum. The gentle touch makes his penis stand hard against the water. Aaron takes his cock in his hand and runs his fingers over the head of his penis. His entire body shivers. His breath grow heavy. In his mind's eye, Jake takes control of Aaron's body. He strokes along his penis letting his imagination take control. The water laps at the edge of the bath as he shudders and ejaculates.

Holy fuck, what was that? Aaron marvels to himself, caught between the quivering breaths of his excitement and a ragged sigh of release. His hand slips away from his penis and his head relaxes back down onto the edge of the bath. His eyelids droop completely closed. His thoughts dissipate into a cool darkness.

8.

AARON WAKES UP SHIVERING. The cooled water of the bathtub has sucked the remaining heat from him. The soapy foam he fell asleep to has languished into a grimy film on top of the water. As he sluggishly heaves his body from the bath to dry himself, his foot collects the forgotten wine glass on the floor, sending it skittering to shatter against the wall.

'Shit,' Aaron mutters.

Aaron grabs for a towel and vigorously rubs the water off him. He ignores the glass while he dresses and warms up enough to be able to hold the bannister broom steady. Still shivering from the chill of the bath, he retrieves the dustpan from the kitchen and scoops up the fragments, wrapped only in a towel. His body greedily soaks in any warmth he happens to come in contact with, though there's precious little of it on the bathroom floor.

Once the glass is disposed of Aaron slides himself under

the quilt of his bed. The nest of comfort hugs his body cosily. He opens his eyes one last time before preparing to sleep. A flash from the bedside table catches his attention. He rolls over and starts at the brightness of his phone. A message from Cameron glares up from the screen.

> Wanna hang out 2moz? I'm gonna go meet a guy and need moral support b4hand.

Aaron texts his answer.

> Yep sure :D when?

> Ill b there @ 10 and we can take it from there

Aaron locks his phone and places it back on the bedside table. *I'm seeing a lot of the Cameron and Jake lately*, he thinks as he drifts off to sleep.

The next morning the rattle of Aaron's phone vibrating on the bedside table wakes him. He opens the screen expecting a message from Cameron. The screen flickers alight with an unknown number.

> Meetings until five. Post-work drinks with CEO. Dinner with Executive Co-Chair. Prep of figures for shareholder ballot until late.

Timothy, Aaron thinks. *This must be David's schedule for the day. It's kind of vague, but at least I know he won't be home tonight.* Aaron rolls out of the bed and heads to the kitchen to make himself a coffee. The familiarity of the machine comforts him through the early stages of waking. The motions of grinding and pouring the coffee bless his senses with its fresh aroma. He sighs through the first sip. Outside the window the city is awake already. The fierce sound of peak hour traffic is dying down to a casual drone of cars.

The doorbell rings out behind Aaron. He startles involuntarily. Gosh, is it ten o'clock already? He heads to the door knowing Cameron will be standing behind it.

'Sorry I'm a bit early but I couldn't sleep. Some guy downstairs buzzed me in,' Cameron says when Aaron opens the door. 'Coffee would be great. May I have one?'

'Sure, come on in.'

Aaron swiftly prepares a coffee for Cameron. Cameron takes it eagerly and sips loudly on the rim.

'You really need a fix, huh?' Aaron asks.

'Absolutely. I think I may need more than this to get through the day.'

Cameron is wearing a tight tank top and shorts that look like something he would have owned in high school. Aaron notices Cameron is moving strangely and a slight paleness in his Cameron's cheeks.

'Is everything okay with you? Do you need to sit down or something?' Aaron suggests.

'No thanks. If I sit I think I might freak out more. Thanks for coming with me today. I suppose I should explain why I need moral support.'

'That would be helpful, yes,' Aaron smiles, trying to keep the mood in the room elevated.

'You remember that guy at DD?'

'The hanging man? How could I forget?'

'No, the one outside. The one that said he loved my work. Well it turns out he's connected to a producer, who now wants to meet today to discuss doing some extra work.

I'm so nervous. I haven't done a gig like this in ages.'

'Of course, you're an actor as well,' Aaron exclaims. 'Why would I think that your three other jobs would be enough.

'I've only had a couple roles with a small company. It has some weird hours but makes great money. My screen name is Mickey Dukes.'

Cameron paces in the kitchen, his thongs slapping on the tiles with each step. He gulps at his coffee between strides.

'I can understand why you'd be nervous. Just the thought of all those people watching you and judging you makes me sick.'

'It's not that. I really enjoy that, it allows me to express myself in front of people,' Cameron dismisses with a wave of his hand. 'It's the fact that if I land this gig it might give me the final chunk of money I need in an instant. I've been working towards this for a long time. It's better paying than any role I've ever been offered.'

'What will you have to do?'

'Smile, flirt, maybe suck the producer off. I don't know. That's why I needed you, for support in the studio, and then to take me out drinking afterwards if it all goes wrong.'

'I meant what will you have to do in the role,' Aaron clarifies, taken aback. 'Would the producer really make you give him sex to give you a job?'

'I want this gig pretty bad. And it's not like that would be unheard of in this industry.'

Cameron downs the dregs of his coffee and smacks the mug down on the counter. Aaron shrugs at Cameron's request, just glad that it wasn't him that had to go through all this.

'Sure, I'll come what could go wrong?' Aaron says.

'Anything could go wrong.' Cameron's usual composure evaporates into anxiety.

'No, I meant that's probably something I could cope with.

Look, you're the most charismatic person I know. I'm sure that you'll get the part, and you probably won't even have to resort to sex.'

'Um... yeah. I think I'm practically the only charismatic person you know. But thank you,' Cameron resumes his pacing. 'Can we leave now and walk there? I don't think I can cope staying in the one place for too long.'

'Sure, just let me get changed.'

Aaron rushes out of the room. He changes into the first outfit that comes to hand so that he doesn't leave Cameron alone in the kitchen long enough to wear a trench into the tiles.

The outside air hangs onto the last of the morning briskness. Cameron marches off in the direction of the production company office. Aaron jogs to catch up and match pace with Cameron.

'Can't we just catch a taxi?' Aaron asks between puffs. 'I only just woke up and I'm not ready for physical exercise.

'Nope, if we get there too early that just leaves me more time to stress and pace around the parking lot.'

'Okay, but can we go a bit slower. I don't want to be too puffed to talk.'

Cameron slows himself down. Aaron watches Cameron rein in his breathing and resume a semblance of control. Cameron's steps become regular and smooth.

'Talking, yes, I can do that,' Cameron says. 'It will help me get my mind off the audition. I'm glad you're coming with me and you get to see more of my life. I think it will help us be closer, and we probably should be close, given that you feel comfortable enough having sex with my brother.'

Aaron gasps. He throws his hand to his mouth but he is too late to stop the obvious shock from appearing on his face. Cameron laughs. His pace begins to slow and his usual calm demeanour reappears.

'I had just assumed you were sleeping with him. I mean, why else would you appear together so often? But now you've just confirmed it.'

'But, how? We made sure no-one else was around. We can't let anyone know.'

'Don't worry. I don't plan on telling anyone. I may play Jake a bit to see what I can get out of him but otherwise your secret's safe with me.'

'Thank you. I think,' Aaron's shoulders relax slightly. An edge of caution keeps his spine stiff.

'I take it you did something on the first night you met.'

'We just kissed. It was confusing. I really like seeing Jake but I still really love David. It feels right. Especially because I don't have to choose between the two. Jake will have to leave on duty again soon, anyway.'

'That's the same excuse Jake uses. He says that to a lot of guys. I think it's just to protect himself from another Kyle. That guy was crazy. Some free advice, never put your dick in crazy. I bet the sex was fantastic though.'

'Gross! You're talking about your brother.'

'Not as gross as actually sleeping with him. I'm just saying things, not actually imagining them.' Cameron pauses all of a sudden. He stares up at the apartment complex above them. 'We're here,' he nods at the glass doors. 'Are you ready?' he asks.

Cameron walks through the door without waiting for Aaron to answer. Aaron follows across the bland, stained tiles to the elevators. The walls seem to close in on them as they walk across the lobby. The drab browns and greys drain all light out of the room.

'The studio is here? In an apartment building?' Aaron radiates skepticism.

'Yeah, a lot of studios find it easier to remain low-key. I'd keep it quiet too until we're inside the office or back outside. Don't want to blow their cover,' Cameron winks.

Aaron swallows back any questions that pop into his mind on the elevator ride to the ninth floor. The elevator opens to a blue carpeted hallway that looks like its spent time on the floor of a mechanic. Cameron leads them around the corner to an office with a small gold plaque on the door. *Morgan's Agency*, Aaron reads. The door gives away no further information. Cameron presses the doorbell.

A young, skinny man opens the door with a smile. His pursed lips and curiously eager eyes remind Aaron of a kitten waiting for something to bat away.

'Can I help you?' The man asks.

'Yes, I'm Mickey. I have an appointment with Michael. This is my friend, he came along for the ride.'

'Oh yes, Mickey,' the man straightens up and holds his hand out for Aaron and Cameron to shake. 'It's lovely to meet you. I'm Tim, twenty-one, Libra.'

'Seriously? Another Tim,' Aaron blurts out while shaking his hand.

'What?' Tim asks. Cameron widens his eyes as if to warn Aaron.

'Nothing,' Aaron clarifies. 'It's just you're far too charming to be a Tim.'

'I don't know what that's supposed to mean,' Tim eyes Aaron worriedly.

'Don't worry about it,' Cameron steps in. 'He's a bit weird, he doesn't get out much. Words are a bit difficult for him sometimes.' He places his hand gently on Tim's shoulder. Tim sparks at the physical contact, his eyes lighten up with intense happiness.

'Oh, I see. That's okay then,' Tim says. 'Come with me, I'll take you both through now.'

Tim leads them into the apartment. The interior has been gutted and fresh walls put in. Aaron doesn't recognise the layout. The white of the carpets and walls reflect enough light to stop the apartment crowding over them like a warren. Tim takes them around several corners before a small hallway opens up with a large glass door at the end. A star embossed with Michael Morgan is printed on the glass. Several other plain wooden doors break off the other sides of the hallway. The carpet reeks of cheap bleach.

'If you just wait here for a moment I'll let Michael know you've arrived,' Tim says.

Tim scoots a couple of steps ahead and slips behind the glass door. Cameron bounces agitatedly on the spot. He shakes his hands to remove the nervous tremor. Aaron begins to feel faint, a sudden wave of bleach hits his nostrils. Tim returns quickly and stands in front of them ready to make confirmed announcements.

'Michael is ready to see you Mickey but he would prefer to discuss your audition and contract in private. I can take your friend to the waiting area.'

'That sounds alright,' Cameron says with a sudden note of confidence. Aaron nods, glad he won't be exposed to the casting couch.

Cameron steps over to the semi-open door. He knocks and sticks his head in. Aaron can picture the cheeky face he is presenting to Michael, something a little playful but enough to show knowledge of how things work.

'This way please,' Tim directs.

The tour continues around another two corners to a larger open space with couches pushed against one wall. Large windows stretch across the far wall, a futile attempt at gathering light given the neighbouring apartment block that consumes the entire view. The admittedly very clean soullessness reminds Aaron of the empty shell his apartment has become.

'Take a seat anywhere. Can I get you a drink while you wait?' Tim asks.

'Just some water would be great, thanks.'

Tim nods cautiously and steps out of the room. Aaron walks across to the couch near a coffee table loaded with magazines. He lowers himself softly onto the couch. Scratchy fabric covers the rock hard cushions under his buttocks. He tries to lean back and sink into the couch but it fights him off, holding him upright and uncomfortable. Aaron ignores the awkward couch and scans the magazine titles. Across the glass coffee table are splayed a range of volumes with single-word titles emblazoned above pictures of unusually attractive men. Very scantily clad, unusually attractive men. An assortment of men of different ages and body types, but all of them very attractive and all of them leaving very little to the imagination. This seems very strange to Aaron, but then he wouldn't know what kind of magazines aspiring actors would read. A lot of actors are also models, and they all look like models, he reasons to himself. There is even a few slimmer magazines featuring similarly clad women on the second shelf.

'Here you go,' Tim says when he re-enters the room, interrupting Aaron before he can investigate further.

Tim places a coaster down with a highball glass directly on top. He cracks open a bottle of water with an effervescent hiss. Tim pours half the water and places the rest next to the glass as if explaining to Aaron how to serve oneself a drink.

'Thank you,' Aaron says. He musters the courtesy he usually forces out at dinner parties. 'That's very kind of you.'

'If there is anything else just let me know.'

Before Aaron can open his mouth Tim turns and leaves the room. Aaron takes a sip of his drink. The water feel cleansing and refreshing. He places his glass down next to a magazine with a hairless man winking back up at him.

Aaron picks up the magazine and glances over the cover. The man's tongue rests seductively on his top lip. He perks his buttocks behind him to display his jockstrap. Aaron flicks over the page. Oh gods, I'm not in Kansas anymore. The scantily clad man on the cover is no longer clad at all. His penis is erect and proudly presented to the camera. Or on the next page in the mouth of another hairless man. Aaron scans the pages quickly. *So many penises. They're all weird and different. That one has a piercing in it. Why is there no body hair?* Aaron's thoughts begin to race as he pieces together the discreet location, the seedy apartment, Cameron's ridiculous screen name and private meeting with the producer, and the pornographic magazines into a horrifying conclusion. Cameron is a porn star! Then Aaron is drawn back to his first experience of pornography, right in front of him. *They look too young. That one there doesn't look old enough to be naked in a magazine. Why did they give him a lollypop to suck on? Do people actually prefer people to look so young?* Aaron shakes his head. *I'm a married man having an affair and am currently sitting in a porn studio. I shouldn't judge other people for what they like.* The magazine slumps across Aaron's lap. A young man stares up at Aaron, his face contorted in ecstasy as another young man fucks him from behind. *Do I like having affairs? I love having sex with Jake but does that mean I like affairs in general? What about sex? Am I obsessed with sex just because I enjoy it?*

'All done,' Cameron interrupts Aaron's pondering as he enters the room, Tim riding his heels. 'You can come in now.' Cameron's smile shines with triumph. 'I got the contract but there's a real rush on it. They want to start today. If you want you can stay on set and I'll walk you home afterwards. They're actually on site. Come on, Tim will show us to the studio.'

Aaron drops the open magazine onto the coffee table and marches behind Tim and Cameron.

'Congratulations,' Aaron whispers once he gets closer to Cameron. 'Um, is it normal for it to happen that quickly? I don't think this is a normal film studio.'

'I wasn't sure how quickly they'd need to proceed,' Cameron says. 'Michael said he had a couple of guys lined up because of the tight schedule. I'm glad I didn't douche out for nothing. Why, what seems wrong with it?'

'Er, excuse me. What did you do?'

'You know, flush the chamber. There's going to be close-ups and I need to look good, so I made sure I was clean inside and out.'

Tim turns a corner and opens one side of a double door. Aaron is confronted by a bed surrounded by spotlights in the room beyond. Tim nods and excuses himself. Cameron and Aaron step into the room. Several men bustle around the room playing with cameras of different sizes. Bottles of liquid line up on a shelf above a stack of towels. Aaron recognises a couple of lubricant labels and alcohol cleaners but can't make out the rest. A bulky man stands on the opposite side of the room flicking through a bundle of papers. His muscles threaten to burst out of the tight black material of his shirt.

'That will be my date for the evening,' Cameron says casually. 'I've seen him in a couple of films online. It's going to be great to work with him. I may be sore afterwards, though. He's a big boy.'

Aaron follows the hardness of the actor's stomach down to an obvious outline in his jeans. Aaron's jaw, already hanging lose in bewilderment, drops even further at the length of the man's cock.

'I know right,' Cameron elbows Aaron. 'Oh, Michael's in charge of this one. He's going to direct this film himself. It's kind of a pet project to let Sammy Q over there know that they still want him under contract.'

'Sammy Q is the one in the black shirt over there?'

'You mean that cock riding a pile of muscles? Yeah, that's him. He's the reason they have to film today. If it wasn't for me I think Tim would have to take one for the team, as it were. Which is probably why he's looking so relieved.'

'But Cameron,' Aaron whimpers, anxiety fuelling his sense of urgency, 'I think this is a porn set.'

'Well of course it is, darling. What did you think it was?' Cameron looks at him with concern. 'Oops! Hold that thought. The director's here, I gotta go. Just find a dark corner to sit in, stay quiet, and don't get in the way of anyone holding anything.' The excitement is clear in his voice as he abandons Aaron in a strange and uncomfortable new world.

Michael Morgan charges into the room exuding an air of command. Tim shuts the door behind them and flicks a switch against the wall.

'Right we're now filming,' Michael commands.

Michael sits in a chair close to the bed set-up. His simple jacket and jeans are casual, while the round glasses perched on the bridge of his nose provide an academic aspect. He skims over a pile of papers muttering to himself. His hands run through his thick black hair as he reads.

'Right,' Michael clears his voice. 'Let's get this show on the road. We'll start with the interviews. Mickey, sit yourself on the bed. Lean up against the bedhead. We'll light test as we go.'

Aaron leans against the shelf of lubricant and towels as he watches. Cameron saunters over to the bed and pushes himself up against the bedhead. Aaron watches the proceedings as if floating above a carnal act in a dream. Cameron smiles for the camera, following every direction from Michael. At first there's nothing confronting for Aaron as Cameron, now Mickey, flirts a little as he's asked questions and talks himself like he's giving the audience a chance to get to know him. The next moment Sammy Q lands heavily next to Cameron on the bed. His introduction is short and superficial, as though the audience already know everything about him. Before Aaron can blink Cameron is kissing Sammy Q, his hand is quick to explore the outside of Sammy Q's jeans and run the outline of his cock. A man dressed entirely in black scoots around the edges, his camera flashes incessantly to momentarily blind everyone in the room.

The motions of intercourse seem surreal to Aaron, as though it were a theatrical play performed for his own private benefit, despite the ring of cameras. Michael's constant directions and commentary only add to the pantomime feel. Cameron's fake moans and overacted pleas for more do little to hide the obvious pain of being impaled on Sammy Q's huge cock.

'Have you ever thought about doing this line of work?' Tim whispers close to Aaron.

In the background Cameron continues to moan and

thrash about while Sammy Q pushes harder into him.

'No, I didn't know much about it until today. It's been a real eye-opener,' Aaron says quietly.

'Well, apparently you've got the look for it,' Tim hands a card over to Aaron. Aaron accepts it and spots Michael's name embossed across it. 'Michael would like to consider you for a role on one of his current films. It's an amateur take on this sort of work,' he nods towards the scene on the bed. Cameron is face down as Sammy Q thrusts viciously into him.

'Um, thanks. I'm not sure what to say.'

'You don't have to say anything. Just think about it. It could be a chance for you to have your face on film. Give me a call if you want to meet with Michael.'

Tim struts away. Each of his footsteps slides slightly across the floor, muffling the noise of his movements. Aaron looks back down at the card. *Me in porn?* He thinks. *They think I would be good for it. What's in it for me? That looks painful for Cameron. Maybe the money is that good. Why else would he do it? I guess it would help me increase my allowance. More than that, I'd have my own income. I could do whatever I wanted without David keeping tabs on me. He could cut my allowance completely and I wouldn't be dependent on him. But I guess I would have to have sex on camera. Am I willing to risk being found out?*

Aaron puts the card into his pocket. He feels the ends of the cardboard crinkle into the bottom of his pocket. The scene around him draws to a rough close. Cameron lies on the bed covered in glistening liquid. A cameraman moves close. Cameron smiles at the lens, muttering something Aaron can't quite hear. Tim charges past Aaron again. He snatches towels from the shelf.

'And that's done,' Michael declares. 'That was a quick one

guys, we got it all in one take. Good work. I'll check the footage today. We'll call if we need you to reshoot anything.'

Cameron smiles and accepts the towel from Tim. He lifts himself off the bed to wipe himself down. A strange titillation passes through Aaron as he watches the familiar broad shoulders over a V-shaped torso leading down to the recognisably shaped uncut penis. *It's almost like Jake's body but skinnier*, Aaron thinks. He recognises the same pattern of chest hair running a thin trail down to his pubes, except groomed to highlight the shape of Cameron's trim muscles.

The handshake between Cameron and Sammy Q as they part ways seems strangely formal after such public intimacy. Cameron hobbles over to Aaron holding a bottle of water in one hand and a towel in the other. His legs sit apart as if is still being penetrated.

'What did you think?' he asks Aaron. He wraps the towel around his waist. A fine film of semen still shines on his skin.

'Well, it was something,' Aaron answers, his tongue burning with questions he doesn't know to ask.

'You can say that again. He was big. I think it went well. Either way, I'll have my money now to head overseas and stay there for ages before having to find work, especially if the royalties become a steady flow. Though I'll probably stay around for a little while in case they do call me back. I don't want to seem unprofessional when this could be my big break.'

'It was weird to watch. Does it usually go for that long?'

'Nah, that was a quick one. I think Sammy Q's contract must end soon, so they're squeezing as much out of him. Pun intended. That might also be why they were happy to pay a little bit more for someone with a name already in the porn industry, even if it is a small name.'

'They can't be too picky, they offered me a card.'

'What card?'

Aaron pulls Michael's card from his pocket and shows it to Cameron.

'What did they offer you?' Cameron asks.

'An amateur role. Tim didn't say what exactly it was.'

'Well, you're attractive, and you've got a fit body. I'm sure there's a market for you.' Cameron takes a sip of his water. 'Do you have a porn name picked out?'

'No. I don't think I would do it,' Aaron says. 'I don't think I can do what you just did. Having sex on camera doesn't feel like my sort of thing. I like to keep it private.'

'Well, if you wanted to expand your sexual experience that would be a really quick way to do it.'

'It's not hard to expand it beyond two,' Aaron laughs to himself.

'You've changed,' Cameron pats Aaron on the shoulder. 'Well, I definitely need a quick shower. I'll catch you in the waiting room in five. It shouldn't take long to clean myself up.'

Cameron saunters from the room, his chest still bare from the film shoot. He gathers his clothes up from a man in the doorway. By the bed Tim pats the sweat off Sammy Q's chest. Sammy sits back, an arm behind his head, chatting aimlessly to Tim.

'My assistant gave you my card, then?' Michael says stepping up next to Aaron. His husky voice demonstrates a smooth mastery in his words.

'Yes he did. I have it with me,' Aaron replies courteously.

'Good. I spotted you across the room straight away. What Tim may not have told you is that I recruit for more than just the porn industry. I'm sure I have a position for you within my company if you're ever after some extra money.'

'As in reception sort of work?' Aaron asks plainly. Michael smirks back.

'Very good. There's a huge market for innocence of that calibre. I also run a successful escort business. People watch porn and want a piece of what they see. I think I can do the same for you.'

'Escorting? You want to pay me to go on dates with other guys?'

'Yes, in a manner of speaking. Of course legally I can't endorse any sexual encounters but it is implied that escorts screw their companions.'

'I don't know. I definitely can't do porn. That's not right for me.'

'I could do wonders with you just as an escort. Think about it. Call me if you want in.' Michael steps away before Aaron can protest.

Wow, this is intense, Aaron thinks. He wanders out of the studio and into the musty hallway. Cameron is already standing in the waiting area when Aaron walks out.

'You were quick,' Aaron comments.

'Yeah it doesn't take much to wash up. I was clean walking in. Just the few spots to scrub,' Cameron takes Aaron's arm and walks him to the door. 'I need a drink. Are you up for one?'

'Definitely,' Aaron nods. 'Why did you start doing porn?' he asks once they've walked a few blocks from the film studio.

'For the money,' Cameron says without thinking.

'But you have to have sex in front of a camera. That's recorded forever.'

'Yeah, but it's just sex. I could have sex all the time and never be paid for it. Shove a camera and production crew in the room and all of a sudden there's a solid pay cheque waiting for me at the end of it.'

'Is the money really that good that you would expose yourself like that? Don't you feel under pressure to do whatever they say because they paid you?'

'Not at all,' Cameron says. 'That's why they do up contracts before they start filming. Most companies also seem to like having a little recorded one on one interview at the beginning of the films. They sell it as getting the audience acquainted with the actors but I reckon it's to show that the actors are sane and know what they're doing.'

'I suppose so,' Aaron shrugs. 'I guess I've never seen one to know what any of it is like.'

'Porn is great to watch. To make it can be a lot of hard work. Sometimes it ends really quickly. Other times you can spend hours in the one position to make sure that they get the right lighting. I think it helps that I'm fairly fluid sexually so can take on whatever role they need for the film.'

'It's good to get to know you more,' Aaron tries at sarcasm.

'I'm assuming it will soon be mutual,' Cameron plays along. 'I'm assuming that we are friends now or at least close enough that you are comfortable having sex with my brother.'

Aaron's attention shifts from their discussion to the prospect of drinking alcohol as they arrive at the bar where he'd first met Cameron. Cameron nods to the woman behind the bar before stepping behind the counter and grabbing a couple of beers for him and Aaron.

'On your tab then?' the woman frowns at Cameron.

'Of course. I wouldn't want to rip you off.'

Aaron and Cameron sit at the end of the bar. Cameron

positions himself uncomfortably on the hard stool. He ups his beer and Aaron matches him with his own drink as they toast with a clink of their glasses.

'To money,' Cameron announces.

'To new experiences.' Aaron sips on his beer. The cold soothes his throat.

'One morning on the job and I've made more than I do in a few week.'

'Even with all your jobs.'

'Even then.' Cameron gulps down his beer. 'I can't believe after these all years I got picked up by a major studio because a random fan recognised me at work and I almost brushed it off.'

'Where do you think you'll go now you're set for cash?'

'Overseas. Wherever the tide takes me. That's my plan. Anywhere that offers me a chance of work as well so that I can stay away as long as possible.'

'You and your brother aren't that different after all.'

'Take that back,' Cameron playfully pushes Aaron.

'Nope. It's true. You both like working away from home and now that I've seen you both naked I know that there isn't a huge difference between you.'

'Weird,' Cameron cringes. 'I'm not sure I'm comfortable knowing any of that.'

'You said you don't picture it.'

'I don't. It's just weird to think about.'

'He does have more muscles though,' Aaron teases.

'I sure hope so. He spends almost every spare moment training. In my spare moments I travel to my next job where I'm either just sitting around or standing.' Cameron pauses. A happy glow rises on his face. 'So do you think you'll take up Michael's offer?'

'Ugh, I don't think I could ever do porn. And then he goes and offers me a job as an escort.'

'Nice. I hear that pays really well. I would have taken that up but the hours don't suit me and I like to have some variety in the things I do.'

'They offered you escort work as well?' Aaron straightens his posture in indignation.

'What, don't you think I'm hot enough to be an escort?' Cameron retorts as Aaron hangs his head in embarrassment. 'I'm sure they would keep their books as full as possible to cater to any number of tastes at any time it might be required. Well, so I assume. Or it could just be that it's currently between university semesters. Students tend to make up a larger portion of escorts when they're in town to study. They need the money in between their holiday jobs.'

'I need the money. David's cut my allowance back.'

Cameron bursts into a fit of laughter. He places his beer on the bar so it doesn't spill.

'Are you serious? He keeps you on an allowance?'

'Yes, it's how we've worked for years,' Aaron shrugs off Cameron's laughter. 'But now it's a lot less and it just happens to be when I finally want more freedom for myself. I might have to see what this escorting is about. What would I have to do?'

'It's fairly straightforward. Just do what the client wants. Did Michael explain that clients only pay you for your time and company, and not for any particular activity or service?'

'He did. He must just be covering himself, I guess.'

'Well yes, he needs to make sure he keeps his business legal and will withstand scrutiny. So any sex you have with clients is entirely your choice, but kind of expected. Use a condom. Tell Michael what you're willing to do beforehand, otherwise you could end up suspended from the ceiling with shards of glass protruding from your back.' Cameron cackles in another fit of laughter. 'I thought he was going to string you up when you dropped that glass and interrupted his work. I had no idea he would have improvised like that. It's been the talk of the club ever since.'

'I get to decide what I will do and what I won't do?' Aaron distracts himself from Cameron's snickering. 'So I can say that I only do certain things and a client would have to stick to it?'

'Not quite,' Cameron calms himself. 'It's more so that Michael knows which clients you would be suited to. Once you're with a client you can go as far as you choose to with a client. But if you give a client a little something more, then they'll ask to have you back.'

'My biggest fear from doing all of this is that I'll get caught,' Aaron confides. 'That's why I could never feel safe enough having sex on film to do porn. I had only been helping you out in the bookshop cafe for five minutes before David's friend Aubrey walked in and saw me. David acted like it was the end of the world for me to have a job when he found out. Imagine what it would have been like it that job was as an escort!'

'You don't need to worry,' Cameron reassures him. 'The agency is totally discreet. They look after their escorts and vet all of their clients. No-one is going to know what you do in your own private time. Everything is going to be awesome. Of course, once you make a name for yourself and everyone wants a piece of Aaron Jones, that might be a different story. Nobody can help you then.'

Aaron really did appreciate that Cameron was trying to help calm his fears, because it did seem like it could be an amazing new experience, but he wasn't about to let a gibe like that pass unanswered.

'I could just lie there and take it,' Aaron mocks.

'Well, there's always that option. I'm sure there's a market in the banking industry for that.'

Aaron stifles the immediate laughter. Cameron shakes himself into a giddy state. Aaron can't hold it back any longer. He bursts into a fit of laughter. Beer splashes out of the top of the bottle, adding to the stickiness on the floor.

9.

AARON WAKES the next morning lying stiff and straight in bed. His eyes snap wide open and fight an exhaustion that leaves his body screaming. And ringing out over all that commotion like a klaxon is a brooding mix of anticipation and apprehension. After talking it through over drinks with Cameron he had decided he would call Michael to set up a meeting. He reasoned that if he could be paid in cash he wouldn't need to open a bank account and could just hide it around the apartment. *If David finds it I'll just say it's a rainy day fund I've been working on*, Aaron reminds himself of the lie he and Cameron settled on.

Aaron lies awake in bed, waiting. I can't call too early. I don't want to seem too eager. Then the moment the clock ticks over to nine-thirty he pulls back the covers and reaches for the phone next to his bed. He dials the number on Michael's card, his hands shaking.

'Hello Morgan Agency, this is Tim,' Tim chirps down the phone.

'Hi Tim. We met yesterday when my friend Camer—I mean Mickey did some filming. You gave me Michael's card.'

'Ah yes, of course. Good morning. The name was Aaron wasn't it? What can I do for you?'

'Michael offered me some casual work. I was calling to see about taking up that offer.'

'Fantastic. Of course Michael will want to meet with you in person first to go over the arrangements and contract. Can you make it in by eleven today? He has an opening at that time before he heads into the editing suite.'

'Certainly. I'll be there.'

Aaron hangs up the phone and glares out the window. A sudden realisation grips him. *What am I doing?* Aaron asks himself. *I've just set up a meeting to take on sex work. Well, it's not like I can get a job anywhere else. David doesn't want me working. I need something that is discreet and where I definitely won't bump into someone like Aubrey again.* Aaron nods and smiles to break himself out of his statue-like trance.

Aaron tries to remember what Cameron said the day before, the clothes he wore and the way he flirted with people. Aaron shakes the thought of flirtation out of his head. *I can't be Cameron, I'll just have to be me. Cameron said he was clean though, very clean in case he had to work straight away. I guess I can get started there.* Aaron gets in the shower and begins scrubbing every part of his body he can reach. He carefully trims his pubic hair with a pair of scissors from under the basin, reducing the small tuft of coarse hair down to short spikes. He carefully runs the razor over his face, his spare hand following each line to weed out any stray bits of stubble. He doubles back again with the razor until his skin feels smooth and soft. *Should I douche?* Aaron thinks. *I don't even know what douching is.* Aaron shrugs it off. He gently scrubs around his behind. His finger moves in slow circular motions to rub over every part.

In the wardrobe Aaron spots the outfit he wore to try and seduce David at work. The shirt and pants hang defeated in the corner of the wardrobe. He smiles to himself. *Second time lucky then.*

Aaron glances over himself on final time. The same tightness he had expressed to get David's attention bulges revealingly. The detailed lines of his chest press against the partially open shirt. Aaron leaves the apartment once satisfied to hail a cab for Michael's office.

The same smell of bleach and heat greets Aaron when Tim opens the door. He leads Aaron straight into Michael's office. The routine appears practised to Aaron. The exact same words, minus the names, are repeated by Tim as if he were a robotic assistant. The same eagerness twinkles in Tim's eyes. Aaron walks into the office expecting an over-crowded mess, boxes and paper piled up everywhere. To his surprise the office is almost bare. Michael sits behind a simple glass desk. Two spare seats sit facing him. Three filing cabinets stand discreetly behind Michael. The carpet seems less bleached to within an inch of its life and more plush.

'Have a seat,' Michael welcomes him in. The smooth smoke-laden voice calms Aaron's jitters. 'Allow me to introduce myself properly, as I neglected to yesterday. I'm Michael, Leo, thirty-five. I understand you've decided to take me up on my offer?'

'Not entirely,' Aaron clears his throat. 'I'd like to talk to you more about working as an escort, but I have no desire to be on film.' The routine rolls off his tongue with ease.

'Very well,' Michael leans forwards and slides a piece of paper across to Aaron. 'This is a standard contract. I do a fifty-fifty split. I like to treat my escorts well. You'll be charged out by the hour. One hundred and seventy dollars for one hour or four hundred and eighty for three. We don't do the overnight nonsense. Your contract does not stipulate in any capacity that you are required to perform sexual services for clients. You will be required to submit to regular sexual health screening. You must use condoms for all sexual contact. Barebacking is not tolerated no matter whether it's active or passive. You have the right to refuse any client I offer to you, but please do so before you accept a job. Clients will pay you directly in cash and you must immediately return the half you owe me here after each client, or after your shift if you have multiple clients. You will be provided with a driver before and after each client, so making payments should not be a problem. Any delay making payment will result in your termination and that contract will give me the right to retrieve money owed in any way I deem necessary. Any questions?'

Aaron pauses for a moment, the contract in hand. The single page of information is full of words and clauses. He skims over the details. *It just looks like everything he said put more formally, if that's possible. Though I'm not sure what barebacking means.* Aaron signs the contract without asking a single question. A silent confidence sits behind his eyes as he remembers the certainty he felt when talking the idea through with Cameron the night before.

'Very good,' Michael continues. 'I'll take you to get your photos done straight away. Tim will take your profile down as we go.'

'My photos? Why do you need them? I told you I don't want to be caught on film.'

'My dear boy, it's in the contract you just signed,' Michael waves the question off as if it were obvious. 'We need them for clients to be able to decide which escorts they would like. No-one else will see them. Photos are sent to clients via an app that deletes the photo and message after ten seconds. That's all the time they get to choose. Plus my reputation carries a certain weight as to the quality of my escorts. Or for preferred clients I may set up a private viewing. If Tim can upload your profile by lunchtime, I believe I can have you busy before dinner. I have a couple clients who like fresh ones. It's their thing.'

Mint and ash odours follow Michael as he leads Aaron into a room adjacent. A large white backdrop hangs from the ceiling in the middle of the room. Chairs and a rack of clothing hide behind the screen. A camera stands on a tripod aimed at the centre of the white space.

'Stand on the red dot and look at the camera,' Michael instructs.

Tim walks in and shuts the door behind him. He holds a tablet up and starts tapping on the screen.

'I need to work up a profile for you to put on our database,' Tim says. The camera flashes. Aaron blinks the sudden light out of his vision. 'What's your name?'

'Aaron,' he blinks through the light.

'Flirt with the camera, but do it naturally,' Michael instructs.

'Not your real name,' Tim chides. 'Your work name.'

'I don't have one.' Aaron adjusts his position, setting comfortably onto one hip.

'Okay, your name is now Patrick. Congratulations. I need your age, zodiac and any interests or preferences.'

'My preferences?'

'Just things that the client might like to know about you.'

'I don't know. Twenty-four, Sagittarius. I'm a home-maker. I like cooking and making coffee.'

'Good start,' Tim loads that into the profile. 'Young and innocent is in demand. But let's spice things up a bit. You spend a lot of time at home thinking about your next sexual adventure. You don't see your husband often and just want someone to show you that they really appreciate all you do at home. You're a dog person but not allowed one and you like pear cider with a touch of gin to kick it up a bit.'

'Wait what?'

'It's all marketing, stud,' Tim dismisses. 'You can be all of those things or none, the client won't know the difference. Just be prepared to drink a few ciders. Watch out for any extra bubbles in your drink or a weird taste. One of our escorts did get drugged. That ended messily. And... uploaded.'

'What? Drugged? People get drugged doing this?' Aaron stumbles back off the red dot.

'Hold still and unbutton your shirt another couple of notches,' Michael directs. 'What do you think Tim, do we leave more to the imagination than normal? The tight shirt really shows up well in the photos don't you think? And it plays into the innocent angle'

'It does,' Tim says, looking down at the computer screen next to Michael. Tim turns back to Aaron, the words slip of his tongue as if read off a cue. 'Bad things happen in every line of work hotstuff. All we can do is warn you about them so that they don't happen again. Just make sure pay attention and on the job and listen to anything we tell you.'

Tim's words offer little comfort to Aaron. A horrific drugging scenario is already playing out in his mind. Aaron repeats Cameron's words through his mind to block the doubt from taking control.

'Oh, nice,' Tim declares, looking down at his tablet. 'It seems the homemaker persona is in even higher demand than I expected. Someone wants to take you to lunch already, without even seeing a photo.'

'Who is it?' Michael asks from behind the lens.

'Number sixty-four.'

'He must be back in town for work. It's no surprise he's jumped in so quickly. He likes to get onto people first. He's in first with new profiles quite often.'

'Are you free to go to lunch?' Tim asks Aaron.

'I guess, but am I ready to go through with this?'

'Sure you are, tiger. We'll upload the photos while you're gone. I just need a mobile number to contact you if we get a job for you. We never message and we always call from an unknown number to protect your privacy.' Tim pulls out a small notepad and scribbles on the first page. He tears it out. 'Here, this is where you need to go. He's only booked you for an hour. Make sure you time it, get the cash up front, don't be afraid to leave when you're ready, and don't let anyone take advantage of you.'

'Off you pop,' Michael says.

Michael glares down at the computer screen and waves his hand over his back at Aaron. Aaron takes his leave, following Tim out the front door. *It's happening already*, Aaron thinks once the door is shut behind him. The piece of paper in his hands marks the address of a hotel room a couple of blocks away. The promised driver doesn't materialise, but it's only a short walk away, so Aaron double-checks the location on his phone and heads off towards his first client.

The walk to the hotel seems to last forever. Aaron's mind

uses the time to act out various worst case scenarios of what he might find when the client opens the door. An obese opera singer dripping with greasy sweat cavorts across his imagination, a whole fried chicken in the singer's hand oozing fat down his arm. Aaron shakes the images from his mind. *It's probably just going to be lunch*, he reminds himself.

The moment Aaron knocks on the hotel room door, his arm freezes in place with his knuckles stuck at the height of the peephole. A flood of chills engulfs his spine. His legs wobble and demand that he run away. Sweat collects in his palms.

'Is that you, Patrick?' A voice whispers from the other side of the door.

'No, it's Aar—' Aaron cuts himself off and clears his throat. 'Sorry. Yes it is. From Morgan—'

The door snaps open before he can finish the sentence. A sturdy hand snaps out and pulls Aaron into the room. Aaron spins around as the man locks the door and turns to eye Aaron from head to toe.

'Very nice,' he says quietly. 'Sorry about the abruptness. I didn't want you to be seen coming in. A couple of my colleagues are staying here as well.'

The man adjusts his plush dressing gown and waddles over to the bed. His bald head and short stature look as if gravity is squeezing his body into a mound of wrinkles. Aaron notices large moles covering the back of his neck. A stark ring of white skin emerges above the gown in contrast to the sun-damaged skin.

'For the sake of this meeting call me Simon, fifty-two, Scorpio.'

Simon lowers himself back onto the bed on one side of a large tray topped by a metal cloche. Simon pats the bed next to him.

'Come, sit down,' he says. 'Make yourself comfortable.'

Aaron tentatively walks to the other side of the bed. He flicks off his shoes and slides down next to Simon. Simon lifts the cloche, releasing an aroma of roast beef and gravy.

'I ordered us a little something to snack on,' Simon says. 'I'm sorry I don't have any cider but I do have beer. Would you like one?'

Simon strokes the back of his finger down Aaron's cheek. Aaron holds steady, expecting himself to cringe at the un-expected touch. Simon's finger caresses the line of Aaron's jaw. Aaron doesn't move. Simon sighs with each movement. A shiver of pleasure runs up Simon's arm. Aaron surprises himself with his neutrality at the contact. Each movement of Simon's finger fails to provoke a reaction from Aaron. His body relaxes to an accepting slump.

Simon ceases fondling Aaron's face as suddenly as he started. He reaches into the minibar and pulls out a single beer.

'Eat up, lovely,' he nods towards the food.

Aaron reaches out for the cutlery and cuts a small morsel off the roast beef. He is instinctively critical of the dry cut of meat as he chews, observing that the chef has severely overcooked the meat, though he refrains from vocalising his appraisal. Aaron is acutely aware of close scrutiny from Simon, whose lips curl in satisfaction as he watches Aaron chew and swallow. Aaron leans back to take a swig of the beer. The chilled liquid eases the meat down. Simon's hand moves inside Aaron's shirt. His wrinkled hand presses against Aaron's abdomen. Aaron steels his mind to block any realisation that a stranger is touching him. Aaron con-tinues eating, letting Simon take charge.

Simon unbuttons Aaron's shirt and pulls it off. Greed

sparks in Simon's eyes as he begins to kiss Aaron's chest. His tongue traces the line of Aaron's pec and teases the nipple. Aaron's body reacts to the contact but his mind holds firm. Aaron's nipple stands erect and moist from Simon's tongue. Aaron can feel an erection grow in his pants. His thoughts stay still and calm through each suck from Simon's lips. A bland, sterile calm hovers over Aaron's mind.

Simon pushes Aaron backwards onto the bed. The fork drops from Aaron's hand and bounces onto the floor. Simon hastily opens Aaron's fly to retrieve his cock. Aaron lies back, still chewing on the last piece of beef while Simon takes Aaron's penis into his mouth in one gulp. He slurps gluttonously along the shaft and head. Saliva quickly drowns Aaron's penis and testicles. Aaron quietly swallows the last bit of meat in his mouth.

Simon releases Aaron's cock and stands up next to the bed. He drops his dressing gown to the floor, revealing a sagging chest resting on top of a round belly, and beneath that a stumpy penis pokes out above drooping testicles. Grey hair covers Simon in a bushy layer.

'Roll over lovely, pants off,' Simon says.

Aaron follows the command to strip completely. He pulls a pillow under chest to make himself more comfortable. He watches Simon as he rips at the plastic cover of a condom and rolls the latex onto himself. Simon tears a small packet of lubricant and smears it across his cock. Aaron turns to face the bedhead. *The condom is on. Holy fuck! It's happening. What have I got myself into?* his mind races.

Simon drops his full weight onto Aaron's back, slamming Aaron's hips into the rough quilt. Simon's belly drags up and down on Aaron's back while he kisses forcefully on Aaron's shoulder blades. Simon lifts himself back. His knuckles scrape across Aaron's buttocks as he repositions himself above Aaron. Aaron shuts his eyes knowing what to expect next. A prickle itches around his arsehole. Simon removes his hand and drops his weight back down. The prickle intensifies as Simon enters Aaron completely, then promptly dissipates into Aaron's improvised numbness.

Aaron feels Simon's penis move in and out of him, hears his moans and whimpers in his hear with each thrust. Simon's breath heats the back of Aaron's neck. Aaron's mind voids. The usual shudder of pleasure he feels when Jake is inside of him is absent. The physical sensation is still there, but there's not burgeoning pleasure or pressure. Simon heaves himself in steady movements. Aaron feels the rocking of each thrust. Sweat accumulates on Aaron's back where Simon's belly rubs against his skin.

Simon chokes on his orgasm. His leg spasms between Aaron's. Simon's arms give way and his full weight pushes against Aaron's back. Simon rolls off Aaron, his breath still puffed and ragged.

'That was good,' Simon wheezes. 'The money's on the counter there,' he points towards the television cabinet. Aaron spots the small pile of cash. 'Get dressed and get out. I'm done,' Simon spits in disdain.

Aaron follows the instructions. He slips his clothes back on without bothering to wipe himself off first, counts the money and hurries from the room as swiftly as he can manage. The air outside the hotel greets him as an old friend, refreshing after the stuffiness of the hotel room. *That was easy*, Aaron thinks. *I can't believe I got paid for just eating and letting someone fuck me. I did it. How the fuck did I do it? It was just sex, wasn't it? Fucking hell it's too much.* Aaron breathes deeply to calm his thoughts. *I finally made my own money*. He pats his pocket, feeling for the cash folded away inside.

Aaron makes his way straight back to Michael's office to hand over half of the money. Tim opens the door to the office in his usual form.

'Hi Patrick, come on in,' he chirps. 'How did it all go?'

'Well enough,' Aaron confirms. 'Is Michael in? I've got his money from the booking.'

'Michael's in a meeting at the moment. Come with me, I can process that for you.'

Tim leads Aaron around the maze-like apartment to a small office near Michael's. Tim's office mimics Michael's in its minimalism. An identical glass table occupies the middle of the room with three chairs surrounding it. Several framed photos hang above the filing cabinets. Tim's tablet lays on the table top with its power cord hanging over the side.

'Have a seat,' Tim pulls out one of the seats for Aaron. He takes his place at the far side of the desk. 'It was a one hour booking, which means you should have eighty-five dollars for us.'

Aaron hands over the money. Tim scoops it up and shoves it into the top drawer of a filing cabinet. He pulls a book out of the same drawer and opens it onto the table. He fingers through the columns until he finds the right date. Aaron watches Tim add the numbers in the ledger and place the book back into the drawer.

'Michael was right about you,' Tim says. 'There's currently a huge demand for purity among escorts. Weird, I know. But your innocence and naivety has resulted in a flood of messages. We have several bookings listed for you for the rest of the week.' He pushes a small piece of paper over to Aaron. 'Be strict with the times. We'll advise you if any cancel. Oh, and before I forget,' Tim passes a business card over, these are the contact details for a doctor, very discreet. He never asks what sort of work you do. We recommend all our escorts receive sexual health screenings through him. The public health clinics ask too many indelicate questions.'

Aaron holds the card and paper up to say thank you to Tim. He lets himself out of the office. *Eighty-five dollars, what could I possibly do with that?* Aaron pushes the cash deeper into his pocket, letting the corners dig into his skin. The small scratch of the money makes Aaron feel like he's accomplished something. He hails the first taxi he sees and directs it over to Jake's house. He doesn't message ahead, assuming Jake is home.

Aaron's prediction is proven correct when Jake answers the door in his underwear. Aaron is instantly aroused by the proud swell of Jake's chest and the outline of his cock through the thin jocks. He throws himself at Jake and they stumble backwards into the living room. Their lips press together through the sudden wave of passion. Jake kicks the door shut before letting himself drop completely to the floor. Without words they strip each other and tumble into the flow of sex. Aaron shudders through the pressure building in his groin. Jake ducks into the bedroom for a condom and returns before Aaron's enthusiasm ebbs. Aaron rolls over, holding his body in the same position as he did in the hotel room. Jake eases himself inside Aaron. This time however a rush of pleasure bursts through Aaron with each thrust. He rocks back against Jake's cock. Their skin rubs together and bounces apart in a primal dance. They climax together and collapse into a heaving mound on the floor before either of them speak.

'It's nice to see you too,' Jake eventually says.

'I knew you'd want to see me,' Aaron nuzzles himself into

Jake's arm. They twist their limbs together on the floor.

'How did you know I would be home?'

'I guessed. I just really felt like coming over.'

'This floor is gross,' Jake says.

Jake untangles himself from Aaron, the condom still flopping off the end of his penis. He scoops Aaron up in his arms. Aaron giggles at his helplessness as Jake's muscles hold him tightly against his chest. Jake drops them both onto the bed and curls up under the covers. Aaron's eyelids droop in a sudden heaviness.

'Has it been a long day for you?' Jake runs his finger over Aaron's cheek.

'No, just an interesting one, I really needed that,' Aaron purrs into Jake's hand.

'I'm glad I could be of assistance. Are you happy to nap for a while? I'm feeling a little pooped as well.'

'What have you been doing to make you so exhausted?'

'Wouldn't you like to know,' Jake teases.

'Sure, why not? I'm sure you do get up to other interesting things besides just having sex with me.'

'Well—' Jake pauses. His voice crackles as he continues. 'I just had someone over. They just left before you arrived.'

Aaron's eyes snap open. *Someone over? Someone other than me?* His breathing and the weight of his eyelids calm the initial stab of betrayal. *This is an affair*, he reminds himself. *And I did just sleep with someone for money.*

'Is it someone I know?' Aaron asks calmly.

'No, I don't think so. It's someone I see casually every now and then.'

'Is he better than me?'

'Feeling a little jealous, are we?' Jake jabs Aaron in his ribs.

'You wish,' Aaron teases.

'He's cute, but he's all about the sex. It's fun while he's here but he never hangs around afterwards for a drink or cuddling or anything like that. He walks in, we have sex and then he leaves.'

'You should charge him for that,' Aaron says without thinking.

'That'll be the day,' Jake laughs. 'We're both young and attractive enough to have men lining up to sleep with us without having to pay them to do it. Besides, you saw that little sideshow at DD. Even the weirdest of fetishists can find someone to have sex with.'

Aaron's mind begins to fog. Glee fills his dreams as he dozes off in Jake's arms. The knowledge that people are willing to pay for sex with him adds to the new sense of pride growing within him.

AARON STRUGGLES TO adjust to each week passing with such velocity. Where once every day had dragged waiting around for David to come home, now time seems a blur of work and naked bodies. The varying bodies, faces and sexual preferences slowly meld into a single nondescript amalgam of flesh to Aaron. Each evening Aaron blows through Michael's office to surrender half of the takings. The other half he stashes around the apartment, repurposing some old coffee tins and hiding them in multiple rooms. Aaron deliberately loses track of how much he's earned to maintain plausible deniability in case David finds out and asks exactly how much there is.

The opportunity to earn money wakes Aaron each morning early and excited. He waits patiently for Timothy to message through David's itinerary at nine o'clock before making his plans. *I suppose he's good for something after all,*

Aaron smiles to himself. When he's not with a client Aaron wraps himself up in Jake's body or hangs out with Cameron helping him map out an itinerary of international travel, at times a vexing task.

'What's the point of visiting somewhere if you're not going to truly live it?' Cameron debates each time Aaron tries to press him into a time schedule. 'I want to be able to work and experience anywhere I visit and live just like the locals.'

Aaron's attitude towards sex becomes increasingly blasé, almost to the point where it becomes a joke. Each encounter seems to Aaron like some strange distorted parody of a dinner party. The welcome is warm and charming. Names, zodiacs and ages are exchanged with perfect etiquette. The meal (Aaron relishes the metaphor of his body as the main course, and sometimes also dessert) is devoured hungrily. The whole time Aaron maintains the façade of an ideal host, ensuring his guest's needs are served before his own and smiling graciously at compliments and other gestures of appreciation. But like every other dinner party Aaron ever hosted, the guests are never his own, never people he knows or really cares about. The succession of men blur together to a point where they're indistinguishable from each other and it feels like he's once again with David, the commands arrogant, the belly protruding, the cock uninspiring and the sex void of true passion.

Immediately after each shift, Aaron washes himself and launches himself into the ball of sexual inspirations Jake and he have become. At every encounter Aaron discovers a new part of their bodies. Jake even introduces toys into their sex life.

'Nothing extreme,' Jake ensures as he presents a slick pink

dildo. Aaron relaxes into every new sensation and sexual role Jake offers him.

The mornings always cycle around again. If David is home there are food and clothes for him. The guestroom wardrobe is crammed ever more full as Aaron's free time trickles away into work and each spare moment is given to Jake. Strangely to Aaron, he hasn't seen any client more than once. Michael assures him that's normal.

'Don't sweat it kiddo. A lot of our clients are in business,' Michael says, 'so they fly in and out and want someone different each time they're in a new city. And our regulars already have their favourites. You'll develop your own client base soon enough.'

Aaron shrugs off the lack of reoccurring clients. Each new body looks the same to him as the last.

❋

Aaron holds his knuckles up and knocks on the hotel room door of another new client. He stands close to the door expecting another whispered call to enter.

'Come in Patrick. Shut the door behind you,' the client says with an unusual certainty.

He's done this before, Aaron thinks. He slips inside the darkened room and shuts the door behind him.

'Hello,' Aaron calls.

The curtains are drawn. A faint glimpse of sunlight sneaks out the borders of the windows. Aaron steps forward, his arms out feeling for any obstacles. Aaron jumps at the sound of footsteps behind him and the click of the lock. The client switches the lights on, blinding Aaron's unadjusted eyes. He blinks through the instant tears filling his sight.

The client steps in front of Aaron. His polo shirt and shorts add colour to the otherwise drab room. As Aaron's eyes clear he starts to make out the man before him. His small stature is amplified by the tightness of his clothes. His tanned skin and straightened hair give him an air of control Aaron hasn't seen with other clients.

'You're quite young,' Aaron says before he can stop himself.

The client looks younger than Aaron. His soft skin shows no blemishes. A small streak of fluff imitates facial hair under his lip.

'That I am, Aaron,' the client scowls.

'What? Who?' Aaron blurts, startled at hearing his own name. 'Do I know you?' He asks instinctively. He wipes the final streak of tears from his cheek and stands straight in front of the short client.

'No, I don't suspect you do,' the client says menacingly. He starts pacing in front of Aaron, his eyes searching the length of Aaron for all his imperfections. 'But I certainly know you and what you've been up to.' Aaron remains silent, lips pressed hard together. 'I've been watching you for a while, waiting for you to screw up. It didn't take me long to find dirt on you.'

'Who are you working for? David?' Aaron snaps, anger searing red into his cheeks.

'Who's David? I bet that's another interesting story. Is he another one of your men you fuck for money? Disgusting,' he spits. 'No, I don't work for anyone. I'm here for myself. You stole my man and I want him back. I'll get you out of the picture one way or another and you've made it easier than ever.'

Aaron squints down at the petite stature of the man before him. His bones protrude his skin.

'You're Kyle,' Aaron's shoulders drop. Understanding cools the worst of the tension gripping his spine and he squares himself ready to fight back.

'Yes, I'm Kyle, twenty-two, Taurus, and you're the slut keeping me from Jake. Well, not anymore.'

'What do you want from me?' Aaron cuts in.

'Isn't that obvious? I want you to leave Jake alone,' Kyle marches to under Aaron's nose. He stares up. Aaron ignores Kyle's gaze. 'And you're going to do it. Once you're gone it's just going to be me and him again. We love each other. You can't get in the way of that.'

'Well, that will be easy enough soon,' Aaron counters nonchalantly. 'Jake's about to leave for duty again. I'm sure since you love each other you'd know he's been recalled early to fill a shortage.'

'Of course I know that,' Kyle hisses. 'And because of you I haven't spent any time with him since he's been back. I'm not going to let that happen again.'

'You haven't spent time with him because you don't work well together.'

'Liar! Whatever Jake has told you is a lie. We haven't spent time together because he's never free from your sticky little fingers.'

'Cut to the chase already. I have work to do.'

'I know you do, and if you want to continue working you need to stay the fuck away from Jake.'

'That's not going to happen.'

'Oh yeah? You leave him or I'll tell him and anyone else you're close to that you're a filthy prostitute.' Chills run down Aaron's spine. *David can never know.* 'I see that's caught your attention. I'll take that as a sign of agreement.' Kyle turns away from Aaron. Aaron remains frozen on the spot. His mind hunts for any possible escape. 'And just so you don't forget, here's a little something to remember our agreement by.'

Before Aaron can flinch a burning pain explodes in his upper thigh. He looks down to see Kyle's fist clutching a fountain pen, the nib red with blood.

'What the hell?' Aaron stumbles backwards. His hands clamp down on the wound, small droplets of blood spurting between his fingers.

'Now anytime you think about spreading your legs for Jake my mark will be there.'

'You—You little cunt!' Aaron curses. 'Jake was right, you are a crazy fuck!'

'Whatever. You can get out now you filthy tramp. I've got what I wanted.' Kyle points towards the table by the door. 'There's your money you disgusting whore,' Kyle spits. 'Payment for your tainted body.'

Aaron scoops up the cash and dashes from the room. His leg burns with each step towards the elevator. It's difficult for Aaron to inspect the wound through his pants, but it doesn't seem too deep. When he examines his hand Aaron notices a black stain mixed among the red. *Of fuck, this is not how I imagined it would be the first time I got inked*, he curses.

Aaron leaves the hotel as fast as he can. Each step pulls at his pants, yanking the drying blood away from the wound. He cringes as the movement stretches the laceration open again. Aaron's driver is startled at the quick re-emergence, but is otherwise unfazed. Aaron directs him to return immediately to the agency.

'What is that?' Tim demands as soon as Aaron steps into the office.

'I'll tell you what that is,' Aaron yelps. 'That last client you sent me to was a psycho and he stabbed me in the leg.'

'Oh snap, you're bleeding,' exclaims Tim. He taps out a quick message on his tablet then turns back to Aaron. 'Come with me, Stud, I'll sort you out.'

Before Aaron has a chance to protest, Tim grabs him by the hand and drags him limping into his office. He unearths a first aid kit from a corner somewhere and directs Aaron to sit upon the desk.

'Pants off, tiger, so I can get a proper look.'

Aaron complies, suddenly uncomfortable with getting undressed in front of Tim, who waits, patiently eyeing him. Then, once Aaron's pants are around his ankles, Tim moves boldly between his legs, and strokes the skin around the wound gently and lingering, though his eyes appear to be more focussed on Aaron's crotch.

'My my, your little whackjob certainly did a number on you, didn't he?' Tim scolds. 'You're going to need stitches. Luckily for you,' he continues as he removes a needle and nylon thread from among the bandages, 'I know how to do that. Unluckily for you the only thing I have by way of pain-killer is some chilled champagne.'

'Oh no,' Aaron declines, 'you're not coming anywhere near me with sharp objects.' He leans forwards to try to re-trieve his pants, which only brought him further into Tim's embrace. Aaron backed off again when Tim took the oppor-tunity for a quick grope.

'Sorry Sexy, I'm the best offer you've got right now. I can't take you to a hospital, so there's just me.'

'Fine,' Aaron concedes. 'I'll take that champagne then.'

'Of course.' Tim leaves the room and returns moments later with a glass and a glittery bottle. 'It's the expensive stuff from Michael's room,' he confides. 'Don't tell the boss.'

Aaron tackles the cork and pours some calming booze

for himself while Tim occupies himself with threading the needle and prepares the wound to be sutured. Aaron bites his lip as he tries to ignore the stinging pain in his leg and the face in his crotch.

Moments later another person enters the room. Aaron tries not to flinch at the sudden roar of anger. 'What the bloody hell is going on in here?' Michael yells. 'I hear tales of one of my prize escorts stupidly getting himself mauled by a client, and then here I find you Tim, head firmly planted between his legs and treating him to my finest champagne!'

'Oh, Michael,' Aaron ignores the rage in his voice. 'It was terrible. I—'

'You can shut up,' Michael interrupts. 'It's your job to make sure my merchandise doesn't get damaged, and now you've gone and got yourself stabbed. How am I supposed to market you as innocent when you're all scarred up?!'

'No, I'm okay Michael,' Aaron tries to calm him. 'It's just a small cut.'

'The fuck it is!' Michael roars. 'You're supposed to be unblemished, immaculate. And you had such promise, too, my best homemaker escort. Now I'm going to have to start from scratch.'

'What!? You can't blame this on me, Michael,' Aaron tries to look indignant, a hard act to pull off in his underwear. 'The Agency booked a crazy client. I've been injured by your oversight.'

'It's not our job to vet clients. We only ask questions relevant to their needs and wants. We will blacklist him from the Agency, though,' he nods to Tim, who immediately starts tapping on his tablet.

'You've solved the problem then,' Aaron bargains. 'He won't be back and I can keep working.'

'You're still damaged goods, though.' Michael shakes his head. 'I'm going to have to let you go. It's a shame, I saw big things for you.'

'But I need the money. What am I going to do for cash?' Aaron's voice is bitter. 'So much for looking after your escorts.'

'I look after my escorts for as long as they are valuable to me,' Michael snorts. 'but you are no longer my problem.' With that Michael turns and marches from the room. Numbly, Aaron can only stare at the closed door and fumble for his pants. Tim grabs Aaron by the elbow and slips a bandage into his hand. 'Here you go,' Tim murmurs as he guides Aaron from the office. 'You can finish yourself off outside. I'm really sorry, tiger, it's been great working with you but the boss has spoken. I'm sure you understand. You can keep all of the final payment for your severance. Goodbye.'

Tim pushes Aaron out of the office and shuts the door behind him. Aaron turns ready to pound on the door but stops himself. A sense of hopelessness saps Aaron's confidence. *Some nutter attacks me and now I'm on my own?* he shakes his head. He touches the stitches on his thigh through the hole in his pants, too shaken to even try the bandage. *There's one thing to do about this.* Aaron marches out of the building heading for Jake's house.

✳

'We have to call the police,' Jake says when Aaron shows him the wound.

'No, we can't,' Aaron says, defeated. 'What do we tell them? I was selling my body for money and got stabbed by my lover's possessive ex. We can't. They'll call David and everything will turn out worse. I can't risk it.'

'I still can't believe you didn't tell me that you were escorting. As if I would care.'

'I couldn't know how you'd react?' Aaron fires up. 'I've never done any of this before. I kept myself so hidden from everyone's opinions and thoughts that I didn't even know what fun or sex or happiness was until I met you. I was so fucking sheltered and had no experience with anything. How else would I get any employment? And fucking David would have seen any payments go into our bank account, so I needed to be paid in cash. You're just a root on the side. Why should I tell you anything like that?' Tears well in Jake's eyes. Aaron feels a sharp pain in his chest. 'I'm sorry. I didn't mean any of that.'

'I know. It's just hard to hear when it's put so bluntly,' Jake says.

'You're special to me in your own way, but I'm married. I'm with David.'

'Then what am I?'

'You're my closest friend,' Aaron chokes on his own rising tears. 'I've never had anyone like you. I've only ever concerned myself with David and our relationship and his success. I've never known an intimacy or connection like this. I'm scared,' Aaron's voice drifts into a mumble.

Jake pulls him in. His arms squeeze against Aaron's chest. The strength of his embrace crackles Aaron's ribs.

'I'm so sorry,' Jake whispers. 'I never thought Kyle would do something as mad as that. He must have been stalking you for some time. It's all my fault.'

Warm drips of moisture trickle onto the back of Aaron's neck. Aaron feels his own eyes spill over as tears stream down his cheeks. His sobs combine the anguish of secrecy and the release of confession. He pulls Jake in as hard as he can, Jake's chest heaving in rhythm with his own.

Jake pulls back and kisses Aaron hard on his lips, lubricated with salty tears. They fall back further into the bed. Their bodies stumble together in a heap of arms and legs pulling each other closer together. Aaron drags his pants off with barely a wince and pulls Jake's down to his ankles. Jake reaches across to the drawer for the condoms.

Jake's eyes flicker from sorrow to desire. Several tears sneak out the corner of his eyes. Jake pushes against Aaron's lips for one last kiss before pulling back, reaching back into the drawer for lube and squirting some into his hand. His hand disappears down to moisten his erection. Aaron holds firmly onto Jake's face to keep their eyes aligned while Jake enters him. Jake's mouth drops open in pleasure, and he pushes forwards wanting to kiss again. Aaron shakes his head. His hands hold Jake's head directly above his. Jake starts rocking, his hips pushing his cock in and out. Aaron and Jake stare into each other's eyes. Their mouths quiver with each thrust. The rhythm intensifies. Aaron moans to the pressure of each plunge into him. Jake's jaw begins to grind on its joints. Aaron feels the pulsing of Jake's cock as he fires into him. The intensity causes Aaron to respond in kind. Hot fluid projects onto his stomach. Their tears leave dry streaks across their cheeks.

Their bodies heave through the final throws of climax. Aaron releases Jake's face to let him lower down for a kiss. They peck each other gently into the withdrawal.

'I am going to miss you,' Jake admits. 'I really care for you. You're not just a root. That's why I'm so sorry that you've been hurt by my past mistakes.'

'I know. You leaving will be a void I'll have to fill some-how. I wish things could be different. I wish I could be with you, but I have too much with David. It's not a life that can easily be given up.'

'Neither is the army. I love what I do too much to give it up.'

'Lovers then?' Aaron smiles. His cheeks glow red from the heat.

'Lovers we are.' Jake pauses. He holds himself up on one elbow. 'On the condition though that you never stab anyone else I decide to sleep with.'

'I can guarantee you that. You can sleep with anyone you want.' Aaron holds his hand up. Jake shakes it in his own rough fingers.

'And you can sleep with anyone you want for money.'

'Thank you, but I doubt that will happen again any time soon. This was my last gig. They said I'm damaged goods.'

'What fuckers. What will you do for money now?'

'I don't know. I'll think of something. I've got some cash saved away. If worse comes to worst I can manage on the al-lowance David gives me. It's mostly for the running of the apartment, but I can scrounge a bit for myself.'

'As long as you'll be okay.'

'If it comes to it, I think I can survive even without David. Probably. I should be able to.'

'You don't need to worry about that. I'm sure the two of you will be together forever.'

'Cheers,' Aaron snickers. 'A very comforting thought. We hardly know each other anymore and yet we're married.'

'I would say that's normal, but my mums know every-thing about each other. It's weird to watch. They may as well be the one person.'

'Every marriage is different then.'

'That's true. My mums are identical. You and David are completely different.' Jake pauses and repositions himself on the bed. 'Are you coming to see me off tomorrow?'

'I think I can free up some time for that,' Aaron smiles.

'Good. It's nothing fancy. Lots of hugs. The families usually hang around to watch the plane take off and then I have no idea what actually happens.'

'I'll find out for you,' Aaron kisses Jake. Aaron takes control, leading his tongue into Jake's mouth.

II.

AARON WAKES EARLY on the day of Jake's departure, a hollow knot writhing in his stomach. He knows from the invite that Cameron had messaged through the evening before that Jake's family all plan to be at the airport. He and Jake plan to meet first thing in the morning for a personal goodbye before the whole family drives to the airport.

Aaron lies in bed with his eyes open, staring at the ceiling. David left an hour ago. *I think it's safe to get up*, he tells himself. Tiredness latches onto his mind but sorrow pumps him awake as soon as he starts to doze. He shuts his eyes and shakes his head. *I'm not going to get any sleep here.* He pulls himself out of bed and showers. He knows it's early but doesn't care.

Aaron dresses casually with pocket space for handkerchiefs. He charges out of the apartment without worrying about his morning coffee. The swirling in his gut threatens to purge bile whenever he thinks of food or drink.

The taxi ride to Jake's house drags. Each set of traffic lights blocks Aaron from where he truly wants to be. His leg shudders into the carpet of the car floor every time the taxi slows down. A sudden chill rushes through him. *This might be the last time I see him*, chimes a panicked voice through his mind. The thought of being stuck in the car a moment longer than required irritates him. His leg shakes with greater intensity.

The taxi pulls up out the front of Jake's house. Aaron throws money across to the driver and dashes out of the car. He carelessly pushes through the gate. The noise of the latch scraping echoes against the chill of early morning. Aaron ignores the sound. His sight tunnels, a door the only object within his field of vision. He glares at it. His breath catches with each step forwards. He feels himself puffing by the time he reaches the door to Jake's house.

Aaron lets himself in quietly. The cold door handle freezes the sweat on his palms. The familiar stale warmth evaporates Aaron's unease and he boldly enters Jake's room. Jake is sprawled out on the bed wearing only his jocks. Jake's chest lifts and drops in time with his dreams. His legs are spread out towards Aaron. Aaron eyes off the bulge presented before him. The black of Jake's jocks outlines the morning growth.

'Huh, what's happening?' Jake mumbles. He squints himself to a state of semi-arousal.

Aaron stares silently down at Jake. He strips himself down and slides onto the bed next to Jake. He presses his lips directly onto to Jake's mouth, the musty taste of morning breath filling Aaron's lungs. His sensitivities are erased by the desire to pull Jake's chest against him and feel the tickle of Jake's chest hair against his skin. Jake's obvious erection nudges against Aaron's leg.

Aaron throws himself on top of Jake, tugging on the underwear that impedes his path. Aaron relieves Jake of his jocks in an awkward wrestle. The black material flops off the end of Jake's foot. Aaron positions himself directly over Jake's cock. The head of Jake's dick teases the entrance of Aaron's arse. Aaron feels the wetness of Jake's excitement.

'Should I get a condom?' Jake whispers.

Aaron pushes in harder against Jake's lips. His tongue explores the slightly cracked edges of Jake's mouth, the smoothness of his teeth.

'No,' Aaron answers. 'I want this to be more meaningful than any other time we've been together. I want there to be nothing separating me from you.'

'Are you sure?' Jake pulls back, he takes Aaron's cheeks in his hands. Heat builds between Jake's palms and Aaron's skin. The warmth comforts Aaron in his decision.

'Yes,' Aaron nods. 'I don't want David to be the only one inside of me naturally. There's no-one else I would want to share that part of me with.'

A smirk slithers out one side of Jake's mouth. Jake nods, his eyes tracing Aaron's face. Aaron drops himself down, his kisses turn to gentle pecks as he handles Jake's erection into position. Aaron spits into his fingers and rubs the slick saliva along the shaft of Jake's cock. The slide down onto Jake pulls against Aaron's skin. The tightness fills him with raw excitement. Jake's body shudders with pleasure underneath him. Aaron removes his hand and makes the final drop. Jake's eyes light up, his jaw drops and quivers. Aaron's body fills with a rush of pressure that builds in his pelvis. The heat of each rise and fall on top of Jake's body floods blood into his own throbbing erection.

Aaron pushes his hands onto Jake's chest to hold himself

securely. He begins to lift and slide his hips down in controlled motions. Redness glows in Jake's chest under the grip of Aaron's hands. Aaron's nails dig into Jake's skin. Hair slides into Aaron's finger nails with each movement. Sweat slips under Aaron's thighs as the friction builds.

Aaron positions himself so Jake can watch him ride his cock. Their eyes stare intently into each other's unbroken by the rocking of Aaron's hips. Jake's eyes twinkle, his jaw twitches to the side. Aaron recognises the clenching of Jake's face. Aaron latches onto his own cock and strokes across its head. Jake's body tenses. The muscles under Aaron's hand ripple into spasms. A sudden pulsation inside of Aaron snaps him into his own climax. Jake groans through his ejaculation. Aaron matches the orgasm. Liquid spurts out across Jake's chest. Aaron's moans echo through the room. Jake's legs twitch as he looses the last of his load into Aaron.

Aaron glances down. Sadness floods into him to fill the void left as the ecstasy drains away. He strokes the back of his finger along the bristles of Jake's whiskers.

'That was unexpected,' Jake sighs. 'I didn't think you would be here so early.'

'I didn't want our final farewell to be rushed,' Aaron lowers himself onto Jake's chest. The rapid beating of their hearts contrasts the slowing rhythm of their breaths.

Aaron senses Jake smiling. He moves completely off Jake's hips and drops himself down next to Jake on the bed. His leg stretches across Jake's hips and tense into a solid embrace.

Aaron's mind discovers a vacantness and drifts into the happiness it presents. His body relaxes against Jake's. Within moments Aaron can hear the calm, cycling breaths of Jake as he falls into a light sleep. Aaron smiles to himself knowing he is truly comfortable. He drifts off into a broken sleep in Jake's arms.

A sharp knock at the door rips Aaron from his dreaming.

'You two had better hurry up and get ready,' Cameron calls into the room. 'Mum said breakfast would be ready soon.'

'Oh shit, your mums,' Aaron groans as he sits upright. 'What will they say about us?'

'Nothing,' Jake says. His knuckle digs the sleep out of his eyes. 'They still think you're here with Cameron. They're of a weird generation. They don't believe in extra-marital sex. It would be a real shock for one of them to do that.'

'How can you say that?' Aaron teases.

'Don't worry. I don't think they actually do anything beyond matchmaking,' Jake sniffs at his armpits. 'I definitely need a shower,' he declares.

Jake grabs onto Aaron's hand and leads him to the door. He carefully pulls on the door to open it just enough for a slither of light to break through. Jake presses his face against the wall and peers through.

'All clear,' he says. He pulls the door wide open and walks nude across to the bathroom with Aaron in tow.

Jake starts the shower and quickly has the room billowing with steam from the heat of the water. Aaron steps into the shower with Jake. *The sex in here was great*, Aaron recalls. Jake pulls Aaron into a wet hug. He fills his hands with liquid soap and rubs it all over Aaron's body. Aaron returns the kindness. The slipperiness eases the slide of his fingers across Jake's body, an action that imprints itself onto Aaron's mind. Aaron focusses on Jake's body, recording the feel of muscles pushing back against his touch. Jake pulls Aaron in closer. Their chest compress together. Air struggles to seep between them. Aaron's head falls onto Jake's shoulder with the water gushing across his back. Jake's shoulder jerks, his breath shortens.

'I need to shave,' he says, pulling himself off Aaron suddenly.

Aaron spots the glistening tear sneak out the corner of Jake's eye.

'Let me,' Aaron says.

Aaron reaches across for the razor and cream. Aaron squirts the white foam into his hand and massages it roughly across Jake's face. He laughs at the sight of Jake before him. The white beard of foam hangs limply from his cheeks.

'Do I look like a miner?' Jake laughs. Shaving foam floats off his lips with each puff of air.

Aaron reaches his hand out to carefully position the blade and eases it through the foam, his finger tracing the smoothness behind the blade as he memorises the lumps and edges of Jake's skin. Each wipe of the blade clears more foam away from Jake until his face emerges clean-shaven. Jake's body stands wet and confident. The last few specks of white trickle off the tip of Jake's nipples and down into the drain.

Jake leans into Aaron, pressing their lips together. Jake's biceps bulge as they draw Aaron in tightly. Aaron's ribs click against the pressure of Jake's muscles. Aaron ignores any pains to reach into Jake's mouth with his tongue one final time.

Jake releases Aaron and switches off the water.

'I guess that was our goodbye,' Aaron smiles.

'Couldn't have been a better one,' Jake nods.

They duck out of the shower and dry themselves quickly. Jake leads them back into the bedroom to change ready to the leave the house. Aaron quickly slips himself into his clothes from the pile he left on the floor. Jake faces away from Aaron. He picks up one piece of clothing at a time from a neat stack in is wardrobe. The green blandness of the outfit is another reminder of the parting soon to come. Jake turns around, fully dressed. His shoulders protrude determinedly from under the weight of the army uniform. Aaron feels a twinge of pride flicker inside of him when he sees how natural the uniform appears on Jake, who stands before him with a purpose that pervades his entire being.

The door swings open behind Jake. Cameron stands behind it, one arm spread wide as if he is presenting himself.

'We better hurry up,' Cameron announces. 'Just so you know I'm going to fix all of these walls while you're away. I could hear everything. There's only so much earphones and a pillow over your head can muffle out.' Jake opens his mouth to protest. 'Aunt Lisa is here so beware. Everyone's a bit on edge.'

Cameron turns to lead the way before anyone can protest.

'Just don't burn anything down while I'm away,' Jake mutters to Cameron as they head to the door.

'Who's Aunt Lisa?' Aaron whispers.

'I think she's had a tough time recently, she may be in one of her moods,' Jake answers.

'What mood is that?'

Before anyone can answer Aaron they're at the main house and within hearing range of their mums. Denise and Susan's eyes light up at the sight of Jake in uniform. A tear shimmers in the corner of Susan's eye.

'You boys are late. Your early breakfast is probably cold now,' Denise says. She leans in and gives Aaron a warm hug. 'It's so lovely of you to come and see Jake off with us.'

A woman sits at the end of the table cuddled in a knitted jumper. A sharpness to her features reminds Aaron of Jake. He glances over her briefly. Her standoffishness is obvious in her huddled state.

'This is my sister Lisa, Aquarius, thirty,' Susan introduces. 'This is Cameron's friend Aaron, Virgo, twenty-six,. Sit down and eat boys before it really goes stale.'

Three dirty plates sit in front of the three seated women. Steam rises from the mugs nestled in their hands. Aaron wrinkles his nose at the acrid scent of instant coffee. Bacon and pancakes are stacked high in the centre of the table. Jake reaches across and serves himself up a large dish of breakfast.

'We're going to miss you,' Denise says as she watches Jake fill his plate. 'At least we'll have more time and space to ourselves. Especially once you're both overseas.'

'Oh gods,' Susan sniffles.

'Mum, please don't,' Cameron implores. 'We've been through this already. You've farewelled Jake many times before. We don't want a repeat of last time.'

'I know,' Susan pats her cheeks with a tissue. 'It doesn't get any easier watching the boys you give birth to disappear into a strange place,' she sobs.

'What happened last time?' Aaron whispers close to Cameron.

'She had to be escorted from the airport,' Cameron says calmly so everyone could hear. 'She was wailing so much that she needed to leave. I can't go through that again. Jake will be back in a couple of months mum, same as always. He's a glorified gardener, remember. It's not like he's going into combat.' The table rises with a thud. Cameron yelps and reaches down for his leg. 'I mean that like it's a good thing,' Cameron says to Jake. 'No need to get violent with me.'

'We should change the topic,' Denise directs. 'How are things going with Andrew?' she asks Cameron.

'Who?' Cameron pauses. 'Oh him. I haven't seen him in ages. It's going nowhere mum. He was fun but definitely not my type. Besides, now that I saved enough to go overseas I don't think it's a good idea to get into a serious relationship.'

Susan gasps for air.

'Right, another new topic,' Denise tries. 'Aaron,' she glares intently at Aaron. 'How are you and your husband? Looking forwards to kids sometime soon?'

'Well, no,' Aaron chokes on his cold bacon. 'David's in line for another promotion, which will change his executive level. I don't know what that means but apparently a lot is changing for him, too much to be thinking about having family. I'm not even sure I want one. We kind of spoke about it but I don't think children are the way for us to go.'

Lisa scoffs over the top of her coffee mug.

'Great distraction Denise,' Lisa mumbles.

'Oh my, I'm so sorry Lisa. I wasn't thinking, I just wanted to change the topic of away from our children leaving us.'

Aaron stares around confused. Jake shrugs his shoulders to Aaron and shoves another piece of pancake into his mouth.

'I've been trying to have a child,' Lisa says. 'But it's getting nowhere.'

'That's right,' Cameron tries to explain the situation. 'You've been trying to conceive as a single mother. Have you had another setback?' Curiosity flashes in his eyes.

'Yes, the clinic won't accept me unless I have a partner,' Lisa looks as if she is about to swear.

'It's nonsense,' Susan perks up. 'There's nothing about your life that says you won't be a great mother.'

'I know that,' Lisa says. 'But apparently there are risks involved in dealing with a single woman.'

Aaron glances quickly around the room. Everyone nods in agreement. He searches their faces for an answer.

'Breeders,' Cameron says, noting his confusion.

'Yep, breeders,' Lisa says. She lines up Aaron as new target to vent at. 'Apparently they've had issues with women pretending to be single to access reproductive clinics when in reality they're breeders who haven't been able to conceive on their own ways so they try the natural course of things.'

'And because of that you can't have children of your own?' Aaron asks.

'It looks that way,' Lisa downs the rest of her coffee. 'Weren't we supposed to leave ten minutes ago?'

'Oh yes,' Susan sparks into motion.

Susan and Denise jump out of their seats and snatch up the dirty plates from the table. Aaron's mind blanks as the realisation that the airport is the next stop jerks him out of his seat. He instinctively falls back on domestic mode. Susan and Denise shuffle about, too distracted to stop Aaron from loading their dishwasher and clearing the table with them.

Aaron feels outside his body. The will to perform each step towards the car forms solely out of necessity. His numbness fails to save him from the approach of the inevitable. All six of them pile into the family car, Lisa slipping into the front between Susan and Denise. The car shudders under the weight of Jake's rucksack as he throws it into the boot.

'You should probably sit in the middle,' Cameron suggests. 'You're the shortest. Plus you can keep Jake and me from fighting.'

'Isn't that true,' Denise says from the driver's seat. 'Every trip in the car they would have an argument. It was usually from Cameron stirring things up once he got bored of sitting still.'

Aaron shrugs at the instruction and eases into the middle seat. Denise starts the car and drives in silence out of the driveway. No-one speaks on the trip to the freeway. The rumble of the engine blurs into a neutral rhythm. Trees flash by unnoticed. A firm hand presses against the side of Aaron's leg. He looks down to see Jake's finger teasing at the side of his thigh. Jake stares out the window as if nothing is happening. Aaron glances around the car, his eyes widen in embarrassment, but the women in front glare forwards, consumed by the white lines whizzing past. Cameron smirks down at Aaron.

'You're welcome,' he mouths, nodding down at Jake's hand.

Aaron smiles his thanks and intertwines his fingers with Jake's. The roughness of his hand moulds into Aaron's memory. The growing sweat between their palms fails to distract Aaron from tracing the outside of each of Jake's fingers with his own.

The car grumbles up the ramp of the airport carpark. Jake squeezes Aaron's hand one last time and releases when the car enters the darkness of the multi-storey carpark.

'Are you sure you don't want us to get you a trolley for that?' Denise asks when Jake heaves the rucksack over his shoulder.

'No, that's okay mum. We're not allowed to take anything with us that we can't carry ourselves.'

'Why are we at a public airport?' Lisa glares around at the parking spaces. 'Shouldn't you be taking off from an army base or something?'

'That's all up north,' Jake explains. 'This is just a domestic flight. We'll then be shipped to base and take off from there.'

'Gods, so do you need to start loading the plane once you get there?' she mutters.

'Hopefully not,' Jake responds. 'We're the last flight to land up north. The plane should be full of supplies before we get there. This is the army, not a commercial airline, we know how to run things on time.'

'How will mums' roses survive without such precision?' Cameron teases.

'Knock it off boys,' Denise commands.

The echoing steps as they enter the airport reverberate through Aaron. The mindless conversation between the family hisses as background noise while Jake checks his bag in and collects his ticket. Aaron huddles close to the family for the trek towards the gate. The sight of uniforms similar to Jake's littered throughout the airport causes Aaron's heart to skip a beat, the palpitations heavy in his chest. Other members of Jake's troop cluster in small groups in a mixture of uniforms and civilian clothes. To one side two men stand in a warm embrace, smiling as they kiss. Aaron can detect no sorrow or loss in their gaze, just a certainty that their separation won't be forever. Next to them a woman in uniform hugs onto two small children who blink through glistening eyes. A second woman rubs the back of the woman in uniform. She visibly chokes back her tears when the children are looking the other way.

'Well, this is it,' Jake turns around and announces. 'I should fall in with the rest of them.'

Cameron steps in front of Susan, who suddenly turns pale. Cameron pulls Jake into a matey embrace. Aaron stands back, watching the muttering whispers between Cameron and Jake. Cameron unlatches himself and lets

Lisa move in for a quick squeeze before she steps back. Jake holds his arms out and his mums dive in knowing it's their turn. They latch into the back of Jake's ribs together. Once his mums are buried in his chest he wraps his arms around them. Susan's back bounces through her muffled sobs. As they detach themselves from Jake, Susan sneaks a final run down Jake's chest with the back of her hand.

'Thanks for coming to see me off,' Jake says, looking at Aaron. A smug grin pops onto his face. 'Come here.'

Jake struts over to Aaron and drags him into a bear hug. Jake's scent is thrust into Aaron. The dry odour of his uniform blends in with the sweet smell of his sweat. The rough pockets of Jake's uniform scratch against Aaron's shoulder. Jake releases Aaron and pats him on the arm in the heartiest manner he can without hurting Aaron.

'I'll see you all in a few months,' Jake waves.

Jake turns and heads towards the queue moving out the boarding gate. Aaron stares at the back of his head and listens to the squeak of his shoes on the tiles fade. His memory soaks in every detail he can. Jake doesn't look back. His head remains steadily looking forwards. Aaron imagines that Jake is hiding his tears from his family, sobbing silently as he walks away from those who love him.

Aaron stands with Jake's family as they watch the line of people disappear into the plane. They stare blankly out the window at the plane as it pulls out and shuttles to the runway. Their heads rise as they watch the plane take flight until the ceiling blocks their view.

'Well, I need a drink,' Lisa declares to break the silence. She rubs a hand up Susan's arm. Susan dabs at the last of the wetness on her cheeks.

'I second that. You coming Aaron?' Cameron asks.

'Sure, a stiff one would be great. Where are we going?'

'Somewhere grotty. Farewells are always drab affairs,' Lisa says.

'I see how you're related now,' Aaron attempts to joke.

'We sure are,' Cameron pats Aaron's shoulder.

'We're out,' Denise says. 'We have a lot of housework to get done.' Cameron nods as if he's understood a special code from his mother. 'We can drop you off somewhere on the way though.'

Cameron takes charge in the car. He directs Denise as she drives them into the city and pulls up at a kerb. Lisa and Aaron climb out of the car to wait for Cameron's directions. Aaron glances around the street. Nothing stands out to him again. *Cameron's in usual form then*, he thinks. Denise and Susan pull away and disappear down the road.

'About time. I have no idea how I ever lived with them for so long,' Lisa says. Her shoulders drop. Her closed demeanour opens up from her defensive state. The new strength of her pose reminds Aaron of Jake. 'So, what dump are you taking us to, Cameron?' she asks.

'It's just a little dive bar. I know the owners. Spirits are really cheap and nasty there. Hangovers are the price you pay for entry.'

'Hangovers are the price you pay for living with your mothers,' Lisa smirks. 'First round's on me.'

Cameron leads the way into the bar. The door weighs heavily against Aaron's hand as he holds it open for Lisa to enter. The stench of stale beer is rank throughout the room. The bar floor sticks to the bottom of Aaron's shoes with each step. Aaron's eyes adjust to the darkness after a few squints into the bleak gloom.

'Cameron, long time no see,' the barman greets. 'What's

been happening? Tough day I guess, otherwise you wouldn't be here.'

'So true, but not as bad as normal,' Cameron says.

'Speak for yourself,' Lisa cuts in. 'Three vodkas on ice. What do you guys want?' Cameron and Aaron shrug. 'Make that six.'

'This is John,' Cameron says. 'Fifty-seven, Taurus.'

'Fifty-eight now,' John says. 'Rough start to the day for you lot?' Aaron gives a glazed nod. 'Don't worry about sharing the gory details. There should be a booth for you in the back. I'll bring the drinks out for you.'

Cameron nods and leads the way to the back of the room embraced in darkness. An analogue television crackles static through the room. Flies dive at the floor as if swooping in on their last feast. The leather of the booth seats is cracked to the point it may as well have been made of dried mud.

'How, may I ask, did you find a place like this?' Lisa asks as they sit down. She sits uncomfortably on the seat.

'You know me. I get around.'

'I know that's way too true. I can't believe you would come here often enough to be known by name. At my local they still think my name is Trudy. I have no idea why but I go with it. It somehow scores me a lot of free drinks.'

Aaron sits in silence. The gloom of the room around him dampens his mood. The loss of Jake from his routine and freedom trashes any sense of hope that remained after Kyle lost him his job.

'Cheers John,' Cameron salutes when John drops a tray of drinks in front of them. 'Here's to being alone in the house again.' Cameron holds up a glass of vodka.

'Here's to happy singledom,' Lisa says.

They both look at Aaron, waiting. *Gods what am I sup-*

posed to say, he thinks. *Here's to the loss of the second love in my life. I'm sorry he's gone but I don't want to miss him. What do they want to hear?* Aaron raises his glass ready to clink it against theirs.

'Here's to whatever the future holds,' Aaron submits.

They clink their glasses together. Cameron and Lisa hold the straws out of their way and down the contents of their glasses. They barely flinch at the alcoholic burn. Aaron relaxes his throat and pours the liquid down, bracing himself against the bite of the vodka.

'What have you done to him?' Lisa suddenly asks Cameron.

'Nothing, I just introduced him to a couple of new things.'

'So, Aaron, Why are you here? What have you done to score our family?' Lisa rests her chin on top her interlinked fingers.

Aaron's back arches. He instinctively retreats to a defensive attitude that had provided effective sanctuary against David's friends. However, a glint of humour in Lisa's eyes gives him pause, and he examines her demeanour a little closer. There Aaron sees that same desire for connection that had drawn him to Cameron and Jake. The directness of her question now seems charming rather than interrogating, and Aaron relaxes enough to give a candid answer.

'I met Aaron randomly at one of his many jobs, and he seemed to make it his mission to bring me out of my shell. And then I met Jake when he returned from his last tour of duty and we've been sleeping together these past few months,' Aaron casually states.

'Thought so,' Lisa sips on her second glass of vodka. 'You're lucky Susan hasn't pushed for you to marry into the family yet. Damn it, they're too traditional. It's hard to believe Susan and I have the same dads sometimes.'

'They're just obsessed with seeing their sons married off. They spent the last few months trying to set me up with this army bloke named Andrew, when all I was interested in was a shag,' Cameron explains.

'Was that they one they were talking about this morning? I think your words were he was great for sex but completely stupid.'

'That's the one. If I didn't give him directions he didn't know what to do. It was a change for me so somewhat fun.'

Lisa downs the remainder of her second glass and starts clicking her fingers at John. The sharpness in her mannerisms and calmness around Cameron rests strangely with Aaron.

'Aren't you aunt and nephew?' Aaron squints over his glass.

'Cameron and Jake don't give much away, do they?' Lisa shakes her head. 'I'm Susan's much younger sister. I spent a lot of time with her and Denise through to my later teens when dads decided to take on more work hours with the plan of saving for a better retirement. Well, it worked for one, the other died trying. Cameron and Jake are more like brothers to me. We spent a lot of time together when they were young. I was practically living in Susan's house when Jake was born. There's a lot less time together now with our work schedules.'

'Jake and I have always felt closer to Aunt Lisa than each other. The age gap must help that,' Cameron says.

'You two are weirdly similar,' Aaron says, an alcoholic haze begins to drift across his mind. 'I've been spotting it all day.'

Cameron orders extra drinks over Aaron's shoulder.

'That's biology for you. Susan, I and our older brother have the same genetics. Jake and Cameron have the same genetics. The dominant genes are going to make their way through somehow. It just happens to be the damn eyes and nose that keeps popping up between us all. Oh thank you John, you are too kind,' Lisa turns her attention to the fresh round of vodka placed before her.

'I thought I'd save myself the trip,' John says, placing a full bottle of vodka and a bucket of ice in the middle of the table.

'Thanks John, you're a champion. I feel this will become a good old session before too long,' Cameron says.

'I guessed that's why you're here,' John smiles and walks back to behind the bar.

'How often do you come here?' Aaron asks Cameron.

'Often enough. Usually to celebrate or mourn.'

'What's today for you then?'

'Let's go with both,' Cameron raises his glass. 'Jake's nice to have around but he cramps my style.'

'I'm happy just to go with the mourning thing,' Lisa clinks her glass against Cameron's. 'Although knowing I won't have the burden of children leaves me free to do whatever I want.' Lisa wipes away the tear that sneaks onto her cheek.

'Is it very recently you found out?' Aaron asks. 'I didn't mean—I'm sorry you don't have to answer that.'

'No, it's all good,' Lisa composes herself. 'It's why I'm here now, to let it all out. I found out yesterday afternoon. That's why I was over at Susan's house. I stayed the night because I didn't want to be alone.'

'Is it over for you then?' Cameron cuts to the point.

'Yeah, unless I can find a partner who's happy to have kids with me. But we both know that it won't be happening any time soon.'

'Why not? You're still young and hot.'

'I know,' Lisa laughs. 'But I've never gotten along with any of the ladies I've dated. It's been fun but I don't think relationships are for me. I get bored of them after a while.'

Aaron glances between Cameron and Lisa. The conversation cycles through talks he and Cameron have had in the past. He hides his smile behind the condensation on his glass.

'I know that feeling,' Cameron says.

'The worst part is it would all be perfectly fine if I was a man,' Lisa's aches up. 'They can pay for a surrogate and keep it all on the books with the surrogacy screening program. But because I have a vagina they assume that I could be screwing the system over.'

'That's bullshit,' Cameron spits. 'A single man could easily game the system and then go back home to his female partner with a fresh baby.'

'I know. I tried telling them that but they refused to listen. They just said that's the law and I would have to change the law if I wanted to have a baby through them without a partner.'

'Why don't you just do it yourself?' Aaron mumbles.

'How do you mean?' Lisa asks. 'Find myself a sperm donor and do it at home? That's a bit out there. Who knows what sort of kid you could end up with?'

'Why not?' Aaron says. 'Breeders do it.'

'Yeah and look at what their lives are like. That's not what I would want for a kid,' Lisa says.

'You don't have to tell anyone,' Aaron adds. 'When David was thinking about us having children he didn't want to go through the surrogacy program because of the potential for the mother to seek access. He wanted as little interference as possible. He made it sound as if he found a way to keep it off the books. If a man could do it I'm sure a woman could with greater ease.'

'So you'd think, but it's easier to hide a pregnancy when you're not carrying it around for nine months. You can just say it came from a surrogate. Eventually someone would ask me where the sperm came from.'

'Could just say it came from a reproductive clinic and not go into detail.'

'It's not that easy, but thanks for the encouragement. It's actually picked my mood up. Well, it's either that or this vodka. It tastes so cheap but it's working wonders,' Lisa grins. 'Who knows? I might try again and get all crafty like David.'

'Ah crap,' Aaron says. He drops back into the sticky seat. 'David. His diary says we're hosting a dinner party tonight. I've been trying not to think about it. I'd better get home and actually cook something. He's only just calmed down about the last time I didn't cook. I was out drinking vodka then as well.'

Aaron cringes through the burn of the last of his vodka. His chest heaves with the ice-cold weight pressing against his ribs.

'Well you'd better head off,' Cameron says. 'If it finishes early you'll know where to find us.'

'I'll probably crash in Jake's bed,' Lisa adds. 'There's no way I'm going into the main house completely wasted. Denise doesn't let things like that slide very easily. She still thinks you boys are impressionable youth,' she laughs.

'Right, got to go. Nice to meet you Lisa. I'll see you around, no doubt.'

Cameron and Lisa wave tipsily from their seats as Aaron walks from the bar and hails a taxi. A wave of pity flushes through Aaron as the car begins to move towards the apartment. *Poor Lisa*, he thinks over and over again. *The system is messed up. I bet if she was a CEO the path would just fall in front of her. I wish there was something I could do for her. What about my sperm? I don't want to be responsible for a child but she does. Could I just hand it over? I have no idea how but it might help her out, knock down one hurdle. Could she lie, though? Perhaps she could say she went to an overseas clinic? It doesn't seem like that much of a stretch. It could work, but how the hell would I offer something like that to someone.*

12.

AARON DASHES AROUND the kitchen busy with preparations for the dinner party. The roast beef in the oven exudes a juicy garlic aroma through the apartment. Two salads sit in their bowls on the kitchen bench with their dressing to the side. The cutlery and crockery are all counted out awaiting final confirmation of numbers. Almost everything is ready for the arrival of David's guests in half an hour, but David isn't home yet.

Wine, Aaron reminds himself. In this inebriated state the thought of wine has lost its seductiveness, but David's guests will no doubt demand it. He pulls at the heavy door in the cellar and switches on the light. The pinpoints of reflected light in the dimly lit room do little to disguise the pile of empty boxes in the corner of the cellar. *Damn it. I need to order more of the pedestrian plonk.* Aaron crushes the boxes down absentmindedly while he ponders his wine situation.

Then, distressed by the untidy pile of cardboard on the floor but without time to take it to the recycling alcove outside the apartment, Aaron shoves the flattened cardboard into the guestroom wardrobe, now alarmingly full. *I'll have to remember to clear this out eventually*, he thinks as he shoves the last box in with his foot.

Aaron heads back to the cellar and stares blankly at the line-up of vintages before him. *Screw it. One red, one white, one in between. That should get them through the first hour.* Aaron selects from the least dusty bottles along the top rack. *Chardonnay, rosé, shiraz. Done, easy.*

Aaron pours the red wine into a decanter and places the shimmering glass container in the centre of the table. He puts the other two bottles in ice-filled steel wine chillers next to the shiraz. The vases are quickly dripping with condensation.

The apartment door slams shut.

'I know I'm late,' David shouts from the hallway. 'I'll be ready in five.'

Aaron acknowledges the signal and marches around the table placing the salad and candles.

'How many tonight?' Aaron calls to David.

'Six,' David's yell is muffled by the bedroom door.

Aaron clutches the stack of plates, placing them evenly around the table to give everyone as much space as possible. He matches the plates with three glasses per person. *Gods, I'd better do some washing*, he thinks when he notices one glass missing. He puts two glasses in front of his seat at the end of the table. *I'll just pretend I already have a glass with me in the kitchen.* He ruffles the napkin at his seat to make it look already used as a signal not to sit there.

Aaron places the last water jug down as David turns

the corner into the dining room. David stands in a freshly pressed suit, his stomach bulging against the buttons more than Aaron remembers.

'Is it all straight and tidy?' David asks with a spin.

Aaron moves over and stands behind David's back. He pretends to straighten the collar on the jacket. *Here's that little confidence boost you need*, Aaron thinks. *You knew it was fine. You just needed the confirmation. God, what's that smell? It's so fruity*. Aaron sniffs closer to David's next. His nostrils are blasted with the scent of berries.

'Did you get a new cologne?' Aaron asks.

'Yeah, Timothy gave it to me as a thank you for his pay rise. He says it has a fresher scent about it.'

'It's certainly something,' Aaron says.

David pours himself a glass of chardonnay and downs half of it in a single gulp while Aaron returns to the kitchen. *I might be needing to force some of that down as well to last the night*, Aaron thinks. He opens the dishwasher to a rotting compost smell that triggers his gag reflex. Godsdamnit, that's disgusting. I must eventually deal with that as well. He blocks his nose and grabs the first wine glass within reach. He slams the door shut and starts rinsing the glass just as David enters the kitchen, his almost empty glass in hand.

'Dinner smells great,' David says. 'Is it going to be ready on time?' Aaron nods, swallowing down the lumps blocking his throat.

'Yes. Mains will be done in an hour. I can stretch it out if needed. There's cheese to start and port to finish.'

David nods his satisfaction and leaves Aaron alone in the kitchen. Aaron inhales the meaty air down as fast as he can. The fresher odour dislodges the compost smell from his memory. With Aaron's renewed composure comes a revelation about the evening ahead. *A godsdamn dinner party*, he swears. He grumbles on his way to the cellar. He seizes the first red wine he sees and hauls it back to the kitchen. The cork slips out with a pop. The deep scent of the wine tickles Aaron's senses. He pours himself a glass and sips heavily, knowing the night could be a long one.

The sound of the doorbell rouses Aaron into an automated state. He switches from his slumped position into robotic movements.

'Aaron,' Aubrey greets with a smile. She opens her arms wide and pecks a lipstick smear onto his cheek. 'It's been ages. I missed you last time. David's cooking definitely isn't the same. You were sick weren't you?'

'Yeah, he was,' David cuts in. 'Couldn't move out of bed.'

'Yes, it wasn't pretty,' Aaron nods politely. 'I didn't want to contaminate any of your food,' he lies. The calmness of his voice oozes David into a more relaxed state.

'You remember my partner Jennifer, forty-five, Aquarius,' Aubrey says.

'Yes, of course. How are you Jennifer?' Aaron holds his hand out.

'Great to see you again,' Jennifer takes his hand and pecks his cheek as well. 'You have no idea how much I've been hanging out for another one of your famous roasts. Aubrey is always exulting on it.'

'And these are our friends Greg, forty-six, Capricorn and his husband Robert, fifty, Libra.'

Aaron continues through the pleasantries. Greg looks like someone who has worked hard his entire life. Deep stress lines trace down his forehead to his jaw. Robert seems the much younger of the couple. A slick mop of black hair with a grey tinge waves thickly across his scalp. Aaron admires the smoothness of Robert's skin, remarking on the clear use of gentle moisturiser glowing on his cheeks.

'Greg and Jennifer went to school together,' Aubrey continues. 'He now works as an advisor to the Finance Minister.'

'Nice to meet you both,' Aaron says. *That would be why he's invited. Robert must be a homemaker as well.* 'Please have a seat and help yourself to the wine. I'll bring the cheeses out.'

The room quickly fills with complimentary chatter.

'Such a lovely view,' Aaron hears Robert say before the kitchen door shuts.

Aaron dawdles in the kitchen. He fills his glass with more wine and leans against the bench. His eyes drift to the view outside. *I wonder where Jake is now*, he thinks. *He must be on his way out of the country. I wish I could message him. Gods, I'm going to have to distract myself until he gets back. Do I miss him already? He was just a fling, wasn't he? I should be at ease now that he's gone. No more sneaking. Right, distract myself, I can do that.* He takes a gulp of wine. *I wonder how Lisa and Cameron are going.* The image of the pair sobbing over each other crying alcohol instead of tears makes Aaron smile.

'Oh right, the cheese,' Aaron startles himself back into action.

Aaron takes the prepared plate of cheeses and crackers and places it in the middle of the table. Aubrey dives in the moment the plate touches the tablecloth. David follows her lead and scoops a large chunk of blue onto a single cracker. He shoves it into his mouth while listening to Jennifer.

'The office has still been rumbling since we switched to the newer computer system,' she says. 'It was time for an upgrade. The operating systems constantly crashed and to fix it entirely we had to move onto the new computers with debugging software.'

'That's a sneaky trick,' Robert smiles. 'Computer and technology companies do that all the time. Instead of fixing the current versions and improving them they introduce a new product. It forces people to spend more money if they want to be able to continue to use system.'

'It doesn't bother me,' Jennifer continues. 'It's not my money they're spending. It's just having to deal with the complaints. Human resources says they've had an increase in stress complaints because people don't know how to use the new computers.'

'Nonsense,' David throws in. 'It's just because they've had their comfortable lives disrupted. No-one likes change.'

Aaron rolls his eyes and lets the conversation float to the back of his mind. He excuses himself from the table to check on the meat. Inside the kitchen he ignores the oven confident that nothing needs to happen for another half an hour. He resumes his position against the bench looking out the window. The dark street is spotted with the last remnant headlights of rush hour zipping along. Aaron sighs into his wine. *They do the same thing every time*, Aaron mocks. *No-one likes change. It's only a matter of time before David will be schmoozing the finance advisor for some insider gossip.*

Aaron carries on the pretence of being busy. He walks in and out of the conversation, smiling politely each time, insisting everyone refill their glasses. He replaces the empty wine bottles with deeper reds to numb their taste buds. Greg's face starts to glow a bright red. *He's plenty drunk now. I suppose I should bring the mains out.* Aaron waiters out the roasted vegetables and a tray of juicy meat. Redness bleeds out of a dark border on the roast.

'I did say you wouldn't be disappointed with the food,' Aubrey brags.

'You weren't wrong there,' Greg says. 'It looks and smells delicious.'

'Help yourself everyone,' Aaron instructs. 'I'll be back in a second with the gravy and join you.'

Aaron returns and takes his seat at the opposite head of the table to David. Aubrey and Jennifer sit to one side with Greg and Robert on the other.

'So you two,' Aubrey says to their hosts through a mouthful of beans. 'What's in store for you guys? Any plans on extending the family?'

Aaron freezes in his seat, fork in mid-air. His eyes look to David, who stiffens into his corporate mode.

'Not at the moment,' David says calmly. Aaron's drops his hand onto the table glad that David is answering. 'It might be on the horizon. I just want to make sure I know where I'm going to be working first. Who knows where my next promotion will take me?'

'Very wise,' Jennifer says. 'I'm glad we waited until we had both secured careers before we had our girls.'

'Everyone is different,' Greg adds, a defensive twitch flares off his eyebrow. 'Children aren't for everyone. We decided not to have our own children. It allows us the freedom needed for politics. I guess it might be similar to banking in that way. I don't know what position I'll have after the next election.'

'Speaking of,' David interjects. 'How is the election looking?'

'Well, preselection is completed,' Greg mutters. 'also it's all down to a matter of timing. The election needs to be held before winter. The Prime Minister will call it eventually.'

'You mean to tell us you don't know the actual date yet?' Jennifer teases.

'I have a rough idea about when it should be, but nothing is set in concrete. I can't rule anything in or out.'

'Politicians, it's so easy to tell when they're lying,' Jennifer laughs.

'It does help that you've known him for forty years,' Aubrey adds.

'You should have some fantastic dirt on Greg, then,' Robert says. His body shoots upright with excitement. 'I know you're hiding something from me. A previous lover maybe?'

'Or a love child?' Jennifer teases. 'Unfortunately, he was a boring then as he is now. It makes perfect sense as to why he was chosen by the Finance Minister. He would always lose himself in maths homework and numbers.'

'I don't believe you, Jen,' Robert stirs. 'I know there's something tucked away. I guess I'll just have to wait until he's promoted or somehow becomes Prime Minister and the tabloids get hold of it?'

'Damn, you ruined my master scheme,' Jennifer laughs.

'Why hasn't anyone challenged the Prime Minister yet?' David drops the conversation to a serious tone. 'He's been in the position for years.'

'The answer is the same as Jen's computer problem,' Greg answers. 'It's difficult for people to accept sudden change, especially in the lead up to the next election. People feel secure with what they know.'

'Wow, this shiraz is good,' Aubrey compliments. 'You wouldn't happen to have any more, would you?'

'We might,' Aaron perks up at the chance to escape the conversation. 'I'll just check.'

Aaron seizes up the decanter and glides from the dining room. He pauses on the kitchen side of the door. A loud exhale escapes him and his muscles soften in the relative safety of his kitchen. His mind numbs into a haze from his half-finished bottle of wine. He puts the decanter on the bench and walks into the cellar and flicks the switch on. He flinches, expecting the light to blow. The shudder through his system jolts him alert. His eyes dart around suddenly aware of what is happening. *It's all the same. Nothing ever changes with them.* A sense of sneaky pleasure seeps into him. *I've changed. I've grown. They're all the same.*

Aaron shakes his head to cool himself down from the strengthening pride within him. He dulls himself back into a man of routine in preparation to return to the dining room.

'What do you think the outlook will be going into the next financial year?' David asks.

Aaron's deadens his mind. Knowledge of the proceedings assists to blank his thoughts. The same questions will be asked. He smiles and nods as appropriate and accepts the compliments about the food as they are thrown at him. The volume of the conversation grows with each bottle of wine. Aaron censors his ear by applying a similar level of alcohol to his system. He repeatedly excuses himself from the table to steadily bring out bottles of wine and finally some port to draw the evening to a close.

Aubrey savours the final drop of the port and slumps into her seat.

'I think this has been a very satisfying evening all round,' she says. She pushes her chair out and stands. 'I think we'd best be off. Another big day tomorrow for all of us.'

The guests all mumble their agreement and make their departing comments. Aaron smiles, kisses cheeks and shakes hands repetitively until it is just him and David standing alone in the dining room. David pours himself another glass of port.

'That was very useful,' David summarises openly. 'It looks like the banking sector will have to contend with some new taxes soon. We will have to make plans to lobby against it. The CEO should be pleased to have some advanced notice if he doesn't know already.' Aaron circles the table collecting dirty dishes. 'I'll let Timothy know in the morning so he can schedule a brief discussion into the agenda for next week. No point rushing. Or should I?' David continues as if Aaron isn't in the room. 'Maybe I should schedule an earlier meeting with the CEO. No I will wait and keep it to myself until a bigger meeting. I don't intend to let anyone else take the credit for it.' David quiets himself by sipping on his port.

Aaron switches the dishwasher on for the first time in a week. The rest of the dishes he stacks neatly in the sink in case David walks in and complains. Aaron progresses through his routine expecting David to leave. He cleans the last of the apartment and heads into the bedroom. He changes into his pyjamas ready for sleep. His body slumps into the comfortable embrace of the quilts. He drags his romance novel out of the bedside table and opens to the folded page. *I have been at this same spot for months*, Aaron thinks. The same sentence describing the door opening and Diego stepping inside for a beer repeats before him. His eyes glaze over, the words on the page blurring before him.

David steps into the room. Aaron's vision clears at the movement. The strange sensation of having someone else in his bedroom snaps him into readiness. David strips naked in front of Aaron. *He's obviously feeling good about tonight*, Aaron thinks. David's eyes look down hungrily upon Aaron's body. Aaron puts the book back into its drawer. He glances over David's body. The belly sags more than he remembers. Grey nipple hairs poke out of the rippling fat of his chest.

The droop of his gut overshadows the stumpy erection that protrudes from a matt of pubic hair. David's foreskin retreats at the rising of his cock to reveal a deep purple head hanging from the shaft.

Aaron rolls to his side to hide his cringe from David. Aaron's concentrates, forcing his body to relax. *This is no different from how it would be with any client*, he thinks. The mattress tilts as David heaves his weight onto it. Aaron steadies himself on his pillow. The squirt of lubricant makes Aaron shiver. He waits for the cold to touch his arse. David carelessly slaps the lubricant around Aaron's cheeks. Aaron's muscles tense ready to take the extra weight.

The penetration doesn't strike Aaron like he remembers. David is thrusting heavily inside of him but the initial burning sensation he is used to doesn't arrive. David grunts, dropping his hips right on top of Aaron. Aaron pushes back rigidly, robotically encouraging David. The bare minute of thrusting and grunting comes to an end with David sighing and retracting from Aaron.

Aaron doesn't roll over to congratulate David on his conquest. His body slumps, devoid of post-sex bliss. He stares directly at the bathroom door. He slips out of bed and follows his line of sight to clean himself up. *I guess I'm the only thing that has changed around here*, he tells himself.

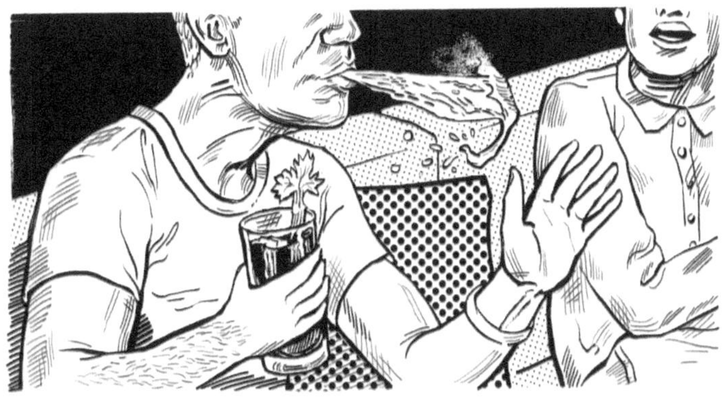

13.

'NOTHING SEEMS TO change in their world,' Aaron complains to Cameron the morning after the dinner party. Cameron squints weakly through his hangover. 'It's like walking into a maze where everything is on loop. There's no change, no way to escape it. The only real difference was the weight David has put on.'

Cameron snickers to himself. He sips on his Bloody Mary and curls himself up tighter on the couch. Aaron senses a change in the feel of Cameron's house. The musty scent that usual welcomes him is gone. The lounge cushions are all neatly lined up. The kitchenette tiles sparkle in the mid-morning light.

'Did you clean?' Aaron asks. He raises an eyebrow suspiciously at Cameron.

'No,' Cameron shrugs off. 'Lisa is a drunk cleaner. I think it's part of the hangover from when she studied nursing.'

'So she came here and cleaned?'

'Yep. She stayed the night but didn't want to wake up with a mess. I was asleep in my room, so it escaped her attention, but everything else is spotless. It has to be one of the strangest things I've seen someone do when they're drunk. Most people have disappointing sex or crash cars but Aunt Lisa has to be different.'

Cameron cradles his head with his arm as he leans back against the couch.

'What were you saying?' Cameron returns the focus. 'Something about David being terrible?'

'Yes, the entire night was terrible. I could write a book about it, except their repetitive behaviours wouldn't make for enthralling reading. The recycled conversation must have made the Finance Minister's advisor feel comfortable otherwise he wouldn't have bragged about the policies they're about to release.'

'He's a politician, a glorified salesperson. Of course he's going to brag.'

'It's not just the conversation. The sex with David just seemed monotonous as well. I used to think I enjoyed sex with David but now I realise it's just not that good.'

'Jake has gone and wrecked you, hasn't he?' Cameron teases.

'More like shown me that's there's more than one position.'

'David's a man of simple tastes, is he? I would have thought that as a straight-laced executive-type he'd have some secret kink to him, but there you go,' Cameron inhales his drink as if it were lifesaving medicine.

'He's definitely a one trick pony with me. I don't know what he does with other people.'

'That's assuming he does anything with other people,' Cameron clarifies.

'Oh, I'm convinced he's doing something. There's definitely something going on with his PA, Timothy.'

'That's just conjecture. You don't have any proof. If he's that terrible at working out what you like in bed then I bet there's a fair chance he can't do it for anyone else either.'

'I suppose you're right. Just because I'm having—I mean had—an affair it doesn't mean that he is. I just want things to change. I want something different. More freedom maybe. My money has been running low and the allowance David is keeping me on is barely enough to cover the catering costs of his dinner parties. He doesn't seem to realise the nicer meat costs more.'

'Ask for more,' Cameron points out.

'He won't listen to me,' Aaron whinges. 'David doesn't see anything I do as essential. He'd rather spend the money on himself instead.'

'Get a job,' Cameron lets his growing irritation emerge through his tone.

'I tried that already, remember. I'm not sure how I'll go getting another one I really don't like the idea of David knowing I'm working. And who knows when Kyle is going to show up again.'

'Well, Jake's psycho fuck of an ex really pulled a number on you, didn't he?'

'Completely. I've even considered asking Michael if he'll take me back for the porn role he originally offered me.'

'Probably not,' Cameron shrugs. 'He's a stubborn bugger and I think after he's dropped you once he won't take you back out of pride as much as anything else. I would try to tease you by saying you've completely aged out of the adult entertainment game but that would be unrealistic given that Michael has a couple of escorts in their eighties on his books.'

'Gross. Why would anyone ever hire them?' Aaron cringes.

'Don't judge. Everyone has their own thing. David likes boring sex. You like it a bit more versatile and secretive. Others are kinkier still.'

Aaron slumps into the couch nodding. He knows what Cameron has said is true.

'What should I do?' Aaron's voice wavers close to begging. 'I've never been so confused.'

'Be happy,' Cameron answered plainly. 'Everything else will fall into place.'

'You're right again,' Aaron admits.

'Of course I am. That's just who I am,' he raises his glass to toast his own confidence.

Lisa stumbles out of Jake's bedroom. Her hair stands up in random shapes behind her head. Dark rings encircle her eyes. She glares between Aaron and Cameron. Her throat spasms ready to talk but struggles to produce any sound. Her eyes catch sight of Cameron's glass held in the air and she drags her feet over and snatches the glass from his hand.

'Good morning Aunt Lisa,' Cameron sings like a schoolchild. 'Feeling a bit rough? What time did you finally put the mop down?'

'No—' Lisa pauses to down the entire bloody Mary. 'Idea,' she finishes. 'Hi Aaron,' she mumbles on her way to the bathroom.

'It's strange seeing her come out of Jake's room,' Aaron says.

'Not for me. When Jake's not home she spends a lot of time crashing here after long nights. Her house is much further out from the city. I cut her a key. My mums don't know about it. They might get overprotective if they did. Or hurt because they're out of the loop. Who knows?' Cameron glances at the celery stalk that now garnishes an empty glass. He gets up, his hangover now soaked in enough alcohol for his usual perkiness to rise to the top. 'I think I finally feel my buzz returning. Do you want one? I'm getting another.'

'Sure. I feel like today is going to be another big one. I need something exciting to happen to make me feel better about going back to the apartment.'

Aaron slouches back into the couch. His careless flop compresses a gust of chemically disinfected air out of the couch cushions. *Jake is really gone*, Aaron thinks. He squints away at the tears trying to form in his eyes. The thought of Jake not being available kicks his stomach up into his throat. His mind races over the memories of Jake. A desire to remove his clothes and climb into Jake's bed tingles along his pubic bone. Aaron crosses his legs to hide an erection that begins to pump between his legs.

'What is that expression?' Cameron asks while handing Aaron the sweating red drink. 'I don't think I've seen that face before.'

'Just realising Jake is actually gone,' Aaron confesses without thinking.

'Say no more. I know the feeling.' Cameron drops himself down next to Aaron. 'It's sad that's he's gone, especially to an active warzone. He might never come home in one piece, or at all.'

'That's not helping,' Aaron glares.

'I know, but it's the reality. That's why when I downplay his role to a gardener. The worse thing he could do then is step on his own rake.'

Aaron's mind gushes with affection for Cameron. *He hides that he truly cares about Jake behind those taunts. He cares more than he's able to cope with, so when Jake does come home is when Cameron can be relaxed about it.*

'Why are you looking so smug?' Cameron interjects into Aaron's thoughts.

'Nothing,' Aaron sips on the watery cocktail. 'I'm just realising how great your family in its own way. It makes me kind of miss mine.'

'You have a phone. Give them a call,' Cameron suggests.

'We aren't that close. I see them at weddings and funerals and other family events, but other than that it's birthday messages if we're lucky.'

'That's sad.'

'Not for me. I've always been too shy to reach out and see that not everyone is like that. I'm sure after another cocktail I'll realise I don't miss them that much. Being the youngest always made me feel like a burden. All my dads' attention went into my older brother. Marrying David sort of freed me from their expectations and apathy. They always fight, especially my dad and my brother. It was always easier to just accept it as normal.'

'No wonder you're so passive,' Cameron says.

'You didn't make me one, then?' Lisa hisses from the bathroom door. She stands in a bath gown, her hair dripping with water.

'You already drank yours, remember,' Cameron waves his glass in the air to remind her.

'Fine I'll make my own,' she snaps from the fridge door as she stares at the empty shelves. 'Brandy coffee it is. I need something to perk me up. So who's passive?' She calls over her shoulder.

'Aaron is, well was,' Cameron says proudly.

'That was obvious, no wonder Jake had a thing for you.

He's not very confident himself,' she says casually.

'So, you're feeling better than you did yesterday about your news?' Aaron flips the target of conversation.

Lisa stumbles over to the couch opposite Aaron and Cameron and eases herself down into it. She hugs onto the mug in the palms of her hands. Her face remains blank while she pours the coffee down her throat.

'Except for the hangover, yes I feel much better thank you for asking,' she says drily.

'Do you still want to have kids?' Aaron asks sharply.

'Timing dude,' Cameron mutters. 'You could have hit that one home a bit softer.'

'Yes *timing dude*,' Lisa pokes her tongue out at Cameron. 'Last night took the edge off. I think I cried enough to flood a desert. After a night like that I'm usually good to go.'

'Are children part of your goals?' Aaron asks more softly. His hands become slippery with sweat. He feels his legs twitch ready to run away.

'Yes they are,' she answers confidently.

'Okay. Good. Would you like my sperm?'

Cameron sprays boozy tomato juice from his lips in a bewildered guffaw and it spatters across the room.

'Cameron! I just cleaned this place,' Lisa complains.

Cameron smacks his hand across his mouth. He wipes the last drops of Bloody Mary with the back of his hand. The whites of his eyes still pop out from under his eyelids.

'I wasn't expecting that,' Cameron says.

'I know right. Shouldn't we at least go for dinner first?' Lisa responds neutrally.

Cameron's body convulses erratically on the couch. He swipes at the drips hanging off his glass. His concentration shifts from Aaron to tidying his cocktail by swirling the celery stalk. His ribs heave out in a final deep breath.

'So,' Cameron begins once composed. 'Where did that come from? You've only just met,' his voice chokes at the end of his question.

'I don't know,' Aaron mimics Cameron usual relaxed shrug. 'I've been thinking about reproduction a lot in the past few months. Especially with David wanting children and then giving up as soon as he found out he couldn't be the biological father. It was just so dismissive of the whole point of having children. And then you pop up and really want to have children, but you've been completely let down by the system. It doesn't seem fair.'

'So your answer is to offer me your sperm?' Lisa asks. 'Just to clarify, you're offering me your sperm because you think the system has been unfair?'

'Yes, pretty much. That and even though I don't want to have children it doesn't mean I can't help someone else achieve the family they want.'

'It's not the worst thing I've heard. It's kind of weird and sweet when you think about it.' Lisa's eyes explore the room. Her pupils flicker, tracing a pattern in her thoughts.

'How do you know your sperm is good to go?' Cameron interjects. 'And Lisa, Aaron's still a stranger to you, would you take a stranger's sperm?'

'At this point, yes, I would take a stranger's sperm,' Lisa fires back. 'But Aaron isn't a complete stranger. If he's good enough to almost be family here then that's enough for me.'

'Fine,' Cameron says. 'So, Aaron, how do you know that your sperm are viable?'

'I don't,' Aaron admits. 'But I'm healthy, much healthier than David. There should be no reason why they wouldn't work.'

'What about your recent employment?' Cameron raises his eyebrows.

'That's all fine,' Aaron dismisses. 'I was always careful and had regular screenings, and all my tests came back clear. There's nothing to worry about there.'

'Screw it, let's do this,' Lisa nods. Cameron's shoulder trembles between a shrug and rigidity. Lisa laughs at Cameron, holding her stomach against the hangover pains. 'I think that's the first time since—I don't know—probably since you were ten that I've seen you completely stumped.'

'But—yes, I—of course, I'm stumped,' Cameron stutters. 'You barely know each other then all of a sudden you want to have a kid together.'

'Why not? It happens the all time. But we're not having a child together, are we Aaron?'

'No,' Aaron's throws his open palms up at Lisa. 'I don't want children. It will be your child, not mine. I'm just a donor.'

'It all seems way too fast. Even for me,' Cameron calms himself. 'But how will it happen? What about the clinic?'

'Screw the reproductive clinics,' Lisa dismisses. 'I tried going about it the right way but they're arseholes who are too blinded by policy to care about me as an individual. I'll just say I went to a clinic. No-one is going to check with them about how I got pregnant.'

Aaron watches the debate between Lisa and Cameron rise and crash. Their cheeks twitch with the same tells that betray their reluctance to admit defeat despite their agreement. Aaron leans back into the couch with the Bloody Mary nursed in his palms.

After ten minutes of arguing Cameron and Lisa start bouncing ideas off each other as their combativeness neutralises into a brainstorming event. Aaron watches the day-dreaming creep across their faces.

'Damn it, you would have a cute child,' Cameron concedes.

'Of course I would. Look at all of us. The nose and eyes are such a strong family trait that I'm sure they baby will have them too, and Aaron might contribute some other features but he's cute enough. He's a bit timid of course, but you've worked wonders helping him with that in a short time. Imagine what a lifetime of such support growing up in our family could achieve.'

Lisa and Cameron both drop back into their couches, caught up in a bliss that both excites and relaxes the two of them. A pleasant satisfaction rises high in their cheeks.

'It might finally happen,' Lisa sighs. 'After all the rigma-role it's going to be a home affair. I know I'm not the first to do it without a clinic but gosh, it's such a relief to avoid the paperwork and needles.'

'So how do we actually do it?' Aaron asks.

Cameron and Lisa freeze and eye Aaron up and down, waiting for Aaron to answer his own question.

'You're up,' Lisa nudges Cameron when the answer doesn't come.

'There are a couple of options. You could have sex with Lisa,' Cameron says. Aaron cringes but then calms himself. *Why does that sound weird to me?* he thinks. *I've had bad sex with men. Could sex with a woman be any worse?* 'Clearly you also agree that's not ideal. The other way is to masturbate into a small container and give it to Lisa to inseminate herself.'

'It has to be timed though,' Lisa adds.

'So, scheduled by clock? Like a dance?' Aaron's eyes light up proudly that he could contribute something.

'More like by calendar,' Cameron nudges.

'What? It takes that long?' Aaron glances between Lisa and Cameron.

A moment of sympathy is shared in a glance between Cameron and Lisa before their faces return to neutral. Aaron sits stiffly between them shifting his attention back and forth to absorb all the information he can.

'Do you know what menstruation is?' Lisa asks calmly.

'I think I've heard of it,' Aaron feigns.

'Okay, so it's a cycle women have,' Lisa continues unperturbed. 'And at a certain point in that cycle is when women are able to fall pregnant. Well, that's if I'm not freaking out from stress. That window is the time I need to get your sperm into me. Where's your calendar Cameron?'

'My what?' he asks, confused.

'Your calendar. You know? It's an item you might hang on the wall to tell you what you need to do each day.'

'I think this is the first time that I've seen you as a different generation to me,' Cameron smiles. 'Us hip young kids just use our phones to keep track of what day it is. I keep my timetables in there as well.'

'Fine, be difficult,' Lisa grumbles. She pulls out her phone and nods her head at the screen while counting. 'So it will be at the end of this week. Shit that's quick. Can you do that Aaron?'

'Do what? You?' Aaron's back stiffens.

Lisa glares at him.

'Are you later this week to masturbate into a cup and give it to me? I'll need to go shopping for some supplies.'

'Yes I can be free then. It's not like I have a job,' Aaron mumbles.

'Good,' Lisa states. 'So from the calendar, tonight is your

last opportunity to ejaculate and after that you'll need to save them up to make sure you produce the most healthy sperm.'

'You should actually make sure you ejaculate tonight or tomorrow morning first thing,' Cameron adds.

Aaron's mind loads into overdrive. *I didn't think there would be that much involved. Why can't she just take my sperm whenever and be pregnant? What if it doesn't work this time? Do I need to do it again?* He breathes in heavily to calm himself. *If it doesn't work this time that's fine. I can do it again. There's no rush.*

'Will you make sure you cum tonight?' Cameron nudges Aaron.

'Sure, I'll handle it.'

'I'm sure you will,' Cameron laughs.

The list of procedures pours knowledgeably out of Cameron and Lisa. Aaron dismisses the thought of them making it up. *Clearly she's been in the system for a while*, he thinks. Within a few minutes his masturbation schedule has been mapped out for this attempt and the next three. Lisa grumbles as she taps the timetable into her phone. Cameron incites her anger by refusing to hand over a pen and paper for her to write a note on. *I wonder if David knew about all these procedures involved in reproduction.* Aaron's mind wanders. *Do we have that much money that he can just pay for someone to ovulate? I can't believe he would go in so blindly. I thought I had some understanding but I know nothing compared to these two. Is it really that hard to have children? All they're going to do is ask me to pleasure myself at specific times. It could be fun for me. What about them? Women's bodies are different and strange. Is insemination like masturbating for her?*

'Will we do it here?' Lisa suggests to Cameron. 'I think it's the best place. You're comfortable for us to do it here aren't you Aaron?' Cameron hides his smirk.

'Yes, here's fine,' Aaron says.

'It does seem like it would work well,' Lisa maps the plan out vocally. 'I'll be in Jake's room you can be in Cameron's. They're right next to each other. You leave *it* out the front of Jake's door and knock. I'll wait a minute so you can duck out and I'll do the rest. That way we can avoid any weird eye contact. This sounds like a plan.'

Aaron and Cameron nod their agreement. *This is all it takes sometimes?* Aaron finds himself backtracking. *Do we actually need reproductive clinics and laws dictating how we have children? No wonder David wanted to use breeders and avoid the system.*

'Let's formalise this,' Lisa stands confidently and holds her hand out. 'I accept your sperm and will have a child that results from it on the condition that I will be the sole parent and you will have no parental rights or responsibilities.'

This is it, Aaron thinks as he stands up. *What am I supposed to say now? This sounds too formal. I didn't think this would be so intense.* Aaron inhales deeply to master his thoughts.

'I undertake to provide you my sperm,' he stumbles through awkwardly. 'I acknowledge that I will not be a parent to any child from any pregnancy that may result from your use of this sperm, and that all decisions, rights and responsibilities as a parent will be yours alone. I'm happy to help but I don't want to be a parent.'

'As your nephew, Aunt Lisa, and your friend, Aaron,' Cameron steps in. 'I am pleased to witness this agreement, with the intention that Lisa will be the sole parent and that Aaron will remain a donor only. But I expect to you say hi to the kid every now and then. Just as a friend of the family,' Cameron stares down at Aaron. Aaron nods his head excessively in agreement to Cameron's demand. 'Awesome. Then it's done. This kid is going to be so cute. So Aaron, you need to ejaculate tonight and then come here on Friday for the real deal. And you, Aunt Lisa, have just quit alcohol for the foreseeable future. Your body needs to be in pristine condition.'

'Fuck off,' Lisa laughs. 'There's no such thing as pristine condition when it comes to the human body. This will be my last drink for now anyway.'

'But you will definitely cut off the alcohol once you're pregnant?' Aaron asks. The concern drops heavily on his gaze.

'Of course,' Lisa says. 'Until then I think we need a toast. Raise your Bloody Marys.' They all lift their hangover cures into the air. 'Here's to having a baby. Gods I hope it works this time.'

They all thrust their glasses together. *Gods, I hope this works first time*, Aaron thinks.

14.

AARON SNEAKS AROUND the apartment while David is on the phone. He keeps himself hidden under constant mindless chores. *He won't want sex in the morning*, Aaron reminds himself. His thoughts do little to comfort his nerves. The niggling possibility that he might ejaculate at any moment and ruin Lisa's best chance this month shivers through him. He finds a strange excitement in having to withhold himself that arouses him. Aaron turns to sweeping the floor, ensuring both hands are on the broom. Any moment a hand is idle he finds it wandering towards his crotch.

David paces in the living room, his hand clutching onto the phone pressed against his ear as though it were a lifeline. Aaron presumes from his calm tone that Timothy is on the other the end walking David through the problems.

'They must be joking. That timeline is impossible,' David mutters. 'I understand. I'll get into the office as soon as I can.

I'll be about twenty minutes. Email me the information and I'll read it in the taxi.'

Aaron ducks through the living room when he hears David fall silent, then shuffles the broom down the hallway and into the laundry. He hopes the cold, tiled room will shelter him from David.

'I'm leaving,' David announces loudly from somewhere in the apartment.

Aaron holds his breath. He stretches his ears towards the front door waiting for the final thud to signal David's departure. Aaron breathes sighs relief when it comes. He leans the broom against the wall and leaves the confines of the laundry.

Aaron whirs the coffee machine to life. The sound of the crunching beans tempts his senses. His body relaxes knowing it will be pumped by caffeine in a couple of minutes. *It will be just me and Lisa*, Aaron prompts himself on the plan. *Masturbate, put the cup by Jake's door and knock. Then leave.* Cameron's erratic work schedule will prevent him from mediating between Lisa and Aaron. Cameron did demand that Aaron go to Driller's Dungeon for a drink afterwards and share the gory details. The way Cameron teases him about the whole process has confused Aaron. *I'm not going to be that involved, he reassures himself. My role pretty much starts and ends with masturbating and I've done that plenty of times before.*

Aaron finishes his coffee and readies himself to leave. He stands facing the wardrobe of clothes glancing over and dismissing the outfits one by one. *Too dressy. I'm not really feeling that colour. Too tight, I'll need access.* His thoughts race.

Aaron shakes his head. He laughs at his own silliness. *I'm not going to some formal event.* He stiffens on the spot. *But it is still an important event. I don't want to be underdressed. Well, I will be partially undressed for a while. Sod it, I'll dress casually for DD.* Aaron puts on a loose shirt and jeans. He stares at his colognes with equal frustration. *Should I even use one? Could it hurt the sperm?* His hand hovers over the bottles, his finger grazing the lids. *No, it contains alcohol,* he decides. For the past few days he has avoided everything in the list Lisa gave him, alcohol, hot baths and sex at the top positions on the list.

Aaron looks at the clock. *David should be well and truly at work. His schedule says he won't be home until after nine. I should be safe.* Aaron hails the first taxi he sees for Cameron's house. The cash he snuck out of the house prickles into his skin, a reminder that the cash will run out eventually.

Aaron walks confidently down the side of Susan and Denise's house. Lisa has ensured they won't be home to interfere with their plans. Aaron has snuck around often enough to feel confident that he can get to the house out back without being caught.

Aaron halts at the sight of Cameron's house. The television flickers colourfully behind the curtain. Lisa sits in the lounge sipping on a tea. *She's not supposed to be out of her room.* Aaron inhales deeply to calm himself and knocks on the door.

'Morning,' Lisa greets with a chirp. 'How are you feeling? Nice and relaxed I hope.'

'Morning. I'm a little nervous but I think I'm good. I did everything you put on the list.'

'Great, I'm all prepared too. Come in, come in. Let's get this show on the road.' Lisa steps back to let Aaron in.

The minty steam rising off Lisa's tea soothes Aaron's nerves. The lounge room is descending back into the messy state Aaron is accustomed to seeing. *I guess that means she hasn't been drinking either*, Aaron thinks confidently. *This all might just work.*

'Cameron said he left his computer open in his room with some encouragement open on the screen in case you need extra help,' Lisa explains.

'Okay, encouragement,' Aaron nods. His mind blurs into a hum of ideas processing. 'Oh, pornography!' he blurts out.

'Yes, that's the one,' Lisa continues. 'There should be some headphones attached as well. I'll be reading in Jake's room waiting for the knock.'

Lisa walks around the lounge piling cushions into the one place. She pats down onto them, squishing the foam as low as possible and watching it rise.

'What are you doing? Aren't you going into Jake's room?' Aaron asks.

'Yes, but once you're gone I'm going to inseminate right away and then sit here with my hips raised and watch a movie. I need to keep my pelvis up in the air for a while afterwards. That's what the internet said to do and it sounds sensible.'

Lisa paces around the room continuing her mission. She places her mug in the sink and picks up a small plastic container and lid resting there upside down to drain. She places the lid on and holds it out like a trophy to Aaron. The opaque plastic masks anything that might be inside the container.

'Make sure you get it all in and secure the lid tightly,' she says. 'We don't want any to get away, particularly if that one is the one to become a child.'

Aaron gulps as he accepts the plastic container.

'Will this work?' his voice wavers.

'There's not much guarantee,' Lisa admits. 'We might have to do this several times. Provided your sperm are viable

I have a good feeling we'll get there. I'm still fertile and I've checked everything to make sure I'm ovulating. Now to do the practical testing.' Lisa's tone slips into a sterile monotone towards the end. Aaron can see her face harden into a stiff shield. She nods the severity out of her forehead and relaxes her jaw to talk. 'Right then. Let's do this. Once you're done remember to knock twice, leave the container at the door and then head off. I'll wait thirty seconds before opening the door so we don't have to do an awkward face-to-face handover.'

Aaron takes his leave into Cameron's room. He is greeted by a familiar stench of staleness and unwashed clothes. The quilt has been hastily thrown on the bed and several bulges still poke out from underneath the fabric. Cameron's laptop sits open on one side of the bed with large headphones next to it. A small piece of paper lies on top of the keyboard. Aaron lowers himself onto the bed.

'Good luck. I hope you enjoy yourself,' the note reads. Aaron smiles picturing the smug grin Cameron would have had while writing the note.

Aaron lies back completely on the bed. He pushes his pants and jocks halfway down his thigh and lifts his shirt up onto his stomach. The lid on the plastic container twists off with ease. Aaron finds a stable spot within easy reach on the quilt to put the open container. The computer flashes to life to an open folder when Aaron switches it on. A list of movies sprawls down the screen. Aaron reads over the terrible names unsure of what each one is. He clicks at the top one. The muffled sound creeps out of the headphones through the opening credits. The words drop from the screen to reveal Cameron sitting casually on the bed. The name Mickey East underlines Cameron's slouching position.

Aaron slams the computer shut with an abrupt snap. *I'm not watching that. It was weird enough to see in person.* Aaron eases his head onto the pillow. He shuts his eyes and takes his flaccid penis in the palm of his hand. He stays motionless, his mind reaching for something to spark him into his duty. A stray finger tickles at the side of his scrotum. His cock twitches to life at the teasing contact. His mind charges to life with offerings from the memory bank of his time with Jake. The musty smell of his room bolsters the familiar scene. The thought of Jake's naked chest pressing against his fuels his cock with blood in an instant.

Aaron starts stroking with his fingers. His hand moves to the image of Jake's arms tensing with each thrust against Aaron's body. Aaron finds himself quickly peaking. His body rushes into his first orgasm in days. His cock tenses ready to explode. *The container!* he remembers. His spare hand reaches across his chest to grab the plastic container. His fingers fumble with the edges to find the opening. His penis thickens with the pulsations of his orgasm. Aaron sees the opening and shoves it onto the end of his cock. He ejaculates hard against the side of the plastic, ignoring the scrape of the container's rim as it digs into the tender skin on the edge of his penis. Aaron's breath eases through the final spurts. He squeezes hard against his dying erection to coax out the last of the semen.

Aaron holds the container up at eye level. *It doesn't look like much*, he thinks when he sees the blob of white liquid sliding across the bottom of the container. He shrugs and screws the lid on tightly. He steadies his hand as he lowers the container carefully onto the bedside table. His hand twitches nervously, fearful of dropping precious life. *Tidy up, knock on Jake's door and leave*, Aaron reminds himself.

Aaron rushes about redressing and flattening out the quilt to remove his body print, returning the bed to its lumpy state. Aaron quietly opens the door and tiptoes into the living room. He doesn't bother to shut Cameron's door to avoid making excess noise.

Aaron presses the container into the carpet by Jake's door. He waits, hand hovering over the lid in case it springs up the moment he steps away. Confident the container is safe he straightens up and stares at the door. *Thirty seconds*, he tells himself. He holds his knuckles at the ready. The hairs on his fingers brush against the wood of the door. His hand twitches, stuttering against the door. *Damn it*. He stands still uncertain what to do. *I've screwed it up. Did she even hear that? Was that two knocks?* His skin begins to shiver. The hairs on his neck stand up. *Screw it*. He knocks loudly twice and rushes from the house. The front door slams behind him in his suddenly noisy escape. His feet pound heavily up the garden path and onto the road. *She definitely would have heard that*. He presses his hands against his knees in a wave of sudden breathlessness. He puffs through the adrenaline and shuts his eyes to concentrate on calming himself down. *It's done. I've done it*, he comforts himself.

Aaron walks casually to the end of the road to hail a taxi. He directs it to DD, where Cameron is expecting him.

'I already know,' Cameron says with a grin when Aaron walks up to the bar. 'Lisa messaged and said it's all up there. Now to play the waiting game. You haven't had a drink in a few days so I bet you're up for one. You can relax now while I keep setting up for tonight.'

Cameron doesn't wait for Aaron to answer. He pushes a cold beer in front of Aaron, who nods his head in thanks.

'It feels anti-climactic,' Aaron says eventually.

'I'm sure it wasn't,' Cameron winks.

Aaron sits quietly on the bar stool. Sunlight creeps through the holes corrugated iron walls of the building and dot the opposite wall. Aaron's shoulders hunch over the bar.

'Come on, I thought that was a really good one,' Cameron wheedles.

'What?' Aaron returns his focus to Cameron.

'It really did take it out of you,' Cameron says. 'I didn't think rubbing one out would be such a big deal.'

'I know, it's not that. It's the sense of completion. I've done my duty now and it's out of my hands. We may have to try again in a month but otherwise it's over.'

'Unless of course Lisa wants another child. But I doubt that will be for at least a few years. I'm not sure she could afford a second child on her salary.'

'But what am I going to do until then?' Aaron picks at the beer label. 'This could be my last drink as well. My cash reserves are running low. I've been sneaking a bit of my allowance into a savings stash in my sock drawer but it's not much.'

'What have you been spending your money on?' Cameron turns his back to Aaron to restock the liquor bottles behind him.

'That's another issue. I don't have anything to show for it. Most of it has been spent on the extra taxis to and from your house.'

'You should have just stayed over.'

'That wouldn't work. David was really cross when that happened last time. I don't want to do that again.'

'So to summarise, you want change but you can't really change too much? The only changes you can have is whatever fits into the schedule of when David's out of the house? And you can't leave him because you can't support yourself financially and also don't want to change things that much.'

'Yep.'

'That's depressing.'

Aaron slumps further into the stool. His shirt sags with his shrinking posture. He sips on the rapidly warming beer, savouring the bitter taste. Cameron spins around to catch the gloom shadowing across Aaron's face.

'Why don't you get a job here? It's not the sort of place you'd find David's friends,' Cameron suggests. He pauses, a sly grin sneaks onto his face. 'I take that back. This is probably the exact place you would find bankers, CEOs and all other kinds of repressed employees, but if anyone spots you here I doubt they'd tell. People hold a code of silence here, particularly the upstairs part.'

'That would be great. What sort of work though? What hours are expects? I'm not going to work upstairs?'

'Oh that's not work. The space is just supplied, or we might bring someone in for special events.'

Aaron shudders. *They were just cutting into each other in public purely for fun.*

'I'll ask the boss. Hold on one sec.' Cameron leans over the bar, his elbows sinking into the bar mat as he stretches further out. 'Alan,' he calls out. 'Alan. Can I borrow you for a minute?'

A short man in a dark suit and slicked back black hair struts over to Aaron and Cameron. Mint and cologne assault Aaron's senses as he gets closer. A heavy gold chain swings menacingly from his neck. Aaron senses the eyes of invisible bouncers staring more intensely down at him the closer Alan gets.

'Hey Cameron,' Alan's voice oozes confidence. 'How can I help you today?'

'This is my friend Aaron, twenty-six, Virgo,' Cameron starts.

'Nice to meet you,' Alan holds out his ring-encrusted hand. Aaron shakes it. 'Alan, forty-eight, Scorpio.'

'He's a good guy. Loves people.'

'I see where this is going,' Alan smirks.

'Exactly,' Cameron says confidently. 'Do you have any jobs you can get him into? He needs something discreet with flexible hours.'

'Interesting story,' Alan says. 'What experience do you have?'

'Well,' Aaron clears away the lump in his throat. 'I don't have anything I can put on a resumé, but I'm very accommodating. And I'm a host as well.' Alan stares blankly at him waiting for the rest of the spiel.

'Homemaker,' Cameron explains. 'Aaron's been running the household for his banker husband and hosting all their swanky dinner parties.'

'That's very impressive. A banker you say.' Alan's phone buzzes against his chest. 'I need to get back to it. Sorry mate,' he says sincerely. 'I'd love to take you on but I don't have a position for you. I have a drawer overflowing with young upstarts who are overqualified but want casual work on the side. No strings attached sort of thing, which works for me. You're competing against that. Sorry, lovely to meet you,' Alan retrieves the phone from his jacket pocket. 'Talk to me,' he says, walking away from the bar.

Aaron slides back into his slump. He downs the rest of his beer in several fast gulps. Boredom grows a hard lump inside the pit of his stomach. Cameron stoops over the bar to meet Aaron eye to eye.

'Look, you just did something awesome today. It's one

of the most generous acts I've ever known someone to do,' Cameron says.

Pride wells in the corner of Aaron's eyes. Realisation smacks him out of his self-pity. He can feel himself inflate again from the limp, exhausted wreck he was becoming.

'You're right. I should be happy,' Aaron says with rising confidence. 'Screw it, I should be happy. I still have a roof over my head. I have freedom to do whatever I want during the day and I may have just helped in the process of creating life. I think I could have another drink.'

'I recommend something sparkling,' Cameron smiles. He pulls two champagne flutes off the rack hanging above the bar. 'My treat, so of course I'll have one with you.'

'Are you allowed to drink at work? That doesn't sound like a safe thing to do.'

Cameron nods his head towards a female bartender bopping erratically at the end of the bar. Her blond braids flop around with her fitful style of wiping down the bar surfaces.

'She's pops a few pills to get her through the shift,' Cameron whispers. 'Everyone has their vice. Here it's more or less ignored as long as you do your work. Alan plays it safe by keeping a good business front. We just can't screw up while enjoying them, otherwise we'll be fired without any chance to explain ourselves. The dancefloor crew is full of professional addicts. Interesting bunch.' Cameron holds his flute full of sparkling wine. Aaron raises his to toast. The bubbles spurt and hiss out the top. 'Well, here's to the next generation. You'll be my niece or nephew's biological father, so you're stuck with us now. Jake won't be able to get rid of you as easily as he did Kyle.'

Aaron's eyes widen at the mention of Kyle. The scar on

his leg itches. He rubs on the outside of his jeans to confirm that the fabric is still intact.

'I hope I'm not like him,' Aaron says coldly.

'I'm sure you're not... yet,' Cameron laughs and steps back out of Aaron's reach. 'Last time you were here you did help someone cut an innocent man with a shard of glass.'

'That wasn't my fault,' Aaron jumps to his own defence, arms waving about glass and all.

'Put. The glass. Down,' Cameron says through a huge grin. Aaron calmly places the flute on the bar top.

'That happened the only other time I've been here.' Aaron's jaw drops in the realisation. 'I completely forgot about that with everything else that's been going on. I still can't believe it happened.'

'I still can't believe a lot of things,' Cameron says smugly. 'That story has done the rounds a few times here. I think in the most recent version of the story you're being charged for assault with a deadly weapon,' Aaron gasps. Cameron holds his hand up for silence. 'You stabbed a guy multiple times with a tile you yanked off the wall during a drug-fuelled mania.'

'How is that possible?' Aaron drops his elbows onto the bar to stop his head from dropping down. 'None of that is true.'

'I know, but that's the way rumours work around here,' Cameron shrugs. 'It's kind of how this place maintains such a grim reputation. Alan doesn't mind. It seems to bring in more business than it loses.'

Aaron smiles. A smug feeling pumps his body into a confident posture. *I've become a story. People are actually talking about something that I did by accident.*

'I feel like a celebrity,' Aaron grins.

'Settle down,' Cameron says over his champagne flute. 'I wouldn't go that far. You're just part of the rumour circuit like the rest of us.'

'Really, what rumours are there about you?' Aaron winks.

'Nothing as good as yours, but apparently I head up an orgy that happens every night on the bar once the club shuts.'

'How much of that is true?'

'Well sex on the bar does happen. I've done it once, though it was too rough on my spine, I came out with bruises. But the bar hasn't hosted any orgies. That all happens upstairs.'

'So, just because you're the cute guy behind the bar they assume that you would be on it as well?' Aaron smirks.

'Wow, we have really trashed you. You were so sweet when we first met and now you think of me in dirty ways.'

'I watched you make a porn movie,' Aaron states blankly.

'Oh yeah, that's right. Did you use any of those for inspiration?' Cameron asks, an eyebrow rises.

'No, I couldn't. That felt weird.'

'Weirder than watching me having sex in person and then masturbating in my bed?' Cameron queries.

'I suppose not,' Aaron shrugs.

Things have really changed for me, Aaron finally admits to himself. *I would have never done any of this if I hadn't walked into Cameron's bar because I felt low after David's rejection.* A glow from happiness and wine heats the inside of his cheeks.

A darkness returns to his thoughts. *Once I go home that might be it. I'll be back in David's routine. Back to the boring romance novels instead of the fun sex. At least for another six months until Jake comes home from duty. I hope he wants to be with me again. I don't think I can last just with David.*

'There's that look again,' Cameron points out. 'All doom and gloom. Things don't have to be that bad.'

'Things do feel that bad though. All the fun of the past few months has come to an end. Where do I take it from here?'

'Tell David,' Cameron states. Aaron freezes in shock. 'Don't panic. I'm sure it isn't that bad.'

'How can you say it isn't that bad?' Aaron's voice wavers. 'Tell David everything? Do you know how he will react?'

'Do you?' Cameron fires back.

Aaron raises a finger to protest again but fails to oppose Cameron's point. *I don't know what David would say. When I missed the dinner party he was only mad that he looked bad and had to do extra work.* Cameron stands confidently behind the bar. Aaron concedes defeat and nods.

'You're right. I don't know how he would react,' Aaron admits.

'That's why you should just talk to him. You probably need to make sure he knows that no-one in his circle knows what you've been up to, but other than that you never know, he might agree to an open relationship, or even letting you find a job during the day.'

'Yeah, and a divorce at night,' Aaron grumbles.

'Would it be that bad? You're happier away from him anyway. Sure it might take a few years to get back on your feet but then you're free. You can do whatever you want.'

'But where will I live? What will I do for money?'

'Don't worry about any of that yet. You might not have to think about it. Nothing may change between you and David except that he knows about your secrets. You might get a few on him anyway.'

Aaron rests on the bar to stop his buzzing mind from knocking him over. The realisation that he will have to tell David everything makes his head spin. His desire for the champagne in his hand evaporates. Aaron's mouth runs dry and his heart beats in his stomach in apprehension. *I'm going to tell him*, Aaron resolves. *But how do you tell a husband you've been cheating?*

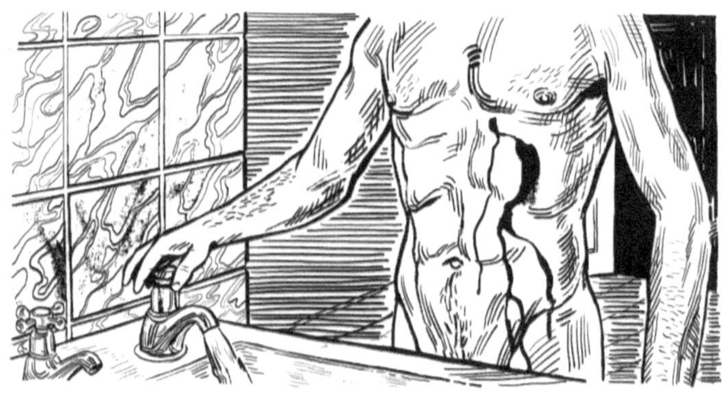

15.

AARON PACES THE apartment late into the night waiting for David to come home. By David's schedule he should have finished his meetings two hours ago. *He might be sleeping at the office again*, Aaron wonders. He feels pumped up ready to launch his confession upon David the moment he walks in the door, but the desire to confess is beginning to fade. Aaron's legs begin to shake from the exhaustion of pacing back and forth through the apartment without a break.

Aaron's frustration boils over. His whips out his phone and dials David's work number. The irritable voice of Timothy blurts through the phone.

'Can I help you, Aaron?' Timothy moans.

'I would like to speak to David, please,' Aaron forces a powerful faux confidence down at his phone.

'We all would like that,' Timothy grumbles. 'David's meeting has gone over again. I've got several reports that I need him to read and sign before tomorrow.'

'Damn it.'

'Exactly. I'll tell him you called. It looks like it will be an all-nighter again.'

Timothy hangs up before Aaron can protest, its beeps the only goodbye Timothy offers. Aaron swears and throws his phone into the couch. *I need to calm down. It's not going to happen tonight. I need to do something to distract myself.*

Aaron marches to the cellar and grabs the first bottle he spots. His arm sways with the bottle hanging from his fist. His spare hand grips a glass and corkscrew. He charges straight into the bathroom and quickly has water streaming out of the tap for a bath. Aaron throws random shakes of bath salts and soothing balms into the water. He tears off his clothes in frustration and shoves the pile of material into the corner of the bathroom. His teeth rip at the top of wine bottle, removing the foil covering. He roughly handles the corkscrew and throws his full concentration behind opening the bottle.

A splash of red wine shoots out the top of the bottle behind the cork as Aaron rips it from the bottle. The chill of the wine flowing down his naked body doesn't register inside his sphere of concentration. The liquid thins into a dull purple while tracing down his skin, its flow barely disrupted by sparse hairs.

Aaron drops the cork still impaled on the screw onto the ground. The tiles object to the harsh treatment with a loud clatter that echoes around the room. Aaron ignores everything else to fill his glass all the way to the brim, then places the bottle down next to the bath. The steam from the water and salts seep into his skin as he stands over the bath. Aaron climbs into the water and drops completely down into the burning bottom of the tub. His skin prickles in the heat. He moans and shivers through the hot pressure dragging along his skin, lowering himself ever deeper. The water rushing from the tap splashes against his bare chest. It rises quickly over his nipples and tickles at the base of his neck. Aaron turns off the taps. The room falls into an echoing quiet as the sound of the last drops of water ripples against the chill of the empty room.

This is working, Aaron smiles. The hot water reddens his skin pleasingly. The dry hiss of bubbles bursting on top of the water releases the scent of lavender. Aaron shoves the red wine under his nose and inhales deeply. *I won't be able to tell David tonight. I have time to plan this better*. He pours the wine down his throat. The water laps against fresh skin with each movement around the tub. *I could have a dinner ready for him. No that won't work. I do that already anyway. There's no guarantee he would be there, or that he would be alone. Maybe I could go to his office? No, that won't work. Damn Timothy. He'll get in the way. I don't know what to do*. Aaron tips the rest of the wine into his mouth. He gags through the acidic burn on his tongue.. He refills his glass and forces his mind back to planning how to tell David. He shudders against the heat of the water. The nerves gushing through him block the sensation of heat pressing down on him.

Why am I in such a rush to tell David? Aaron thinks once the steam and wine slow his thoughts. His face drips with fresh sweat that lands on the bubbles rising up against his chin. *It's not like I'm looking forward to it. I have enough cash to last the week or more if I'm careful. I can stash away more of my allowance before then in case he kicks me out. He won't kick me out, surely. Not straight away anyway. He can't. Not until I'm ready and he knows where everything is. But if he's already screwing Timothy David might get him to move in and take my place right away*. Aaron shudders at the images of Timothy making himself at home, playing with Aaron's coffee machine. Each stroke of Timothy's hand on the coffee handle is accompanied by a suggestive stroking of his tongue across his lips.

Aaron shakes his mind free from the image. The bubbles burst in protest to his sudden movements. *Timothy wouldn't move in that quickly. David can't allow any bad impressions of himself.* Aaron straightens up at the realisation presenting in his mind. *David can't ruin his image*, he repeats to himself. *A divorce is a bad image. David would put in extra effort to hide what I have done. I'm so stupid, why didn't I think of that before?*

The smile growing on Aaron's face quickly fades. *He wouldn't pay me off. He'd just impose more rules just like last time. Why the hell am I with a guy I don't even get to see but tries to control my life? Because you need him*, Aaron tells himself. *For some reason I still love him and I like having some form of life with him. Pathetic.*

Aaron pours out half the bottle of wine into his glass and drinks heavily until it's gone and his stomach feels like it's about to explode. The heat and pressure tense in his gut. Aaron relishes the sickness within. It distracts him from the onslaught of mixed emotions. The rumbling of thoughts is forced out of his mind by the weight of the wine. *I'll have this conversation next time I see David*, Aaron decides. He relaxes himself, content with the outcome of this idea. The nausea slowly dissipates into a floating drunkenness.

'I did try,' Aaron tells Cameron the next day at the bookshop café as he cradles a mug of coffee. 'But I doubt I'll see him for a while.'

'Are you sure you actually tried?' Cameron asks over the coffee machine. He fiddles at the knobs to make the last coffee of the morning rush. 'Here you go Tammy. Have a great day.'

The frizzy-haired woman smiles and ducks out of the shop with the coffee in hand.

'Yeah, he never even came home last night and Timothy refused to disturb him in his meeting,' Aaron says. 'It's impossible to get hold of him when the work cycles around like it does. I've tried going into the office but that snooty Timothy always gets in the way.'

'Is he David's suspected lover?' Cameron steps out from behind the coffee machine and leans on the counter. 'I'm sorry, I mean personal assistant?'

'That's him. Little, snooty organised manipulative control freak. I swear he's more of a husband to David than I am sometimes.'

'You mean a lot of the time?' Cameron teases.

'Fine, yes. A lot. Timothy probably wouldn't cheat on David, either. It's like I'm the apartment husband, he's the office husband and we aren't allowed to switch roles.'

'You are the apartment husband. That's your job.'

Aaron's shoulders slump. He stares blankly at the dying froth in his cup. The brown stain of the coffee clings to the sides as a reminder of how long he's been standing around chatting to Cameron.

'I suppose it's one of my jobs. Well, it's my only job now.'

'You should ask for a raise.'

'Definitely,' a smile returns to Aaron's face. 'Then I won't have to look for a day job.'

'Maybe you could volunteer?' Cameron suggests. 'There's a shelter up the road that's always on the lookout for people to serve lunch to the homeless. It would mean you get to cook for people who would actually appreciate what you do for them.'

'I wish. I don't think David likes anything happening in

either of our lives without him giving his blessing for it first. It would be good for his image but he doesn't give up his things without a fight.'

'Did you just call yourself one of David's things?' Cameron squints a worried look at Aaron.

'No, not in that way. I'm his husband not his possession. He just likes things in order. If I take shifts somewhere there's a chance that I won't be around when he needs me—well needs my food—to secure a good deal.'

'Which is different from what you've been doing recently?'

'Recently I could leave at the drop of a hat in most cases and get home within an hour or two. It would look bad to bail on a shift volunteering at a shelter.'

'That sounds like David's reasoning.'

Aaron nods and drinks the last of his coffee.

'It's more I would feel bad than it would look bad,' Aaron says. 'We've been together for a while now. We have a system in place that seems to work for us.'

'You need to find yourself some more side-candy to keep that system going,' Cameron winks. 'You were much happier when you were sleeping with Jake. Now it's all mope.'

'I know. It's all confusing now that Jake has left. I knew all along that it wasn't a permanent arrangement so I didn't worry about getting too attached, but I think I did become attached. It's not just sex that I'm missing. I think it's sex with Jake. It was freeing and awesome.'

'You don't need to be too graphic. Remember that's my brother you're talking about,' Cameron holds his hand up as a warning. He smirks down at Aaron while feigning horror.

'I don't think I can be more graphic than you. It's a skill you have.'

'Thank you,' Cameron returns to leaning on the counter.

'I don't think having a random affair with someone is the sort of thing I want to do. I would much prefer to have what Jake and I had but with more security.'

'So, another husband?'

'No, just someone who sticks around. David's never home. Jake will constantly be flying out. I have no idea where I'll be living in the next few months. I might end up alone. David could get another promotion and move us both to another city. He could freak out when I tell him everything and kill me.'

A couple sitting at a nearby table snap their heads around, concern plastered on their faces. Their hands halt mid-air with coffee cups hanging from their fingers.

'He's speaking figuratively,' Cameron says in a calm, assertive tone. 'No-one is actually going to kill anyone.'

The couple visibly sighs their relief and return to their quiet conversation.

'We hope not,' Aaron whispers carefully. 'I'm just saying I want the fun and connection I had with Jake but to have him around for longer and still be married to David but with more open communication so I don't have to resent hiding things from him. Am I asking for too much?'

'Probably,' Cameron states. 'You have to remember that you are dealing with people. People are real and unpredictable and have their own needs. People change as well, even if they don't want to. I thought you have a good thing going. You have the security of marriage to a rich guy and the fun of having sex with someone you know is going to leave eventually, so there's no risk of him getting too attached and demanding you leave David. It's Jake we are talking about so he probably wouldn't ask for commitment from you anyway, not after Kyle.'

A bizarre haze floats into Aaron's head. A dreamlike happiness coats his mind and lightens his thoughts. *Cameron is right*, he thinks. *I did have a good thing going. I probably still do. I just need to wait for Jake to get back and things will be back to normal. Well, that's if everything goes well with David.*

'Do you think Jake would come home partnered to someone from the army?' Aaron asks to distract his thoughts.

Cameron bursts into a fit of laughter. The couple on the couch snap their heads around again. They come to their senses as quick as they can to look away from Cameron's hysterics and stare at each other in silence. Tears creep out the corners of Cameron's eyes. He breathes heavily, clutching his stomach.

'Where did that come from?' Cameron coughs out. He composes himself enough to inhale without gasping. 'One minute you're gloomy, the next you're checking up on my brother. Are you getting jealous?'

'No,' Aaron blushes. 'It's not that. I was just thinking about what you said. I did have everything going well. But I'm curious if I should consider the possibility that Jake might not be free again when he returns from duty.'

'Sure, why not? We can go with that.' Cameron cools himself down to lean on the counter again and lowers his voice. 'There's no way Jake will be with someone from his troop. He doesn't get along with them that well. He says he likes working with them but that's it. Also, I think he's more into skinnier guys, not the meat heads. So, like you. He likes your type.'

'My type? What is my type? Married?' Aaron asks confused.

'Lean and trimmed. Not completely scrawny but not enough bulk to compete with him.'

'Oh, I guess I've never really thought about it. I suppose you're right. Kyle did seem to have a similar build to me, just shorter.'

'Yeah, along with every other guy I've ever seen sneaking out of the house. Unless he had a big night that is, in which case I don't want to see what walks out.'

Aaron feels as if his insides have suddenly been cut. The bottom of his stomach sits like it is about to fall out from him. *You idiot*, Aaron tells himself. *You knew he sees other people. It shouldn't hurt like that.* Aaron pushes his coffee mug across to Cameron to distract himself.

'Do you have a type?' Aaron asks Cameron.

'Don't know,' Cameron shrugs. 'I used to think I had a type because I was always dating footballers in high school, but once I left I found I liked all sorts of different guys. It's a bit like everything else for me, I don't stick to the same thing for too long. I like variety.'

'I've only ever been with two people, what type is that?' Aaron mumbles his realisation. 'They're both bigger than me, definitely stronger.'

'I imagine you like a bit of power,' Cameron winks. 'David has the financial power. Jake had physical strength. I bet they both made the first moves as well.'

Aaron pauses to recollect his memories. He traces his time with David back. The image of the lake in their hometown flashes behind his eyes. David leaned in for the kiss while Aaron was staring out at the water. He turned just quick enough to smack his nose with David's. David powered through, shoving his tongue into Aaron's mouth as soon as their lips met. He recalls back to their wedding night, their first time in bed together. Aaron lay there waiting. David did all the work, directing Aaron's movements for the seconds of pleasure David had with his body. He remembers glowing afterwards, knowing his life-long goals had been achieved.

'I take that as a yes,' Cameron says. Aaron nods. 'That could be your type then.'

'I thought David was the only type for me. That's changed,' Aaron replies.

'That's very sweet and innocent of you,' Cameron smirks.

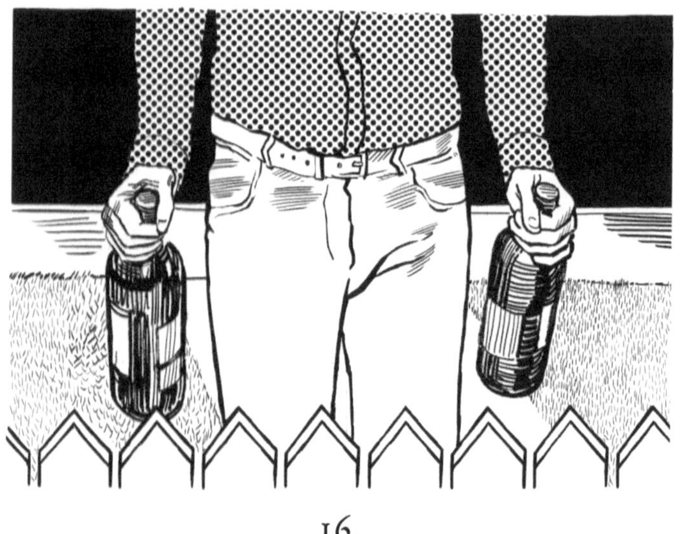

16.

AARON STANDS OUTSIDE the front door to Susan and Denise's house. Insects chirp in the garden around his feet. His dress shirt clings to him by the cold sweat seeping from his skin. Two bottles of wine dangle heavily from his fists. He readjusts his grip on the glass to stop the bottles slipping through his grasp.

Weeks have passed without Aaron catching hold of David for long enough to confess all his secrets and concerns. Those moments when David is in the house his head is glued to his phone or he's charging around trying to pack enough clean shirts for the latest bender of reports or intercity conferences. Each time Aaron works himself up to tell David his voice is cut off mid-sentence as soon as David enters the same room.

'I'm leaving,' becomes the only conversation David is willing to enter into with Aaron. *I won't ever be able to tell him at this rate*, Aaron concedes the situation seems hopeless.

The message from Lisa yesterday had pulled Aaron out of his repetitive slump. Despite being a simple dinner invitation to Susan and Denise's house, Aaron isn't convinced that there isn't an ulterior purpose. *It will be about the baby*, Aaron thinks confidently and nervously. Otherwise Lisa wouldn't have cancelled the next scheduled attempt to conceive. Cameron confirms that he'll be there but doesn't reveal any further information even under Aaron's probing.

'You're looking very handsome tonight,' Denise greets him with a hug. 'I wasn't expecting it to be such a formal event. Ah, you shouldn't have,' she adds upon spotting the wine.

'I felt like wearing something a little nicer,' Aaron says. *It could be a big event tonight*, he adds silently.

'Come on through, we're having martinis to start. Lisa has gone ahead and planned an entire night for us. But somehow she's also gotten herself into one of her energetic moods.'

Denise leads the way into the kitchen. As Aaron enters the house it feels like a familiar embrace. His muscles ease in the warmth of the overcrowded rooms. An excessively large collection of family photos smile down from the walls as Aaron walks through. The scent of freshly baked bread wafts through the house, drawing Aaron towards the dining room.

Cameron, Lisa and Susan are standing around the dining room. Lisa pours martinis into glasses and passes them around to everyone. Aaron greets each of them with the usual pleasantries. Lisa meanders over last, her eyes shifting from side to side to confirm everyone has returned to their own conversations. She pulls Aaron in for a deep hug, her arms lingering around his midriff.

'Thank you,' she whispers directly into Aaron's ear.

Lisa turns away without catching Aaron's eye. Aaron forces his beaming smile to disappear so as to not give the surprise away. He blinks away at a single proud tear forming in his eye. He rubs at it pretending to remove an eyelash. Cameron smirks his usual delight next to his mums. *He's been watching and he knows already*, Aaron raises his glass and winks at Cameron. Susan and Denise converse rapidly, words spilling continuously from their mouths. *I can't imagine Lisa hosts dinner parties very often. How haven't they worked out something is up?* Aaron thinks.

'So, Aaron, how is everything going on the home front? David must be busy as per usual.' Susan asks when Aaron joins their conversation next to the table.

'Everything is going really well actually,' Aaron lies, not wanting to bring the mood down. 'David is incredibly busy at the moment. He looks in line for that promotion, it's all but confirmed. We're just waiting to see if the position will be here or interstate. It's looks positive here, three of the executives have recently moved to international offices,' the story rolls of Aaron's tongue like a practised speech.

'Fantastic,' Denise responds. 'That would mean you two will truly be able to settle down and think about having a family.'

'Of course,' Aaron plays along. 'We'll be able to make definite decisions then, especially if we know we can stay within the same school zone for twenty years. I don't like the idea of moving schools. I think it's really important to provide stability as much as possible.'

'Oh yes, but if you must move schools you need to do it while they're younger,' Susan adds. 'We moved house when Jake was in first year. The cliques hadn't formed yet and so switching schools wasn't like breaking him out of a strong support network.'

Cameron's smirk shines over his mums' heads, shaking his head at Aaron while his nod in polite interest.

'Did Cameron tell you he's postponed his trip?' Denise asks while Aaron exults in the poetic justice of the shift in focus.

'No, he didn't,' Aaron admits. *Hey, that's actually the truth. We're back on track.*

'He's not planning on leaving until late next autumn, and then he'll follow summer around for a year. And he promised to buy a return ticket, so I'm feeling much happier about the prospect of his departure.'

Next autumn? Aaron thinks. *That's a little over nine months. I wonder if he's waiting around for something.*

'I'm sorry if I got a bit emotional at the airport,' Susan says.

'Oh no, of course that's perfectly fine,' Aaron smiles. 'I can understand. It must be such a relief to know Cameron plans to return from his travels.'

'For now, tonight might change my mind,' Cameron scowls.

'Don't be silly dear,' Susan says playfully. 'As a mother it's just a nice feeling to know that you'll come home. It means the goodbye at the airport won't feel like the last goodbye. Unless of course you find a nice young man and settle down overseas, I can probably cope with that.'

'And if you must find your husband anywhere other than here, can he at least be from somewhere tropical near some good resorts, and we'll make sure to visit you regularly,' Denise chuckles to herself.

'I'll make sure it's the resort owner,' Cameron shakes his head. 'That way the drinks will be free as well.'

'Don't be silly. We'll be happy with anyone you bring home to us,' Denise dismisses with a wave of her hand.

'You see, back home, there it is again,' Cameron points out. 'It's second nature to you.'

'I know. I struggle with the idea of an empty nest.'

'You're almost there,' Cameron retorts drily. 'Jake is overseas a lot of the time and I live pretty much independently. I only get to see you on weekends and for special events.'

Lisa paces the room, suddenly making everyone aware that she's in charge. She places her full martini glass down at the table.

'Sit everyone, I can smell the entrée getting close,' she instructs. 'I'll bring out a corkscrew as well. Does anyone want anything other than red?'

When no-one voices any objection Lisa herds her guests in the direction of the dining table before she darts from the room. *This is impressive*, Aaron thinks, breaking away from the conversation to observe the table setting. *Lisa has put a lot more effort in than I used to do.* The table shines of cutlery in the candlelight. Napkins lay perfectly pressed on the table. Small arrangement of red flowers sit in shallow vases around the table, the highest petals reach just far enough to cover the sight of each other's wine glasses.

Lisa bounces into the dining room with plates laden with soup. The salty smell of herbs makes Aaron's mouth burst with saliva. Lisa ducks from the room and returns with a board of fresh cut bread and places it in the centre of the table, within reach of everyone.

'Dig in everyone,' Lisa says as she takes her seat.

'You really have gone all out,' Denise says. 'We haven't seen you in this sort of a mood for a while, not since...' Denise's voice trails off. Her eyes squint suspiciously at Lisa.

'There's nothing to worry about,' Lisa says playfully. 'It's nothing like last time. This is all good news.'

'Last time?' Aaron asks. Cameron laughs suddenly, causing him to choke on his soup.

'It wasn't funny,' Denise hisses.

'Come on mum,' Cameron wipes the spilt liquid off his lips. 'It's kind of funny now, though I'm sure it wasn't at the time.' Aaron's eyes flick between everyone at the table. They all sit silent, waiting for someone else to begin the story.

'It was nothing,' Lisa says casually. 'When I used to live here I just happened to spend a night with one of Denise's colleagues.'

'My boss,' Denise grumbles over a full spoon.

'And they may have bumped into each other in the hallway dashing to the toilet. See it was nothing to be worried about.'

'Keep going Lisa, you're missing the best details,' Cameron encourages.

'Don't lead her on Cameron,' Susan says.

'She may not have been wearing any clothes when they ran into each other. Her boss was nude, not Denise,' Lisa adds.

'Oh seriously? That would have been an experience for you,' Aaron laughs.

'It was embarrassing,' Denise complains.

'Not for her boss,' Cameron says.

'She just stood there completely naked chatting to me as if we were in the office. I couldn't look at her the same for months,' Denise says.

'It all worked out in the end,' Cameron wraps up the story. 'Lisa never saw mum's boss again, she moved offices and mum got the promotion. I'm sure... er, what was her name again?' Lisa shrugs.

'Kylie,' Denise mumbles.

'I'm sure Kylie would have put in a good word for you to get the promotion,' Cameron continues. 'And all because Aunt Lisa bent over backwards for her.'

'Cameron!' Susan scolds, 'there's no need to talk like that.'

Aaron stares down at his soup and concentrates on scraping his bowl to hide a grin that threatens to explode into laughter. The more Aaron focusses on not smiling the more he feels his stomach tense and shiver ready to gush into an onslaught of hysterics. Cameron watches him over his wine glass, absorbing every detail and waiting for the show to continue.

Lisa breaks away from the looming laughter and excuses herself to clear away the plates. The smell of fresh tomato sauce floats out of the kitchen when Lisa opens the door. *Pasta*, Aaron thinks. His gut grumbles with excitement at thought of fresh pasta.

Lisa reappears momentarily with new plates and bowls before escaping again for the final reveal of the meal. The empty chinaware shimmers at Aaron. *This must only be used for special occasions like this*, he thinks. *It doesn't look like there's so much as a scratch on it.* Lisa returns with a proud grin and a large steaming bowl of pasta covered by an aromatic sauce slowly easing itself amongst the pieces of pasta.

'Lisa made it all herself from scratch,' Susan smiles. 'Even the pasta. It's amazing what she achieves when she puts her mind to it.'

'Thanks for the encouragement,' Lisa rolls her eyes.

Lisa shuffles between the kitchen and dining room several times before sitting herself down. She brings out grated parmesan cheese, serving spoons and a plate filled with prosciutto curled into neat rows. A leafy salad looks enticing but is shadowed by the impressive bowl of pasta. *She is really good at this*, Aaron thinks.

'Eat up everyone,' Lisa encourages. 'I got all the ingredients for the sauce from the old couple up the road that sells tomatoes from their garden in the mornings. The bread is from a small family-run bakery at the end of the street and the ham comes from the deli next to them.'

'We really should shop at those places more often,' Denise says.

'It's a bit hard with our work hours,' Susan says. 'Those specialty shops are only open when we are at work. The supermarket is the only shop still open when I come home. It's either that or online.'

'That's a pity,' Lisa adds. 'They all have a lot of great food in there. And the olive range in the deli was huge. I might go back there and stock up.'

'You'll have to hide them from Cameron,' Susan smirks.

'I think you mean Jake, mum. He's the one that can sniff out olives at forty paces.'

The conversation meanders on through a number of light affairs. The highest point of controversy remains the number of glasses that should be set for a formal dinner setting. Aaron and Cameron exchange a number of glances as they wait for the real news to penetrate the conversation. Susan and Denise absorb themselves in the conversation about the rituals of a dinner party. Lisa nudges them further down the dreary spiral of social practises. *At least this is a change from banking and politics*, Aaron thinks. *I mustn't be one of those people afraid of change, but I bet Cameron's parents are. Lisa's news might just send them over the edge. I've never thought of being pregnant before marriage as much of an issue before, but who knows how they'll cope?*

'That was delicious,' Denise declares. She drops her napkin onto her empty plate and slouches back into her chair. 'You should do this more often,' she suggests. Her stomach protrudes out in a satisfied bulge.

'I think a toast to the chef is in order,' Susan says as she lifts her glass.

Cameron's eyes widen at the announcement of a toast. His hand twitches out towards his glass, which he fills almost to the brim and hugs onto it, waiting. Aaron can see Cameron's ears twitch in anticipation. Aaron's heart skips a beat as he observes the change in Lisa and Cameron's body language, which screams that whatever news is coming is about to arrive. Aaron trusts their knowledge of their family enough to fill his own glass, though he leaves his wine glass on the table to conceal the tremble in his hands.

'So, what are we toasting?' Denise asks. 'I think to a fantastic meal with a fantastic family.'

'To a fantastic family,' Susan repeats. She holds her glass in the air and takes a drink once it has clinked with everyone else.

'Speaking of fantastic family. Ours is about to get bigger,' Lisa announces. Her low volume disguises the faltering in her voice.

Susan and Denise exchange confused glances. Aaron sips steadily at his wine to remove the dry lump that keeps forming in his throat. Cameron sits with his back straight, his neck snapping steadily back and forth between his mums and Lisa.

'What are you talking about?' Susan finally breaks the silence. 'Have one of you two started dating without telling us?'

'No, it's not that,' Lisa inhales for confidence. 'I'm pregnant.'

Cameron's smile spread so rapidly on his face his cheeks

look like they're about to catapult off his face. Aaron freezes. He forces his body to remain upright while he repulses the instinct to shrink away.

'How?' Susan asks. 'The clinic said they couldn't legally accept you.'

'No, I couldn't go through a reproductive clinic. There are other ways,' Lisa responds calmly.

'Other ways, there aren't that many other ways,' Denise mumbles. 'Oh you can't be. Surely you're not a—?' Denise accuses.

'No Denise, I'm not a breeder,' Lisa states coldly.

'But then how? How do you even know you're pregnant?' Susan asks.

'It's not secret information, it only takes a simple blood test to confirm it. And it has been confirmed, I'm on my way to becoming a mum.'

'That doesn't answer anything Lisa,' Susan's voice turns sharp. 'How did you get pregnant?'

'With help from a donor.'

'How did you do it? Did he—' Denise cuts herself off.

'No Denise. I did not have sex with a man. It was through artificial insemination.'

'How can you be sure that it's safe? A reproductive clinic is the safest and natural way to do things. You know that. You should have just waited until you found a nice wife to have children. How are you even going to raise a child on your income?' Susan rattles off. 'And you better not be drinking if you're pregnant.'

'I'm not. I thought you would have noticed I haven't touched my drink,' Lisa holds up her warm, full martini. 'And I'll manage financially. I have a great family leave plan and all the money I've had saved up to pay for pregnancy through a clinic is just sitting there. I only want the one child for now but I've been saving for almost ten years so I could easily have more. Plus I was hoping that as my family you would be supportive just as I've helped you out.'

'Helped us out? We've spent all this time taking care of you,' Denise hisses.

'I spent many years babysitting so you both could work. Who taught Jake to read at night when you went on date nights or to pottery classes?'

'You were earning your keep.'

'Mum, don't,' Cameron cuts in. 'Lisa has helped us a lot, even recently she's been there to help me out with things when I couldn't come to you.'

'What things? You can talk to us about anything.' Susan asks, hurt glistening in her eyes.

'Sex mum, I don't feel comfortable talking to you about sex.'

Susan's hurt evaporates in embarrassment.

'Well, fair enough, as long as you are talking to someone,' Susan nods. She turns back to her sister. 'We will of course support you. We're just shocked, that's all. Last we heard you had stopped pursuing pregnancy because the clinic had refused you. We weren't expecting this, especially in such an unusual manner. No-one in our generation falls pregnant in any other way than through a reproductive clinic. It's natural to us.' Susan says while ignoring Denise's scowl as she glowers at Lisa.

'What is it Denise?' Lisa cracks. 'Didn't I do something according to your plans? Didn't you get to play matchmaker on this one? Is that why you're pissed? Are you finally realising that I'm not one of your children? I'm an adult and I've never been under your control.'

'Thank you for a lovely dinner,' Denise seethes through her teeth. 'I'm going to bed. You lot can sort this out without me.'

Denise shoves her chair back and storms out of the room leaving her dirty dishes stacked on the table. The chair leans back precariously from the force and Susan places her hand on the chair to settle it firmly back onto the carpet. Aaron locks eyes with Cameron, who gently shakes his head.

'Don't worry about that,' Cameron says calmly. 'She does this every now and then with big news. More so with Lisa.'

'Will she be okay?' Aaron asks through short breaths.

'Yes, she will be fine dear. I'll talk her through it tonight in bed,' Susan says. Her tone drops down to a comfortable curiosity with Denise now out of the room, her eyes crinkling into a smile. 'If you planned to tell us this news tonight, why did you invite Aaron?'

'I was important to me for him to be here when I first announced my pregnancy,' Lisa says flatly.

'He's the donor, isn't he?' Susan cuts through. Lisa simply nods. 'What about David? What about having your own children?' Susan asks softly.

'David doesn't know,' Aaron sighs. 'I don't really want him to know either. I haven't been completely honest with you. David found out he's unable to have his own biological children. Since then he's refused the idea completely. He didn't even ask if I wanted children in the first place. He just decreed it would happen and then moved on when he realised it wouldn't happen the way he wanted it to.'

'What a horrible man,' Susan mumbles. 'There are plenty of other ways to have children. You could adopt and obviously you could be the biological father.'

'I know that, more so now,' Aaron adds plainly. 'But

I don't want to raise children. I've tried to tell David this many times but he never listens. I just have to accept what he wants around the house.'

'You should leave him,' Cameron interjects.

'Cameron, none of that,' Susan cuts him off. 'That's not your choice to make. Aaron has to decide how his marriage works. So, who approached who about this child? Did Lisa persuade you to do it?' Lisa rolls her eyes but doesn't protest further.

'Actually no,' Aaron says. 'It was my idea. After I saw the heartache she had gone through being excluded by the system I thought that there has to be something I could do. I suggested it to her and then we took it from there.'

'How did you do it? Was it sanitary?' Susan's curiosity continues.

'Well, Aaron had all the necessary health screenings, and we planned out timing around my ovulation,' Lisa explains. 'And then when it came to it he left his donation in a cup outside the door and then left so that I could do the rest in private. He was very gentlemanly about it. And I fell pregnant on the first go, which was incredibly lucky. We had planned several attempts.'

'Are you going to raise the child together?'

'No,' Aaron says sharply. His clears his throat to remove the harshness from his voice. 'I agreed beforehand that I would only be a donor. I don't want to raise any children and I won't interfere with Lisa as a parent.'

'You must be around though. You can't avoid being in the child's life, especially if you keep visiting us frequently.'

'Of course I'll be happy to watch the baby grow up, but that's because I'm a friend of the family, not because I'm the donor. I like hanging out here. It feels like a second home to me. But I won't have any input into how Lisa raises her child.'

Susan sniffles suddenly. Her tears flow freely down the lines of her face. She moves around the table to Aaron, openly sobbing, and latches onto him with both arms before he's able to stand up. Aaron tenses under the strong embrace as warm drops of tears splash on his shoulder.

'Mum, release him,' Cameron says drily. 'Mum. Mum. Stop.'

Susan detaches herself from Aaron, who remains put in the seat afraid to move in case he startles someone.

'I'm sorry Aaron,' Susan says as she sits back down. 'It just became clear to me what this must mean to my sister. Thank you for what you have done. It's beautiful. Not everyone could do something like that.'

'So you're in a better mood about me being pregnant then?' Lisa carefully asks.

Susan springs from her seat again. The others at the table jump back in surprise. Aaron clutches the end of the table-cloth to stop his nails cutting into his palms.

'Of course,' Susan lines up Lisa as her next target and drags her into a bear hug. Lisa cringes and pats her sister lightly on the back. 'Congratulations. This is fantastic news. Of course I worry for you but this is just great news. There's going to be a baby in the family again. I'm finally going to be an aunt.'

'But what about—' Cameron is cut off by a wave of Susan's hand.

'My brother's kids don't count. We never see them.'

'So you're fine if I move overseas now there's a baby on the way?' Cameron moves to capitalise on his mother's joy.

'You're not going to steal the focus,' Susan smiles. Her cheeks shine from the fresh tears as she takes her seat again. 'Now I understand everything I can see how wonderful this is. Denise will be fine once she understands too. Oh, but what will you tell everyone else?'

'I've been overseas recently,' Lisa returns to her script. 'I was thinking I'd just say I attended a reproductive clinic there. And I'd only bother to explain myself if someone asks. Otherwise I just won't discuss it. It's no-one else's business anyway.'

'I can work with this. This sounds good,' Susan nods. 'And what about David?'

'It's none of his business, either' Aaron says bitterly. 'But there's a list of things we need to talk about. If it comes up I'll tell him then.'

'You're pregnant,' Susan repeats to herself. 'This is happening. You're pregnant. Do you know what the gender is? Oh, if it's a girl I saw this beautiful bassinet we can get her. I love my boys, and I loved raising them, but it would be exciting to have some lovely little girl things around the house. I think I have some paint samples in storage if you want to repaint the one of the bedrooms here.'

'Susan, let's not get too far ahead of ourselves,' Lisa pats her stomach. 'One thing at a time. I've only just confirmed that I'm pregnant, and I've only just told those closest to me. I've got plenty of time to plan and prepare.'

'I know, I know, it's just so exciting.'

The evening continues with a buzz of irrepressible ideas from Susan. A happy glow warms Aaron as he sits back and takes in their conversation. Cameron leans back also, continuously sipping at his wine until his teeth become a purple shadow. The jubilation of Lisa's news drains from Cameron's expression as other thoughts appear to cloud his mind. *Lisa and Susan are so excited about bringing a new life into the world*, Aaron thinks behind the adrenaline whirring in his head. *I helped with this. I didn't realise I would see so much of the effect it has on Cameron's family. They're so happy to have a child come into their life.* His mood drops with sudden doubts. *Why don't I want that happiness? It is wrong that I don't want to be like them? Am I jealous of their new opportunity for happiness?* Aaron shoves the thoughts from his mind. *No, I'm happy for them. I know I don't want children. It's not for me. I want my space and my freedom.*

'Well, I think I'm done for the night,' Cameron announces, the boredom apparent in his voice. 'It has been a fantastic evening. I'll see you all later.'

'I think I might go as well, it's getting late,' Aaron excuses himself from the table.

'I'll walk you out,' Cameron offers.

Aaron circles around the table thanking the hosts. He has to battle to hold his feet through the fierce hugs from both Lisa and Susan. They openly state their thanks for all to hear. *That's one secret out*, Aaron smiles to himself.

'Well, that was an eventful evening,' Cameron says after he shuts the door behind them. 'It did begin to drag towards the end though.'

'I didn't realise so many different baby products exist. Why?' Aaron laughs.

'I know. I was surprised mum got that clucky so quickly. Oh well, at least she'll be too distracted to set me up with anyone for a while. I imagine Lisa will probably spend more time hiding out in Jake's room to escape all the fussing, especially once she gets too big to run away.'

They walk slowly up the stone path towards the road. Their breath mists in the brisk air.

'That resort job doesn't sound so bad now, does it?' Aaron teases.

'To you maybe. I love winter. Well not so much that as I love having that change in seasons. I don't think I could cope living somewhere tropical where the days are all the same. I think that's what has been so great about having you in our lives. Each day is different. I think that's why we're friends. We both like the comfort of knowing we can always return home but we also strive to do new things we've never done before.'

'I think you're right,' Aaron admits. 'It's completely strange to me now but I still love David.'

'I can't see why. I haven't met the man but he sounds horrible. You'd be better off marrying Jake,' Cameron says. The bitterness rolls of his tongue.

'I doubt that. David is boring and predictable, but I know him better than anything else, well, I think I do. He's the structure that holds the roof up over my life. He feels like he's conquering the world and I'm happy exploring my own experiences that he remains blind to. If I had a more present husband I would have to do everything with him and that would cramp my style.'

'Cramp your style? You have officially turned to the dark side. The prim and proper man I met all depressed in the bar wouldn't have used words like that.'

'I blame you for everything,' Aaron bumps softly into Cameron's shoulder.

'Well, you're happier now, so I can accept blame for that. Even if a lot of it came from fucking my brother,' Cameron pushes back with his open palm. His voice turns sombre. 'How will David take all of this?'

'I don't know.' Aaron hangs his head.

'You know if it all goes bad you can stay here until you get back on your feet. The house doesn't look like much but there are so many rooms hidden in there you could move in without anyone noticing.'

'Thanks, that helps a lot. I don't think it will come to that in the end. David would want to know where I am even if we break up so he can control everything. So I hope, anyway. I don't want to hurt him or his career at all, but he's so protective of it that's what he will prioritise.'

'What are you going to say?'

'I have no idea,' Aaron confesses.

17.

THERE ARE EXTRA lights on when Aaron returns to the apartment and his heart sinks as he realises that David is home. The cloying odour of David's fruity cologne mixed with sweat hangs sourly in the air. Aaron spots David's briefcase leaning against the wall under the coat rack. The faint smell of wine emanates from behind the kitchen door.

'In here, now!' David barks from the far end of the apartment.

Aaron's body moves rigidly towards the brightly lit hallway. David's shadow paces back and forth on the hallway wall. Before he even sees David Aaron recognises the wine-filled fist stain the shadow makes with each step. *He's on the red. Well, I'm glad he's managed to find it himself without me waiting on him*, Aaron tries to distract himself from the conversation ahead.

'Get in here,' David shouts again down the hallway. 'You need to explain yourself.'

Aaron groans internally. *This was bound to happen eventually, and it's happening now. Let's get this over with.* An odd confidence bursts through him. He walks boldly down the hallway, the smack of his heels on the tiles echoing off the cold walls. His eyes glare straight ahead, focussed on a single point in front of him. The shadow continues to flicker across the wall.

Aaron rounds the end of the hallway into the doorway of the guestroom. David stands at the far wall, wine glass in hand and frowning at Aaron. Aaron meets his steely glaze with his own bored façade. The wardrobe door stands open, its overstuffed contents flooding out and spilling onto the carpet. A path has been paced through the overflow of cardboard pieces and dirty laundry.

'What is this?' David shouts. 'What the hell is this? I come home early, expecting you to be home but you weren't. I had to get my own dinner out of the fridge and I even went to clean up the dishes but then I found that monstrosity in the dishwasher. I thought surely that would be the worst of it, that you wouldn't take everything I provide for you for granted and there couldn't possibly be anything more than that. But then I decided to tour the rest of the house. You weren't in the laundry, you weren't in the bathroom and you weren't in the guestroom, but this was. What the hell do you call this?'

Aaron steps into the room. The walls radiate the harsh glow of the light bulb and Aaron feels heat from his body push outwards into the stale air. Stained bedsheets and other items from the wardrobe are also strewn over the bed. *He's been here for a while*, Aaron thinks.

'I call this the storeroom, or the guestroom, depending on the day,' Aaron states.

David paces back and forth, taking intermittent sips on

his wine. Aaron watches David's eyes twitch. He has seen the same calculation before. *He's scoping what the next step is.*

'David, we need to talk,' Aaron seizes the initiative as he sits himself down on the edge of the bed. 'We haven't been completely honest with each other recently.'

David stops pacing at the corner of the room. The mess of the floor marks a line between David and Aaron. David glares down at Aaron and Aaron feels his determination rise in response. He doesn't shy aware from David's intensity and merely stares back, waiting patiently.

'I know we need to talk,' David says plainly.

'We've needed to talk for a while now,' Aaron says. 'Things have changed between us. We've both changed. We can't continue like this unless we are open with each other.'

'You've been having an affair haven't you?'

'Haven't we both?' Aaron responds.

'No, I haven't been having an affair,' David fires back. 'How dare you say something like that?'

'What about Timothy?'

'What about him?'

'Are you seriously telling me that you've never fucked Timothy?'

'No, well, I don't know,' David drifts off into a mumble. 'You've had an affair?' David reasserts.

'Yes, I have,' Aaron states. 'I have had sex with other men.'

'Men? Plural?'

'You still haven't answered me, what have you done with Timothy?'

'Nothing, we haven't had sex,' David says defensively.

'Just other things?' Aaron shakes his head.

'Nothing serious. He just pleasured me a couple of times.'

'He sucked your cock?' Aaron blurts out.

David shudders upright. A look of shock slaps across his face.

'Yes,' he mutters through his teeth. 'He did that. But it wasn't sex. It was just late nights, exhausted and he thought he was doing the right thing.'

'And I suppose that makes you feel like the bigger man and in charge? You still allowed it to happen, and it's still cheating on me.'

David presses himself back against the wall. His eyes grow wild at the sound of Aaron's words. The directness of each statement cuts through him. David stares down at his wine. He distracts himself by sipping on the glass as he tries to regain composure.

'That's all of my secrets. What about yours? What do you have to tell me?'

'Have a seat,' Aaron suggests.

'I'm fine, just get on with it.'

'Until recently I've been sleeping with someone else,' Aaron starts. David's chest heaves. A smack of betrayal glimmers in the corner of his eye.

'Who?' David groans.

'Just someone I met. While you've been at work I've started making friends. Things became sexual with one of them.'

'Do I know him?'

'No, you don't know him and no-one you know knows him. He's in the army, so he's overseas a lot of the time.'

'Is that why it ended? Not because you didn't want to keep it going but because he was sent away? Are you going to see him again? Are you?'

'I don't know if I'll see him again,' Aaron surrenders, 'but yes, I wanted to keep sleeping with him and I would again if

I get the chance.' Aaron finds this new experience of speaking his mind without having to hide or perform to be quite gratifying. The urge to spill more of his secrets twists into a ball of knots inside of him and spurs him to reveal more frank truths to David.

'Right, I'll take that as a yes, then,' David states. 'What about us? Is this all over?'

'I don't think so,' Aaron says. 'Aside from our relationship our lives have been going fine recently. You're getting your promotions. I'm no longer lonely around the house. I actually get to spend time connecting with people. This is the happiest I've ever felt.'

'That's all well and good for you,' David spits. 'What if I don't want this to continue? What if I want you out of the house? You've betrayed me.'

'You betray me all the time,' Aaron shuts David down with the unexpected force of determination in his voice. 'You don't value my needs or opinions. You value your career and your reputation over me. You take for granted all the work I do to benefit your life. You ignore me and dismiss me when I try to create special moments in our life. Timothy was only one betrayal among many. You're my husband. I'm your husband. You're supposed to care for me, not lock me up in this apartment to use as you see fit. I have so much more to offer than being a homemaker. I want more from life than to sit around and wait for you for days on end. You've neglected me.'

'Don't blame me for this. You're the one sleeping with other people,' David tries to regain control.

'I don't blame you for that. But I need you to know that you're not faultless in this. I was forced to spend far too long alone. I tried to spend more time with you but you rejected me. You would rather be at work, striving for that next promotion, that little bit more pay and prestige.'

'I did that for us!'

'You did that for you. My life hasn't improved along with your salary. You cut back on the money I had available to spend on running this place. If you spent more time around here then you would have noticed I've been struggling. Anytime you have a dinner party I have to scrimp on my next couple of meals. I've had to take on work to support your lifestyle and your dinner parties.'

David's shoulders drop. The face of betrayal dissipates into a look of shame. His eyes drop to stare into his wine. Aaron's chest grows lighter. *Small steps*, he tells himself. *That was just one secret. It seems to be going well so far, but I won't be able to blame everything on David.*

'I should have been here more often. I'm sorry I had no idea you were struggling so much on your allowance. We should spend more time together but I don't think we can. If I work less my career will suffer significantly, and both of us will suffer more.'

'I don't expect you to cut down on your work,' Aaron says gently. Calm rises into the air between the couple. 'Not anymore. I used to when you were the only person I really interacted with, but now I have friends and a life outside of you. We both are very busy. I still make sure I'm home when you need me to be, according to the schedule you send me.'

David lifts his eyes and smiles, but doesn't speak. *That's as close to a thank you as I will get*, Aaron smiles back.

'Okay then,' David continues. His voice stays level as he nods to the mess spilling out of the wardrobe. 'Why is this mess here?'

Aaron looks over the piles. Old bedsheets reek of mould.

Cardboard boxes are crumpled and broken. A tangle of dirty clothes sits clumsily on the floor. What started out as problems to be dealt with later has become just a pile of rubbish.

'I've been lazy around the apartment so I could get out of here quicker,' Aaron says plainly. 'Everything I do around here feels pointless and unappreciated. It wasn't like you noticed what I did until I stopped doing it, or even for a long time afterwards. I did the necessities but then shoved the rest in here.'

'How long has this been going on for? It looks like months' worth of stuff. There are a couple shirts in there that I've been looking for.'

'The candles in the back were the firsts thing I put in there.'

'Candles? What candles?' David's face looks blankly at Aaron.

'That's such a perfect example of how you've treated me,' Aaron's anger seeps out again. 'I wanted to spend more time with you and so I made a treasure hunt around the apartment that ended in here. I had the whole room decorated with candles. It was beautiful but all you did was come in here yelling because it was a mess. I wanted to have you and you rebuffed me.'

'It was a mess. There's no need for any of that crap,' David's voice raises to signal his own defence. 'We're not dating any more. We're a married couple. There's no need for any of that. We're intimate when we need and that's it.'

'We are never intimate!' Aaron's frustration boils over. 'You thought we were intimate anytime you shoved your cock in me but that's not intimacy. That's just you getting off. I used to find it pleasant until I discovered what actual pleasure is. You know nothing of pleasure.'

'Is that why you went off to fuck other men? You wanted pleasure. Instead of talking to me about it you just went behind my back.'

Aaron opens his mouth to yell at David. *You're so stupid sometimes*, he shouts in his head. *I couldn't talk to you about anything like that. Even with kissing you cut me down if I hinted at what I wanted.* Aaron inhales deeply to control the fury simmering behind his eyes. David shoves himself off the wall and starts pacing the room. He walks between the bedside table and wall, avoiding the bloated mess on the floor.

'Okay, I think we can work through this,' David mutters. 'This might not be the end of our relationship. I need you still.'

'I'm glad you think so. I need you as well. It's strange, but I love you still.'

'You too,' David mumbles. 'I don't like that you've been sleeping with someone else. I need to get myself tested. Who knows what you've caught?'

'If you've caught something it's not from me. I made sure I was always safe and gotten health checks too,' Aaron affirms.

'Fine. We need better sex and you need to be able to stay home more. How about I increase your allowance?'

'What if I just get a job? I can earn my own money and use that to run the house while you use your money to pay for the apartment and pay the bills.'

'Why would you want your own job? Do you just want to be outside more? Don't you want to try with me to improve our life? You want to flirt your way around the city? Why isn't the house enough for you?'

'Because I'm so lonely here. You're not going to be here

that often. I need contact with people. I need to be able to spend time interacting with more people than just those interested in my roast dinner.'

'Fine, but no full-time work. I'll increase your allowance so that running the apartment is covered. You can just pay for things you want to buy for yourself. I don't want you spending too long outside the apartment, especially when you're not working.'

'This is my life as well, you can't control me. I will leave the apartment whenever I want and I'll see whoever I want. You need to come to terms with that.'

David's eyes widen. He pauses mid-step, his body twitching as he thinks. Realisation slowly crawls across his face.

'We're never going to be the same again, are we?' David asks, defeated.

'No. I want this to make us stronger and more open and more equal as a couple,' Aaron says sympathetically.

'Does that mean you intend to continue to have sex with other men?'

'Maybe, I don't want to be cut off from the things I enjoy. You should be open to it as well.'

'I don't want to have sex with other men. Timothy has offered but I've restricted him to just oral sex.'

'That's still sex. It's a pointless restriction.'

'I have to for work. I can get away with oral sex but actual intercourse with an employee could get nasty for me.' David's eyes turn calculating. 'Fine, do whatever you want when I'm not home. But don't bring anyone here and I don't want to know anything about it. I need to be able to protect my reputation if it comes out and blows up our marriage. And get tested regularly. Not with our doctor though. Keep it all away from anything connected with my life.'

Aaron begins to glow. *It's going well so far. I can still see Jake when he returns.* Aaron pushes his lips together to stop a smile rising between them. He chokes back the tear of joy that sneaks out the corner of his eye. But only for a moment before a dark awareness blocks the light of Aaron's moment of happiness.

'There's more,' Aaron stutters out.

'How can there be more? Isn't an affair and this mess enough.'

'I—I did have a job for a while,' Aaron fiddles the quilt into small ripples.

'In the coffee shop. I know. Aubrey saw you there.'

'No, I never worked in the coffee shop. I was just spending time with a friend there. No, I found work having sex with men for money.'

David's face drains of all colour until his skin matches the bleached white of his shirt. Pure rage trembles the wine glass in his hand.

'You—you had sex—Sex!—for money?' David forces out through his teeth. Aaron nods fearfully. 'How could you!?' David bellows. 'How could you do that? That's disgusting. I've been sharing a bed and a house with a—with a whore!'

Aaron braces himself, holding his body rigid. He feels like he has left his body to watch a disaster from a safer distance floating in the farthermost corner from David. Words creep out of him robotically.

'I needed money,' Aaron's voice croaks. 'I had no experience and no training, and this paid really well for doing very little. I could earn all the money I needed for a week in two hours and be home to cook dinner.'

David paces again, his steps agitated.

'You're a whore.'

'I was a sex worker,' Aaron continues. 'I needed to find a job that you wouldn't find out about. I was allowed to reject clients, which I did, if I didn't like them or they were too close to you. There's no way that you would have found out about it if I didn't tell you.'

'Again you push the blame onto me. I didn't make you have sex for money. I didn't turn you into such a slut. I didn't make you become a whore. You did that. You did all of that.'

'I know. I'm not blaming you. All you did was isolate me and forbid me from working and force me to find a job I needed to keep secret. I kept the escorting a secret from everyone. I used the cash I earned to do other things around the city without you knowing. I went to clubs. I met people. I saw things I never would have if I sat around the apartment all day waiting for you.'

'This is it. I can't deal with this,' David throws his arms up. 'How can we go on after this? Not only are you cheating but you have sex for money in dirty hotels.'

'It was never like that. They were always clean. I always used protection.'

'Did you enjoy it? Did they give you better sex than me?'

About the same, Aaron stops himself from saying. He shakes his head calmly.

'I didn't really like it but it was the only chance for me to earn money without anyone knowing. I wanted a job. I wanted to get out more and that opportunity came up. And you don't have to worry about anyone else knowing. I used a fake name and all the transactions were in cash. No-one but me and the client knew where we were and what we got up to.' *And Jake, but that's not going to help now.* 'It doesn't affect us and our relationship. I wanted you to know so that we can go forwards honestly.'

'Honestly. I do one thing wrong and you do this to me.'

It was more than one thing, Aaron reminds himself but holds back. Instead he says, 'I didn't do this to you, I did it for me.'

'And so this has all stopped now? Why did it end?'

'I got stalked by some crazy guy who stabbed me in the leg, and so the agency dropped me.'

'You were stabbed?' David's eyes flick quickly over Aaron in search of the damage. 'Are you okay? Why didn't you tell me then? I could have protected you. We could have arrested the man who did this to you.'

David still cares, Aaron thinks spotting the concerned panic in his eyes where previously there had just been anger. Aaron unbuckles his pants and pushes them down past his thigh and points at a small pink scar on his leg.

'See, it's fine. That's all that happened. He's gone now and I'm not escorting any more. There's nothing that can be done about it now. Life has just moved on.'

'I never thought I'd ever be able to move on from something like that. I would have thought divorce was the only possible outcome after learning that you slept with men for money. It was just men, right?' David braces himself for even further scandal. Aaron nods. David returns to his pacing. 'I can't divorce you because a failed marriage is not the image I wish to present, particularly now that I'm investigating membership with some of the more exclusive social clubs so I can mingle with more CEOs. A divorce will not help my application.'

'We can still do all of that,' Aaron encourages.

'I don't know what I can do. I hated you for a moment knowing you had sex for money, but hearing you were stabbed hurt me. And knowing that you couldn't tell me you were stabbed hurt me more You should be able to come to me with anything and I should be there to protect you. I'm your husband. It doesn't matter what work you do. I now know that I can move past you being a sex worker. It might take time. I'll probably still be angry every now and then.'

'I understand. Take as long as you need.'

'I will, but I need to know that you won't do that kind of work again. If I give this blessing for you to do casual work will you promise that it will at least be something that I'll feel happy to talk about at dinner parties?'

'I promise,' Aaron says honestly. 'I don't want to go back to that. I just want something steady that I don't have to hide from you. I may need do some study so that I have some employable skills.'

'I think that's a great idea, so long as you still have time to do things around the house,' David says. A confident glow rises in him again. 'This could actually work. If you have a successful career and we still have a functioning home, it shows that we both work really hard and can manage a lot together. I'll have to make sure the district manager is around for dinner once you get a job. I'll keep a look out for some work for you. The sooner you get a job the better.'

Aaron sighs quietly. He pulls his pants back up knowing the conversation has moved beyond the injury. *It's straight back to spinning the situation for another promotion*, Aaron thinks. *But it still works out for me. I can get out of the house and David can promote his image further. It's what we've both wanted.*

David calms himself. He drinks the rest of his wine but clings onto the glass stem. The glass moves up and around with his thought process as ideas flicker behind David's eyes. Aaron imagines an entire timetable and map being planned out inside David's mind. The old schedule would be erased with fire, the confidential information shredded out of his memory and a freshly inked guide to their future would grow out of the ruins, looking crisp and clean as if it is the only plan they've ever had. David sits down on the opposite side of the bed.

'We can get through this,' David states with a nod. 'I think we can get through this. It just doesn't make sense to divorce and we won't. We just need to be more open with each other. You keep your sexual activities private though, and we could soon be on the high road.' David's face snaps out of his enthusiastic twitching. 'That is everything isn't it? I don't think there could be anything worse than you being a sex worker. Please say that's there's nothing else that can get in the way of our marriage.'

'There is one more thing,' Aaron says coolly. 'Do you remember how we spoke about having children and then you didn't want to when you found out your sperm wouldn't work?'

'Yes,' David answers coldly.

'Well, I donated sperm to a woman I know. I found out tonight that she's pregnant. She's having my biological child.'

'How could you?' David seethes. 'Why would you do that? I'd just managed to see some way of making this work, and now this. Why would you sneak behind my back?'

'I didn't think you wanted children anymore. It's not going to be an issue for us anyway.' Aaron states.

'You're an idiot to think that,' David fires back. 'I hope you went through a clinic with the right paperwork to make sure we're protected.' Aaron glares down and shakes his head. 'You idiot. How did you do it then? Did you have sex with her?'

'Of course not,' Aaron whispers. 'I gave her my sperm in a cup and she inserted it herself. And then I haven't seen her again until tonight when she told me she's pregnant.'

'How could you?' David continues to shake his head. 'This won't be over. It never is. That's why people always go through a clinic, or at least have a breeder surrogate. It's the natural way. It's how everyone protects themselves and the children stay safe. Who knows what she will do now?'

'Nothing, she will do nothing. She doesn't need anything from us. Our reproductive laws are backwards and they screw her over so that no reproductive clinic will help her,' Aaron jumps to Lisa's defence.

'What's wrong with her? Why wouldn't a clinic take her?'

'There's nothing wrong with her. She's just not married or in a relationship. She's going to raise the child by herself.'

'Great, just great. There has to be a bigger reason for her to avoid using a clinic. She's going to come after you for money, which means she's going to come after me for money.'

'It's so hypocritical for you to talk about avoiding clinics You were going to use a breeder surrogate to avoid any potential maternal access.'

'I was doing that for us,' David objects. 'I was doing all of that for us.'

'You were doing it for your promotion. You needed an extra prop to make yourself look good.'

'Fine, yes, I did it for those reasons as well. What are her reasons? What's she going to do? If you think she's going to stay away from you and not ask for anything then you're lying to yourself.'

'She did it because she wants to have a child, to have a family of her own. I can promise that she won't ask for anything from me. That was part of our deal.'

'Did you sign anything?' David asks. Aaron doesn't answer. 'I can't be tied up with this. If she turns on you, as she no doubt will, then she'll be after money. We need to sort this out now or I'm out completely. I'll cop the divorce just to avoid a crazy woman dragging a child out and parading it through the media.'

'We're staying out of it,' Aaron says feebly. 'I donated the sperm. We are not getting involved beyond that. She doesn't need anything from us.'

'You say that now but people change. You've changed. I barely recognise you anymore. You aren't the man I married. You cheated, you prostituted yourself and now you're fathering children. This isn't our marriage anymore.'

David drops back on the bed. He hugs the wine glass to his chest as he lies flat on the mattress. Aaron eases himself down next to David. Their bodies lie rigid, parallel to each other. The air between them retreats into some unfathomable gulf that Aaron can physically feel. The room drifts into silence. A streak of wine escapes from David's glass, dripping onto his shirt. David doesn't flinch, but merely ponders the ceiling as the wine stains his shirt.

Aaron's head buzzes in the silence. Exhaustion overtakes his mind. He concentrates on the lone tick of the clock. They lay stiff, staring directly up. Their gazes avoid acknowledging each other through each second as it approaches and fades away. They just lay there listening to time pass.

Afterglow

Contemporary Western society affords its citizens numerous freedoms that have become so entrenched that they're often taken for granted. And at the same time social conventions from the past that have grown outdated still inform our social values and expectations, our behaviours, and even our laws. It is a sad fact that these outdated conventions still limit the freedoms of those who find themselves in in minority groups within society while they also privilege those already within privileged positons. This is a stain on our culture, a fading tattoo that still leaves its mark on the body politic. The scars of the past still linger.

The concept of laws dictating and censoring our creativity fell unexpectedly within my scope. The idea to write Aaron's story began when I received a wedding gift from a close friend. An artist who works with linoleum cut prints, he is well known for the complex and highly detailed floral designs he regularly produces. In developing the gift he planned, he researched further into the history of wood carving and print making, which lead him to create a unique piece displaying a homoerotic scene. My husband and I loved the gift and display quite proudly, particularly to highlight the complexities of the work. On first glance it is pornographic in content, but beyond that the technique and the storytelling of the piece are accomplished and impressive, a testament to the talent and dedication of the artist. The picture itself is created not through brushstrokes of ink, but through the white space, carved from the medium in a mirror image of the final print.

The meaning and impact of the print deepens further when you consider the subversion of history that the artist conceived. He utilised a historical style of art that was outlawed for its subversive nature and adapted it into a modern, queer work. Shunga, or Japanese erotic woodcarving, is a traditional style that survived in Japanese culture for hundreds of years despite ruling powers attempting to ban it and destroy any prints in existence. They believed the erotic to be a corrupting force on those they ruled over. The general populace had almost the opposite view of the erotic art. The common people believed the art to be an omen of good luck, even for a time hiding prints in the armour of soldiers when they went into battle. All attempts to rid society of the erotic art failed, as historical records attest.

Discussion of the homoerotic print with the artist and the research he undertook to create it fuelled my curiosity. I wanted to discover more about creative works that he been banned or censored. As a queer English-speaking author I focussed on British literature. I started back with one of my favourite books, *Lady Chatterley's Lover*. Banned for its lewd content and only released in full after many revisions, *Lady Chatterley's Lover* is a prime example of written work that was outlawed but continued to thrive and be republished. It also informed the base for the model chosen to write *Homebody*. The dysfunctional marriage and the goal for a family that is ultimately unachievable create fertile territory for the narrative arc.

The exploration of language and the body presented in *Lady Chatterley's Lover* added to the desire to explore the individual self-discovery of one character in a new world. It was from here I created a world based upon ways of life that have were rendered illegal or unsanctioned by the traditional social mores of our own reality. In Aaron's world homosexuality is the norm, having children outside of the help (and confines) of a fertility clinic, donor or surrogate is frowned upon if not outright illegal, and heterosexuality is a minority underclass. Outside of these key changes the world remained close to our world. People still desire marriage. Older generations maintain stronger connections to married life and the family unit. Executives strive for more profits and promotions. Sexuality is still unexplored territory for Aaron. His mind and body remain in a sheltered world. He only knows experiences of marriage and intimacy with the one person.

From this stable but isolated and inexperienced position, Aaron tests the bounds of his cultural sphere and introduces himself to a new and delightfully twisted realm of society.

—ALEX DUNKIN, 2016

Also by Alex Dunkin:

Coming Out Catholic

✳

Visit the author's website:
WWW.ALEXDUNKIN.COM

Buon-Cattivi Press
Adelaide, Australia